I0822450

COMPLICATE

PAM GODWIN

Cover Designer: Pam Godwin
Interior Designer: Pam Godwin

Content Warning

Visit my website at pamgodwin.com

The books in the DELIVER series are standalones, but they should be read in order.

This is the final installment. Cole Hartman's story. But it's not his beginning.
The story of Cole, Danni, and Trace starts in the TANGLED LIES trilogy. You don't have to read TANGLED LIES, but if you want to read it, do so before reading this book.

RECOMMENDED READING ORDER

ONE IS A PROMISE (#1)
TWO IS A LIE (#2)
THREE IS A WAR (#3)
DELIVER (#1)
VANQUISH (#2)
DISCLAIM (#3)
DEVASTATE (#4)
TAKE (#5)
MANIPULATE (#6)
UNSHACKLE (#7)
DOMINATE (#8)
COMPLICATE (#9)

PROLOGUE

Southern Missouri
Seven years ago

Something was missing.

Something significant. Troubling.

Cole Hartman lowered his head to his hands, wrestling with the insidious sense of foreboding. Over the last seven months, it emerged without symptoms, invading gradually, subtly, but with detrimental effects.

Dread was eating him alive.

He sat on the floor in the armory of his safe house, his back to the wall, knees bent, and stomach clenched in knots. Down the hall, his beautiful, free-spirited dancer was likely practicing her choreographic sequences of *the biggest production in the history of wedding dances.*

For as long as he'd known Danni, she'd fantasized about her wedding dance.

Not the dress.

The *dance.*

Hers and his. Their first dance as Mr. and Mrs. Hartman.

Over the past few months, she'd been teaching him the steps. Dancing was her thing, not his, but he didn't mind learning. Hell, rubbing up against her hot little body would never be a hardship. He fucking loved her. So goddamn much it hurt.

But something was missing.

Four years ago, he'd left her to complete a one-year, undercover assignment overseas. They'd only been together for ten months at the time. He shouldn't have gone. He didn't know that year would turn into several more.

Without her knowledge, he'd left her under the protection of his best friend, Trace Savoy. In doing so, he'd inadvertently fucked his fate and shoved his entire world into Trace's arms.

After botching the mission, faking his death, losing Danni to his best friend, and finally, *finally* winning her back, he'd crawled out of hell, alive and victorious.

He'd chosen his job over her, and in the end, she chose him over all else.

His decisions had destroyed her life, and in return, she gave him her heart. *Again.*

The shattered pieces of his miserable existence had been put back together. He didn't deserve her, but when he'd returned from the dead, he put every ounce of life into earning her forgiveness.

He'd fought countless battles through his clandestine career, but seven months ago, he won the only war that mattered.

He won back his dancer.

Fair and square.

She let Trace go.

She chose me.

But something was missing.

The depressing lyrics of James Bay's *Let It Go* trickled through the armory. Racks of guns covered one wall, the rest occupied by file cabinets, desks, computers, phones, and high-tech gear. The kind of equipment that didn't exist outside of his classified unit.

In the corner, her wedding gown hung on a hook. It didn't belong in here. Not in a room crammed with weapons, secrets, and deception.

When he'd taken the dress during their separation, he wanted it in a safe place. He longed to see her wear it as she walked down the aisle, toward him, toward their future together.

Nothing stood in their way now. She'd chosen him. Agreed to marry him. Everything was right in the world.

Except it wasn't.

The soft tread of footsteps approached from the hallway and paused on the threshold.

His pulse quickened as it always did when she was near. His entire being pulled toward her as she entered the room. He didn't move, didn't make a sound, his senses alert, tracking her graceful movements as she floated past his shadowed position on the floor near the door.

She took in the space, lingering on the wall of firearms. This was her first glimpse behind the armory door. He always kept the room locked. Kept her out. She shouldn't be here. Her spirit was too bright, too gentle amid the guns and dangerous evidence of his business.

As if realizing that, she quickly turned back to the

door and paused, startled, her gaze fastened on him. Then she smiled.

The first smile she'd ever given him had been life-altering. She'd stepped in front of his motorcycle at the crack of dawn, wearing almost nothing. Except her smile. It'd been so big and full of life, it softened his insides, turned his brain to butter, and made him weak.

He didn't regret a second of it.

No man with a pulse could regret her. Danni Angelo was a blonde bombshell with a compassionate soul. Beautiful inside and out.

Grey eyes, fair complexion, she glowed with light and stunning sensuality. Her lithe limbs and athletic physique befit her occupation as a professional dancer. But it was her smile that stole the show. And broke hearts. His heart, specifically.

She'd broken him as much as he'd broken her. Crushed. Mended. And soon to be demolished again. He felt it looming—the pain, the devastation, the inevitability of forever's antonym.

Never was coming for him.

Because something was missing.

It was missing in the smile she wore now. Her bowed lips curved like they always had. Her eyes illuminated with angelic beauty. But it wasn't a *Danni* smile. Not the one that had railroaded him the day they met. Definitely not the one that tilted the universe and knocked him off his feet.

It lacked the energy that made his heart rev. It didn't crackle the air and charge his blood. It was low on sunshine, devoid of music, and desperately in need of life.

Her smile cried out for happiness.

There was no contentment in it. No tranquility.

No delirium. Had she been without those things all along?

They'd been inseparable for months, staying here at his lakefront estate, reconnecting, dancing, fucking, focusing on their relationship, and planning their future. They were wrapped up together. On top of the world.

But no amount of planning or intimacy could erase the gaping hole in her heart.

The hole that had been left by another man.

He didn't want to notice it. Didn't want to think about it, talk about it, or do anything to make it real. So he'd ignored it. For seven months, he pretended there wasn't something missing.

They were in love and finally back together, all the while pretending she didn't still love Trace.

It was a point of contention that couldn't be resolved with words or time. Ignoring it wouldn't make it go away. He knew that. They both knew.

It wasn't her fault. She hadn't asked for this. He and Trace had wedged her into a miserable love triangle. Then they'd forced her into a decision.

Choose.

So she had.

Her decision ruined Trace, sentencing him to a life without her.

Her decision left a guilt-ridden hole in her heart.

Her decision yielded only one winner, and he couldn't rejoice in that. But if he was strong enough, he could fix it.

She'd lost him once, and yeah, it had wrecked her. But she'd found happiness again. In his absence, she'd fallen in love again.

The same couldn't be said this time around. She

was surviving without Trace, but she wasn't *living*.

This had everything to do with who she was, not who she chose. The woman he'd shared space with for the last seven months wasn't the Danni he knew.

She'd lost her luster, her vivacity, her effervescent rhythm. His carefree dancer was miserable.

Because love wasn't a choice.

He dangled his arms over his bent knees and leaned his head back against the wall, watching her, memorizing her delicate features, while slowly, painfully, preparing for a decision that would decimate him on a fundamental level.

"I thought you retired." She glanced at the tables of charging phones and running laptops. "What is this?"

"I *am* retired. I only come in here to check my messages." He gave the devices a thoughtful look. "I get a lot of job offers."

"Job offers?" She closed the distance and lowered to the floor beside him, mirroring his pose. "What kind of jobs?"

"The kind that paid for this house. The dangerous kind that send me out of the country for months. Sometimes years."

He missed the work, the challenge in it. The danger. But he gave it all up for her and would gladly continue to do so…if she was happy.

She tensed. "Are you considering—?"

"I would never consider a job away from you." He gathered her beneath his arm and breathed in the unique Nag Champa scent of her hair.

Curling up against his side, she rested her head on his shoulder and hummed. Her fingers stroked his arm. Her silence tried to invoke comfort. All of it felt forced, but not. Tense, but also tender. She was straining for the happiness they'd once shared. And failing to grab hold of it.

Let It Go played again, strumming the air with the glaring truth. The lyrics bemoaned a relationship that was destined to end, no matter how badly two people held on. He'd selected it without thinking, his subconscious sending him a message.

"This song is so sad." She ran a finger along the line of his rigid jaw, unable to coax him to relax. "Why are you listening to it?"

"I know what you're doing," he murmured, his insides sick with unease.

She dropped her hand.

"You're trying so hard to make this work." His voice cracked. "But the heart wants what the heart wants."

She flinched. "No—"

"He's not physically here, but he's here nonetheless, always between us." He met her eyes with a hard stare. "You're settling."

"Damn right, I'm settling." She fisted her hands. "I'm settling into a beautiful life with a man who takes my breath away. I chose *you,* Cole. I'm *with* you."

"Someone told me once that love isn't a choice."

Christ, this hurt. Unlike the bullet that had struck his chest, Danni would leave a lasting, open wound.

"Why do you think I wanted you to wait six months?" He touched her trembling fingers, caressing her engagement band. "I didn't want you to choose. I wanted it to *happen*. I wanted it to rise inside you and become the beat of your heart." He softened his voice, dying inside. "The most decisive actions are the ones with the least consideration."

"What are you saying?"

"The day you forced yourself to decide, I knew. When Trace walked out that door, I saw it in your eyes." He forced resolve into his expression. "You voiced a decision your heart wasn't ready to make."

Her face turned to stone. But beneath the anger, he glimpsed concession. She knew he was right.

"I've watched you fight an inner battle for seven months." He brought her hand to his lips and kissed her knuckles. "You're fighting a war with your heart."

Creases of pain etched around her mouth. "If that's the case, why did I choose you?"

"I was your first. The logical choice. But the heart isn't logical. Sometimes, we don't know what we want until it's gone."

"It doesn't matter." In her usual stubborn fashion, she climbed onto his lap and steeled her voice. "I love you.

"I know you do." He pulled her against him and tucked her head beneath his chin. "But you love him more."

She sank her fingernails into his shoulders, clutching fiercely, holding on, fighting against the inevitable.

For a moment, he fought alongside her. They belonged together. He could work through this, love her hard, harder than any man ever could, and fill the void Trace left behind. There had been a time when he was all she needed.

Until he ruined it.

Agony rose without warning, scraping jagged shards through his throat.

The damage couldn't be undone. He'd left her, let her believe he was dead, and lost her to another man.

Hot prickles stabbed the backs of his eyes. He couldn't swallow. Couldn't breathe.

He'd ruined them.

Dammit, he just wanted her to be happy, and it wasn't fair to either of them to go on pretending. He'd rather be the one with the gutted heart. Instead of fighting for her, he'd rather fight for her wellbeing and take vicarious contentment in that. This wasn't him being a martyr. He simply couldn't find a better way.

He had to let fate play out. Let her go back to Trace. Let her go.

Let it all go.

His vision swarmed with tears. He didn't make a sound, didn't release the air in his lungs, but he couldn't hide his anguish from her.

She leaned back and whimpered at the sight of his tears.

"Don't make that face." A sob escaped her as she frantically dried his cheeks with her hands. "Don't give up on me."

"I lost you, baby. I lost you the morning I got into that cab and left you crying on the porch." He hauled her against him, his embrace constricting and his mouth at her ear. "I'm not giving up. I'm letting you go."

She shattered in his arms, sucking choppy gulps of air. He clung to her, and she clung back, gripping, weeping. He held her through it, crying with her as she came to terms with reality.

Years of friendship, love, and dreams for the future spooled out around them. She would still have those things. Just not with him.

He would never love again. Never find another Danni. He couldn't even fathom it. She was his soul mate.

For endless minutes, they sat in the sadness, deep in their own thoughts, until the tears stopped. Too soon, she raised her head and cupped his face, wearing a look of devastating finality. He wiped away her tears as she dried his.

"No more crying tonight." He kissed her lips, softly lingering.

No words were exchanged as he carried her into the bedroom. No second thoughts were voiced as they undressed. No tears fell as he entered her body for the last time.

They'd been here before. Four years ago, he made love to her and left her. But this time, he wasn't leaving for a job. He was leaving for *her,* and he wouldn't be returning. This time, he stared into her eyes, fucked her achingly slow, and wordlessly said good-bye forever.

After, she lay beside him, studying his face, seemingly dazed. She always admired his looks. Her attraction to him had never been in question. Neither had her love.

The woman loved with her entire being. That was the problem. She loved big enough and deep enough to bind her soul to two men.

"I'm grateful I had you to myself for seven months." He pushed a blonde lock behind her ear. "I'm grateful for every breath, every dance, every memory you gave me."

Sharp, incendiary pain lashed through him, leaching the strength from his body. Fire burned in his chest, searing his breaths and watering his eyes. He couldn't do this. He couldn't let her go.

He wanted to sink into her again and lose himself in her precious warmth. But if he did that, if he stayed the night, he would stay forever. His fragile resolve was splintering. He needed to go.

So he pulled away. Not physically. Not yet. But he pulled his gaze away from her beguiling beauty. He pulled his emotions away from the surface and shoved it all down, growing cold and rigid in the effort.

She seemed to sense his detachment and went still beside him, silent and accepting. There would be no more fighting from her. She knew the score. She would grieve and move on.

Trace was waiting. His best friend would wait for her forever.

As her breathing drifted into the rhythm of sleep, he touched his lips to her forehead one last time.

I love you, Danni Angelo. Be happy.

Without waking her, he slipped the engagement ring from her finger. She didn't need it anymore, but he did. Christ, he needed every memory of her he could carry.

The tightening in his chest was unbearable, his insides hemorrhaging. He pushed through it and pulled away from her sleeping form.

She had Trace, and Cole had enough job offers to keep him distracted for years. He could do this. He had no choice.

In the dark, he slipped out of bed.

Then he slipped out of her life.

ONE

Chihuahuan Desert, West Texas
Present Day

"Ready?" A thrill coursed through Cole as he met Rylee's eyes.

Huge, silver-grey eyes.

Just like Danni's.

Sometimes, it was difficult to hold that stunning stare, for it conjured echoes and aches of the one he let go.

He looked away, directing his attention to the kitchen table, which gleamed in an array of guns, ammo, and other weaponry. Amid the gear lay the high-tech GSM bug he'd pulled from Rylee's house.

The mystery behind who had put it there remained unsolved. After months of investigating, he and his vigilante team didn't have much to go on. But one thing was certain. Someone had bugged her house to fuck with *him*.

Rylee was just collateral. A means to lure him into the open. They wouldn't hesitate to kill her. They'd already tried.

The question was *who?*

Who murdered her next-door neighbor, two innocent motel clerks, and put a hit on her life?

The best clue they had was a word uttered by a dying hitman.

Thurney.

During a mission eleven years ago, Cole had faked his death on Thurney Bridge. Since that detail was classified, it meant he was dealing with someone connected to that assignment. And they wanted him alive. Otherwise, they would've killed him instead of hunting Rylee.

Most likely, they wanted information. Dangerous, top-secret intel from his work in the *activity*. Or maybe this was a revenge plot against him, and they wanted to draw out his death, slowly and excruciatingly.

Time to find out.

Outside, his seven vigilante teammates stood by, waiting for him to set the plan in motion. Most had already moved into position around the perimeter of Tomas' house. The other nine Freedom Fighters, including the Restrepo Cartel's *jefe*, were en route from Colombia to provide backup and reunite with their family.

Family.

The Freedom Fighters were an entangled, dysfunctional mix of blood relations, enemies-turned-lovers, spouses, soul mates, workmates, and above all, loyal friends. They protected and loved one another with a ferocity that made them unstoppable. They killed, waged wars, and sacrificed everything for one another.

And over the past year, he'd become one of them.

It was strange to have a team again after being alone for so long. Even stranger to have a family he could depend on and trust. Criminals or not, he'd grown to care about these people. So much so that he didn't want to put them in harm's way. Didn't want to risk their lives. The thought of losing one of them scared the hell out of him.

That made them liabilities. If his enemies knew what they meant to him, they would use them as leverage.

"I thought I was ready." Rylee tilted her head, studying him. "But I don't like that look on your face. Are we going to die?"

"Everyone dies, darlin'. That's a guarantee."

"Tonight?" Her face paled as she pointed at the high-tech bug. "When you activate that thing and let them know we're here, what are our chances of survival?"

Fifty-percent chance. Sixty, if he was feeling cocky. Which he wasn't. But he wouldn't share those odds with her. This was her first job as a Freedom Fighter, and her fear was palpable, trembling through her willowy limbs.

Nevertheless, she wanted to be part of this. She was committed to the team. More specifically, she was committed to Tomas, one of their longest-standing members.

"You know this is dangerous." He crossed his arms.

Standing over the table, she braced her hands on the surface and leaned in. "A plan that isn't dangerous isn't a plan at all. You can't scare me away."

She wasn't wrong. A few months ago, she drove here alone, with a pocketful of audacity and a reckless plan to meet Tomas Dine, fully aware he was a criminal, a murderer, and livid enough with her to shoot her on the spot.

Her chance of survival had been closer to zero then. Yet here she was, alive, in love with the ruthless vigilante, and ready to fight another fight.

Cole should've kissed her when he had the opportunity. Four months ago, here in the kitchen while Tomas was in the shower, he'd thought about doing more than feeding her breakfast.

It wasn't just her enchanting eyes. She was a remarkable woman. Fierce. Smart. Gorgeous.

Where Danni's hair was blonde, Rylee's was dark brown. Same long, straight style. Same slender, athletic build and graceful mannerisms. Like Danni, she exuded raw, natural beauty. No makeup. No maintenance. No nonsense.

His kind of perfect.

It had been seven years since he'd seen or talked to his dancer. Of course, he noticed beautiful women since then. He craved sex, obsessed over it, and fucked his hand on the regular. He still had a pulse, for Christ's sake. But no one had come close to tempting him.

Not even Rylee.

In seven years, he hadn't felt the luscious curves of a female body. Hadn't tasted soft, warm lips or smelled the sweetness of a soaked pussy. He hadn't encountered anyone who compared to the woman he let go.

But he enjoyed Rylee's company. Perhaps because she looked past his coarse exterior and understood him in a way very few people did. She recognized his pain and seemed to admire him for it.

Her education lent her the ability to see through the bullshit. But he guessed it was her own loss, her ex-husband's betrayal, that helped her relate to him so easily.

"You're staring." She narrowed her eyes. Eyes that made him long for a life he would never have.

"You're beautiful," he said.

"Mm-hmm." She pursed her lips, her expression skeptical. "What's going on, Cole?"

"Just an observation."

"Why *that* observation? Why now?"

"Because Tomas isn't here to take a swing at me."

"Fair enough. Thank you for the compliment." Her cheeks rose. "I'm ready to do this. Are you?"

"Yep." A rush of energy buzzed through him as he grabbed the high-tech bug from the table. "Going live in three, two, one…"

He activated the device and gave her a nod.

Nothing indicated the bug was on, but the moment it detected noise, it would begin recording. Sound clips would be sent to an untraceable phone, and whoever monitored that phone would be alerted of the incoming recording within seconds.

Basic spy technology, but so much more. This bug had been customized with high-speed transmissions, long-reach WIFI, and battery life that exceeded months—all built into a chip the size of a coin.

That level of cutting-edge tech wasn't obtainable outside clandestine groups like NSA and black ops. He'd been retired from the *activity* for so long he wasn't up to speed on the latest tech. Hell, he didn't even know how the bug functioned until he'd taken it apart.

What he did know was that this tiny piece of tech

was the key that would lead him to the threat.

Or rather, it would lead the threat to *him.*

"Where are you going?" he asked Rylee, following the script he'd rehearsed with her.

"I'm sick of hiding, Cole." She stared at the listening device, answering exactly as he'd coached her. "We've been moving around, running for months, and you still don't know who planted those bugs in my house. Now you expect me to sit here in the damn desert and wait for something to happen? You don't even know if they're listening to us now."

While holed up in Missouri for the past four months, he and his team spent that time investigating and planning. Now they were back in Texas, ready to finish this, and she'd just given the enemy their location. On purpose.

"This house is the safest place for us," he said.

"This house holds too many haunting memories for Tommy. We're leaving."

"Where the hell are you going to go?"

"Out of the country. Doesn't matter." She moved toward the door, deliberately distancing her voice from the listening device. "I came here for Tommy. I didn't sign up for this, whatever *this* is."

"Rylee, wait." He followed her out of the house and shut the door behind him, loud enough to be detected by the bug.

The plan was set.

Outside, Tomas sat in a doorless, topless Jeep Wrangler, his arm draped over the steering wheel and his golden stare locked on Rylee. "How did it go?"

"Noticeably contrived." She climbed into the passenger seat and kissed his rigid jaw. "I should've studied acting instead of psychology."

"You did fine." Cole stopped beside the Jeep, sweating in the evening heat. "Doesn't matter if it sounded hokey. They now know where I am, and when they arrive, they'll believe you're gone."

The last part was paramount. Someone tried to kill her once. He couldn't risk her or anyone else getting captured and used as a hostage to control him.

A glance at the Jeep's cargo confirmed Tomas had packed everything they needed to camp in the desert for a few nights. He also had enough artillery to take out an army. Van, Liv, Luke, and Tiago were already in position, far enough away to not be seen, yet close enough to be here at a moment's notice with guns blazing.

Cole turned toward the house and spotted Tate and Lucia sitting in the dark on the flat roof. The instant they heard an approaching car, they would alert the team, aim their rifles, and lie low enough to be undetected from the ground.

If the threat arrived by helicopter, they were all fucked. A view from the sky would mark the positions of his entire team in the desert.

"Get out of here." He tapped the hood and stepped back, watching Tomas drive off.

As the taillights faded into the shadows of sand and desert buttes, he switched on the transmitter in his pocket. "We're live. Do you copy?"

"Loud and clear" came through his earpiece eight times, once for each of his teammates.

They all carried receivers with sensitive microphones and wireless nano earphones that operated over a radio frequency like walkie-talkies. They would sleep in shifts, check in every hour, and wear the earpieces at all times.

"Out." He muted his mic.

Now, they waited.

TWO

Cole returned to the house, keyed up and primed for battle.

He lived for this shit—the tremor of looming danger, the rush of adrenaline, and the thrill in fighting for something meaningful. That was the reason he'd enlisted to become a Navy SEAL all those years ago—a decision that had hurdled him through the ranks and landed him in a unit so covert and off the record that it didn't exist. At least, not to those who didn't have the clearance.

In the kitchen, he holstered a 9mm in the waistband of his jeans. A blade went into his boot. The rifles he set by the door. He left the listening device on the table to record his movements around the house.

It could be days before someone showed up, depending on how far they had to travel. While he was in Missouri for the past few months, he assumed his pursuers had stayed in Texas, waiting for him to reemerge. They wouldn't be far.

He lowered onto the couch and measured his

breathing, taking on the cold, competitive mindset that had accompanied him on every mission over the past fifteen years. He was nothing if not a soldier rooted in grit, preparation, and confidence.

Grit rose from a place of deep purpose. Preparation came only through patience and tenacity. And confidence? That had been drilled into him through experience, training, and resilience.

Kill or be killed. Didn't matter what he faced or how badly the odds stacked against him. He believed in his ability to overcome.

In most missions, he knew his enemies inside and out. But not this one. From this point on, anything could happen.

A retrieval team would likely be sent for him. A few armed men. Maybe a dozen or more. That was the best-case scenario. If an army of thugs tried to take him by gunfire or physical force, the Freedom Fighters would rush in and wipe them out, save one. One breathing man was all they needed to torture for information.

But if only one man showed up, that would mean his enemy wielded something more powerful than bullets. If he had any fear, it lay in that unknown variable, a potential misstep he hadn't calculated, like an unforeseen hostage.

Everyone he cared about was accounted for. Trace Savoy had Danni locked up in the tower of his St. Louis casino, claiming his security was as impenetrable as Cole's safe house in Missouri. It wasn't. Which was why Cole had demanded they stay at his house. Trace's refusal to do so was infuriating and unfounded. Evidently, the uptight bastard didn't trust Cole around his wife.

Was it a valid concern? Maybe. Cole had no idea what he would do if he saw Danni again. Right now, all he cared about was keeping her safe.

As for the rest of his friends, he'd spoken with Matias an hour ago. The cartel boss affirmed they were safely on his plane and on their way to Texas. When they arrived, they would wait at an undisclosed location until Cole gave them the go-ahead to approach.

He hoped he wouldn't need Matias' assistance, but he wouldn't reject it. *Give help and get help.* It was a crucial motto in his line of work.

An hour rolled by, and radio check-ins were made. Then another hour, another check-in.

With the use of a dedicated frequency and encrypted communication, their conversations transmitted over secure lines. As an added layer of protection, everyone used nicknames.

Just before the third hour, Tate's voice came through the earpiece. "Come in, chief."

Cole lurched from the couch and closed himself into the bathroom, where the bug couldn't hear him. "Go ahead."

"Eyes on incoming movement. A single light approaching from the east. Looks like a headlight."

"A motorcycle?"

"Affirmative."

"On it." His pulse kicked up. "Stand by."

"Copy."

One motorcycle.

That wasn't a goddamn retrieval team. It was something far worse.

Returning to the front room, he peered around the window curtain, his neck tense and senses on high-alert.

A bright light bobbed over the horizon and headed straight toward him.

Only one.

Goddammit. His gaze darted to the rifles by the door. Useless. Whatever the biker was armed with couldn't be defeated with gunfire.

His heart rate escalated as he stepped away from the window. Perspiration formed on his brow as he chambered a round in his pistol and returned it to his waistband.

Bullets wouldn't save them. Not from this.

A tremor rippled through his fingers as he removed the necklace that hung beneath his shirt. He couldn't risk losing Danni's engagement ring.

It went into the pack he kept in the back bedroom, safely stowed. Then he drew in a deep breath and stepped outside.

The mic on his transmitter remained on, his team silent and listening, waiting on his command.

The rumble of a single-cylinder engine vibrated the air as a BMW motorcycle approached, taking its time. The rider wore a black helmet and appeared small in stature, at least half his size. He realized why as the bike rolled up beside him.

Slender hands gripped the handlebars, connected to feminine arms sleeved in more tattoos than he had on his entire body. In the moonlight, vivid colors of ink formed so many artful designs it would take him hours to make out all the images.

The biker shut off the engine and left the headlight on, illuminating the desert behind him. No visible weapons. No immediate threats on the horizon. She appeared to be alone.

Three feet of space separated them. He was close

enough to grab her and physically overpower her. Or shoot her point-blank with the 9mm in his hand.

"Right about now, you're calculating your next move." A sultry Russian accent crooned from the helmet as she lowered the kickstand and slid off the motorcycle. "You activated my bug, Cole Hartman, and here I am. But you weren't expecting a woman. This, I know."

You veren't expecting eh voman. Zis, I know.

He certainly wasn't expecting a Russian woman. He didn't have enemies in that part of the world. But he'd worked there. The *activity* operated only outside of the United States, and since all his missions had been overseas, he spoke seven languages with superb fluency. Including hers.

"I'll help you decide your next move." With each syllable, she pulled her tongue to the back of her throat, adding friction to the *H* sounds and hardening the *Rs*. "If you shoot me, your friends will die."

"Which friends?" he asked in Russian. "I don't have many."

The helmet cocked, paused. She seemed startled that he spoke her language.

She was probably a low-ranking myrmidon, a subordinate who carried out orders unquestioningly. Most likely, she was chosen for this task because she was a woman with an attractive figure, her purpose to lure and disarm. She wouldn't know anything about him beyond what they'd given her to complete the job.

"I'm not talking about your two friends on the roof," she said in Russian. "They can lower their rifles. They won't need them."

His scalp tingled. How did she know Tate and Lucia were there? Aerial thermal imaging? If that was the case, the position of his entire team was compromised.

Unease slithered down his spine, but he didn't spare Tate and Lucia a glance.

Instead, he switched back to English so they could follow the conversation. "You have an infrared drone up there?"

"I have eyes everywhere," she purred.

Maybe she was bluffing, but either way, his team knew what to do.

"Come in, *esé*." Lucia's voice barked through the earpiece. "What's your 20?"

"Same," Van said. "All present and standing by."

"Any drones?"

"Eyes on the sky. No bogies in sight. No hostiles on the ground. All clear. Try not to get yourself killed, *mija*."

"Roger," she said. "Out."

Relief swept through Cole as he turned back to the woman. "Tell me who you work for."

"No."

"Remove the helmet."

"This, I can do." She reached up and started unbuckling the straps.

Dark jeans caressed her toned curves, the waistband rising high to her midriff and exposing a sliver of smooth, pale skin. The denim folded into wide cuffs at her ankles, and Gothic boots sported random buckles that served no practical purpose.

Her cropped corset looked more like a strapless bra, with black and white polka-dots that clashed with the colorful artwork on her arms. The bodice clung to the round swells of her tits, clinching an hourglass figure that needed no clinching.

Her top dipped so low it exposed a red bird inked across her breast, its beak lost in her ample cleavage. A swallow bird. Vintage in its design. With vibrant swirls and elaborate filigree, the chest piece looked so fucking enticing on her perfect rack it demanded his stare, ensnared it, and wouldn't let it go.

Until she removed the helmet.

Piles of thick, bright-ass-red hair tumbled out, bouncing off her shoulders and falling around her inked arms. Eyes of sea-green stared out of a face so feminine, so delicately formed, that her flawless ivory complexion didn't appear natural.

Nothing about her appearance looked real. Or soft.

Heavy black eyeliner winged out from the corners of her large eyes. Her lashes were so dense and long he knew they were fake. Even the white stone piercing on her upper lip was an imitation of Marilyn Monroe's beauty mark.

Cherry red gloss stained her lips. Plump, sinful, smiling lips. The longer he stared, the wider she smiled. She damn well knew the effect she had on men.

Her beauty was bold, arresting, and deliberately, garishly exaggerated. With her makeup painted on in aggressive strokes and her mermaid hair so shockingly red, he suspected she spent more time primping than firing a weapon.

From head to toe, she exuded a rockabilly vibe, blending old-school rock with Goth subculture, like a retro Russian pinup girl with a wartime air. She would look right at home sprawled on a Soviet tank, wearing nothing but garters and that ruby red smile. Seductive and freaky and one-hundred-percent artificial.

What did she look like beneath the hair dye and

caked-on cosmetics? He trusted her beauty as much as he trusted *her*.

"While your eyes are bulging from your head," she said in her thick accent, "the clock is ticking. You will come with me now."

Someone had bugged Rylee's house, sent a hitman after her, and killed three innocent people, and this woman was involved.

The plan had been to lure her here. Not get himself captured.

He laughed. "I'm not going anywhere with you."

"You will, Cole Hartman." She removed a large-screen tablet from the pack on her motorcycle and handed it to him. "Turn it on."

His lungs caved in, and alarms rang in his head. He stared at the offered device, unable to move, crippled by memories.

Eleven years ago. Thurney Bridge. He'd faked his death, lost his girl, and destroyed his life—all because of a video on a phone.

He couldn't guess what she would show him on that device, but whatever it was would force him to his knees.

No. Fuck no. Not this.

It couldn't be a threat to Danni's life. Not again. Trace swore she was safe.

The woman huffed with impatience and powered on the screen, displaying a paused video. "Push play."

"Rot in hell." He aimed the pistol at her face, inches from her painted lips.

She didn't flinch or bat a fake eyelash. Instead, her mouth curved up. Her tongue poked out, and she slowly, fearlessly, fucking shamelessly licked the end of the barrel. All the way around the tip she went. Then she drew it between her filthy, lush, red lips.

His dick twitched, heating his anger past the boiling point. He yanked the gun away.

"We're out of time, *tigryenok*." She pouted. "Watch the video."

She pressed play, and as much as he wanted to smack the device from her hand, he was still a soldier. A disciplined operative. Logic over emotion, his mind was in control.

The video showed a tarmac and private airplane hangar, the camera hovering from somewhere overhead. Before it zoomed in on the plane and the people boarding it, he knew exactly what he was looking at.

Matias, Camila, Josh, Amber, Kate, Martin, Ricky, Tula, and Vera. The nine Freedom Fighters who were on their way here.

His throat closed, panic spiking.

How had she obtained this footage? Whoever watched his friends hadn't stopped them from boarding. He'd spoken with Matias after they were in the air. They were safe.

Unless another aircraft was following them.

She switched the screen, displaying a new video. "This is a live feed, streaming from an armed drone."

The drone was in motion, high in a pitch-black sky, and locked onto a target. Equipped with night-vision cameras, it provided an undeniable view of another aircraft coasting at a distance ahead of it.

She tapped on the screen, controlling the drone's camera and zooming in until the tail number on the aircraft's cowling was legible.

He recognized the number instantly and knew it was registered to Matias' plane.

An ache swelled in the back of his throat.

Van's wife, Tiago's wife, Liv's husband, Lucia's sister—every person on that aircraft was irreplaceable. They were family.

The team on the ground was listening through the radio, but they didn't see what he saw. They didn't know their loved ones were in danger.

Didn't matter. They were his people, too.

Cold purpose numbed his chest as he slipped a hand into his pocket and discreetly muted the transmitter, preventing his friends from hearing what came next.

"What's the ordnance on the drone?" he asked calmly.

"Air-to-air hellfire. Enough to take down your friend's plane multiple times."

Fire-and-forget missiles.

Fucking fuck!

The drone didn't need to be in line-of-sight of Matias' plane to hit it with those missiles. They were self-guided. But someone, sitting somewhere in a remote terminal, had to control the drone and pull the trigger.

"Where's the operator?" he growled.

"You'll meet him when we arrive."

"What are the orders?"

"The operator will shoot down the plane at precisely twenty-three hundred."

That was two hours away, which might've felt like plenty of time if she hadn't mentioned a ticking clock more than once.

"Call it off." He tightened his grip on the 9mm. "I'll triple what they're paying you."

"I'm not the one holding the trigger."

Which was why they sent her and not the operator.

"You can make demands, offer bribes, or shoot me with that gun." She shrugged. "The operator will not abort."

"Unless?"

"Unless you and I arrive at his location by twenty-three hundred. No exceptions. If we hurry, we'll make it there with five minutes to spare. I'll even let you watch him call off the strike."

His heart hammered, and adrenaline flooded his system. "Who ordered this?"

"No more questions." She clicked her tongue. "Tick-tock."

If he could get a message to Matias, maybe his pilot could evade the danger. But it was too risky. Matias' luxury aircraft was designed for one purpose only. To transport people. It didn't have the speed or artillery to engage an armed drone.

"I know what you're thinking." She stowed the tablet in the pack on her bike, her accent grating. "If your friends deviate from their course or try to escape the drone, it will fire."

His jaw clenched, his options dwindling with the countdown of the clock.

He would kill for his friends.

But would he hand himself over and endure torture for them?

Would he die for them?

THREE

Eleven years ago, the *activity* deployed Cole overseas to complete a job. His last job. Upon his return, he intended to retire, marry his dancer, and live a normal, innocuous life in the suburbs.

The assignment was standard undercover work. He was sent to infiltrate the Romanian mafia, root out a leak of classified information, and return home. He expected to finish within a year.

But when he discovered the source of the leak was Marie Merivale, his trusted partner and ex-lover, his entire world imploded.

She'd taken a bribe from the mafia, betrayed Cole and her country for money, and because she knew he would figure it out, she made damn sure she was ready for him.

When he caught her in France on Thurney Bridge, they stood in a face-off, guns aimed. Until she held up her phone and showed him a live video of an assassin in Danni's house.

There was no leverage more powerful than a

threat to Danni's life.

He had a split-second to make a decision. Let Marie kill him and save Danni. Or kill Marie and guarantee Danni's death.

Lucky for him, Marie didn't know about the high-tech, bullet-resistant clothing he wore under his jacket.

He let her shoot him.

The bullet hit his chest, fractured his ribs, and sent him crashing into the river below. When he didn't surface, Marie believed he was dead. Everyone believed it. His unit, his employer, Trace, Danni…

Danni grieved his death for three years while he remained hidden, covertly hunting Marie.

The fucking bitch was a trained operative, same as him, and always a step ahead. But he had the element of surprise. She thought he was dead.

Maybe he should've killed her when he caught her, but she wasn't a threat now. It'd taken him three years, but she was finally in prison, serving a life sentence without parole.

All of this flashed through his mind with a horrifying sense of *déjà vu* as he stared at the Russian woman. She'd shown him a video, threatened his friends, and now, in a race against the clock, he had a decision to make.

But this time, it wasn't as simple as kill or be killed. Bullet-resistant clothing and a fake death wouldn't get him out of this.

If he shot the woman, his friends would die. If he died, his friends would die. If he pretended to die, his friends would die.

The only way to save them was to go with her.

But if he did that, he faced gruesome, prolonged torture. They would methodically rip him apart until they extracted what they wanted from his mind.

Unless this was about revenge. In that case, torture would serve no purpose beyond their sick enjoyment. Electrocution, starvation, dismemberment—the ways a man could die were limited only by the imagination.

"It's a two-hour ride." She leaned a hip against the motorcycle and tapped her fingers on the seat. "We're officially late."

There was only one thing he could do in the face of such grim inevitability. He had to trick his brain into fighting for a sense of control and dignity.

Straightening his spine, he pulled in a slow, deep breath.

He wouldn't die for his friends.

He would go with the woman and find a way to survive for them.

"I'm driving." Everything inside him hardened as he regarded the motorcycle, its tires and suspension, and the spare helmet on the back. "I'll get us there in time."

"Leave your weapons and communication equipment."

He ejected the round from his pistol and tossed it. The knife from his boot went next.

With razor-sharp focus, he felt nothing as he switched on the transmitter. "Come in, *esé*."

"Go ahead," Van said.

His entire team was tuned in, listening. Dammit, there was no easy way to say this and no time to mince his words. "Our aircraft has a drone on its tail. Armed with hellfire, it will shoot down our plane at twenty-three hundred unless I arrive at the designated place and time with this Russian cunt."

He glared at her.

She glared back.

The radio went silent. He had to give it to his friends. He'd just delivered the worst news imaginable, and not one of them lost their shit. Not outwardly. They kept it locked down tight. Because they were survivors.

They would survive this, along with every person on that plane.

"I'm going with her," he said. "Listen carefully. This is important. Contact the pilot and tell him not to deviate from his course. I repeat. Do not change course. Do not engage the drone. Or it will strike. Follow these orders, and our aircraft will land safely."

"Copy." Fury leaked through Van's voice. "Do you know who these fuckers are?"

"Negative."

"How do we find you?"

"You don't."

"We will, goddammit. We'll be there with an army."

"When the plane lands, I need you to disappear. All of you. Go somewhere I don't know about."

"They're going to fucking torture you."

"I need you alive, *esé*. Do exactly what I said. Out." He turned off the transmitter and dropped it in the sand. The earpiece followed.

His pulse throbbed in his temples as he shifted toward the house. He couldn't see Tate or Lucia on the roof, but they could see him. They'd heard him on the radio, and they could hear him now as he said, "Stand down."

They weren't stupid enough to interfere, but he wasn't taking chances.

"Now, I will search you for weapons." The

Russian's silky accent whispered against his nape, close enough to raise the hairs there. "It'll be better for you if you arrive unarmed."

"Better how? Less torture?"

"Shh." She smoothed her hands down his stiff back and palmed his ass, searching, teasing. She continued down his legs to his boots. "You're well-built. Strong. Virile." She worked her way back up, circling to his front. "Don't let it give you a false sense of power. Physical strength won't save you."

She stood before him, her intelligent green eyes fixed on his. Then her hand lowered, gliding between his legs and probing his cock through the jeans.

His body reacted, heating his skin and scratching his voice. "Your name?"

"Lydia."

"That your real name?"

"Yes." She closed her fingers around the outline of his semi-hard dick. "Impressive."

"Don't let it give you a false sense of power. It's simple biology. You're not special."

The corner of her flirty lips kicked up, her eyes glimmering with a look that made his skin shiver and heat.

"You don't know where we're going." She stepped back and tossed him the spare helmet. "Without me, you won't reach the destination and save your friends. Remember that before you throw me off the bike."

That was the only reason he hadn't smashed in her face.

Helmet on, he straddled the motorcycle and fired up the engine. The impulse to give Tate and Lucia a parting glance pulled at him, but he didn't give into it.

He focused forward, on the bleak horizon, and steeled himself for the worst.

She slid on behind him, her thighs hugging his hips and hands clasped low on his abdomen. "Head east."

He opened the throttle and shot off into the dark. The uneven terrain hindered his speed. Once he hit pavement, he would have to make up precious time.

The roar of the engine made conversation impossible. Just as well. The ride would give him time to go over things in his head.

For the next twenty minutes, he analyzed everything Lydia had said, looking for clues and hidden meanings. She never mentioned Danni or Trace, and she wouldn't know the *activity* even existed. But whoever she worked for was connected to Thurney Bridge.

He recalled the few interactions he'd had with Russian constituents over his career and couldn't trace any of it back to his last assignment. Lydia's nationality most likely had nothing to do with him. Unless her counterparts were Russian, too. He would find that out soon enough.

The off-road tires sailed across the sand, the desert a graveyard of shadows and scattered holes. Silhouettes of cacti rose up like headstones, the wind warm and invasive. Like her hands.

As his shirt billowed up his torso, her fingers followed, exploring the ridges of his abs. He forced indifference into his posture, neither leaning in nor shoving her away. He refused to give her the satisfaction of a response.

She pressed closer, her hot body flush to his back, as her hand slid between his legs, finding him soft. But not for long.

His lungs expanded with dusty air, his cock thickening. She didn't rub him or open his fly. She simply rested her fingers there, curled around his growing bulge.

It was torture. He wanted her to stroke him, to pull him out and give him a fleeting moment of pleasure before his world became nothing but pain.

But he had far more control than that. In seven years, he hadn't acted on his carnal impulses. Didn't stop his mind from placing her lips around him. He let the fantasy distract him for a few minutes, sinking into images of his cock buried in her throat, her cunt, and deep in her ass.

He had a penchant for anal—the strangling tightness, the forbidden nature of it, and the punishing fear it evoked. Just thinking about it made him hard as a rock.

Lydia squeezed his length, acknowledging his body's reaction. Good for her. If she had any intentions of using sex to manipulate him, she had the wrong guy.

Getting off wasn't high on his personal agenda. His only priority was protecting the people he cared about, and to do that, he needed to arrive at the destination without crashing.

So he shut down the fantasy, shut out the feel of her hand, and concentrated on navigating the sandy land.

She steered him through the darkness, pointing this way and that. No one could find their way out of this desert without a map or GPS. Except Tomas. But she didn't falter in her directions.

Given the high-tech bugs in Rylee's house and the armed drone tracking Matias' aircraft, he assumed

Lydia's helmet was equipped with the necessary communication equipment to guide her back to civilization.

At last, he reached the main road, the pavement giving him license to open the gas and fly. She tightened her arms around his waist, hugging his back with her entire body as he bent into the wind.

If a cop clocked him for speeding, he would just have to ride faster and outrace the patrolman. He wasn't stopping for anyone or anything.

His pulse revved with the roar of the engine, the bike vibrating between his legs. For the next hour or so, he didn't pass another motorist. Vacant fueling stations and diners blurred by. No cop cars in sight.

The dark nothingness pushed his thoughts into dangerous introspection. He had one goal—arrive before twenty-three hundred. Beyond that, he was terrified of what was going to happen.

Torture was barbaric and uncivilized, but it was effective. Whatever these people wanted, he most likely wouldn't be able to surrender it.

They were going to make him hurt.

Would it be more than he could bear? Probably. Would he survive it? Maybe not. But he'd been trained for this. Trained to put labels on his thoughts and compartmentalize his feelings, all in an effort to gain a sense of control in a situation where he had no control over the process or the pain.

Lydia directed him off the main highway. From there, he took narrow back roads through a desolate wasteland. The few buildings he passed were closed-up and crumbling. The skeletal remains of a ghost town.

He wasn't familiar with this part of Texas. While it seemed they'd been traveling southward most of the journey, there had been a number of turns, and he didn't know how much time had passed.

As the clock ticked toward twenty-three hundred, did he have thirty minutes left? Five? None?

The uncertainty pushed him faster, his pulse racing with urgency.

She touched his forearm and motioned to veer right just as a turnoff came into view. It was an entrance to something, the property encircled by a tall, unkempt chain-link fence. The enclosure served more as a boundary marker than a security measure.

Moving closer, he spotted a large industrial building in the distance. No lights or signs of life. *Weird.*

He sped through an unmanned gate and passed several empty parking lots. The property appeared to be vacant. Until he circled the side.

At least a dozen vehicles sat along an old loading dock. She indicated for him to park there, and the moment he turned off the engine, he yanked off the helmet.

"What time is it?" He twisted, hauling her off the motorcycle with him, hurrying her along. "Call off the strike."

She reached around him and grabbed the key from the ignition, pocketing it.

His palms slicked with sweat as she removed her helmet. His mouth dried as she shook out her hair, taking her sweet-ass time. His blood pressure climbed as she pulled the tablet from her pack.

"Look at that." She smiled at the screen, her accent thickening. "Two minutes to spare."

"We're here. Call it off."

Her incisive gaze traveled down his body. "Remove your clothes."

FOUR

Lydia held the smile on her face, but inside she felt cold. Merciless. There was no room for anything else. Cole Hartman was a doorway, and she would cut her way through him to reach the other side.

His nostrils flared, and his neck corded, muscles and veins straining against his skin. He planted his boots wide apart, seething, damn near shaking with fury and fear.

Yes, fear. He was a battle-honed tough guy, but he had a weakness. An aircraft full of weaknesses. In his line of work, he knew better than to get attached to people. That was his own fucking fault.

"We had a deal." He stepped into her space, his rock-hard chest in her face.

Christ, he smelled good. Wild and earthy, like the dusty wind on a dark road. Dangerous and sexy, like the brawn flexing beneath his shirt.

He was gorgeous beyond all sense of the word. With that chiseled body and those fathomless brown eyes, he could crush a perfectly good heart.

Good thing she didn't have one.

She glanced at the clock on the tablet. "One minute."

His lips curled back, baring straight white teeth in the moonlight. And dimples. A pair of them bracketed his enraged scowl, forming deep divots in his beard. Cute. Like a furious grizzly bear.

With a snarl, he reached over his head and grabbed the back of his shirt, yanking it off in that way men did. Tattoos covered his sinewy arms and sculpted chest. Almost as many as she had. But where her ink glowed with color, his were black, the images impossible to make out in the dark.

He held her gaze as he toed off his boots and unbuttoned his jeans. He didn't look away as he shoved down his pants and kicked them off.

"Call off the drone." He regarded her with an unflinching glare, fully nude and chillingly stoic.

As much as she wanted to look down, she didn't check out his body. She refused to break eye contact. Not even as the door opened and armed men spilled outside.

"Your friends are safe." She watched his expression relax a half-second before it hardened again. "Show Mr. Hartman the live video."

Someone appeared at her side. Without glancing, she knew it was Mike. No one looked at her like he did, the heat of his gaze flickering over her, searching for injuries.

He already knew she was unharmed. The technology in her helmet had allowed them to communicate while she was away. But he wasn't rational when it came to her safety.

He was insanely overprotective.

Holding a laptop, he pivoted the screen toward Cole. It showed the Colombian cartel jet coasting at a distance ahead of the drone. A moment later, the drone veered off, changing course, the strike aborted.

Cole stood motionless, except his eyes. They tracked the screen, his expression showing no hint of relief.

It had taken months of digging and a Hail Mary plan to locate the cartel's private aircraft. They had multiple hangars in South America, all of which were monitored for activity by her team. She'd hoped Cole's most powerful ally, Matias Restrepo, would make the journey to Texas, but she hadn't known when or who would be with him.

She'd lucked out when the whole damn crew boarded that plane.

Without a word, she grabbed Cole's clothes and strode toward the building. Her fifteen-man team moved in around him, heavily armed and highly trained. They were hardened soldiers, their backgrounds diverse, spanning from criminal to retired military. But they were all here for the same reason. A paycheck.

Could they be bribed to switch sides? Not easily. But everyone had a price. If Cole made the right offer, maybe he could gain an ally among her crew.

For that reason, no one would be allowed near him unless she or Mike were present.

She entered through the loading dock, confident that Cole wouldn't give them any problems. If he tried to escape, they would shoot to wound, not to kill. He was worthless to her dead.

He was also too smart to run. Without clothes or transportation, he wouldn't get far in the desert.

Past the loading ramps, she turned into a spartan corridor. Dust coated the concrete walls and floors. Overhead, stark fluorescent lights illuminated layers of sand that had crept in from outside and gritty powder left over from the raw materials that had once been hauled in and out of this building.

Years ago, a manufacturing company used this warehouse to split and carve granite blocks into monuments, mausoleums, crypts, and headstones.

She'd needed a secure, out-of-the-way place to do this job, and this was what she got. A building where tombs had been made. *Fitting.*

At the end of the corridor, she passed the factory floor. All that remained were piles of discarded granite and limestone, broken machinery, and dust. Powdery residue clung to everything, each step stirring it into the air and making her sneeze.

She turned away, taking another hallway toward their makeshift quarters.

Over the past four months, they'd converted the storage rooms into private sleeping spaces, hauling in mattresses and other comforts when they weren't hunting and planning and preparing for the right moment to take Cole Hartman.

Getting him here was the easy part. A long, arduous road lay ahead, and by God, she was ready. She'd waited eleven years for this, and she was so close to the end. So fucking close she could taste it.

In her room, she changed into lounge pants and a soft t-shirt. A wobbly old table sat in the corner, covered in cosmetics and beauty supplies. She slumped into the chair and began the mindless task of removing false eyelashes and cleansing away makeup.

That done, she grabbed a bag of Twizzlers and

flopped onto her back on the mattress. Pulling out a long red rope of candy, she chewed on the end, lost in thought.

It was after midnight when the door to her room opened. Mike stepped in, carrying a microwaved burrito on a paper plate.

She shoved the half-eaten bag of candy beneath her. Too late.

He pounced, snatching the Twizzlers and dropping the plate on the bed beside her.

"I'm not eating that." She shoved away the food.

He pushed it back. "You need protein, not empty calories." He tossed the candy on the table.

"There's nothing more unhealthy than a frozen burrito."

"Say that again." He crawled onto the mattress, grinning.

Oh, man. She was a sucker for his crooked Bruce Willis smile. He looked like a younger version of the actor—all cocky and handsome with that indestructible, blue-collar edge that women loved. He also brought a level of warmth and humor that no one saw but her.

Mike was her rock, and every day at his side was a good day to die hard.

"Say what again?" She blinked, playing dumb.

"You know what." He grabbed the burrito and shoved it against her mouth.

"Burrito," she muttered around the dried-out shell.

"I love the way you say those *Rs* in that accent." He tipped his head, biting down on his grin. "Like they're stuck in your throat, and you have to hack them out."

"Shut up."

"Eat." He pressed the burrito to her hand.

She pouted but didn't have many options. The only food around here was either frozen or in a can.

While she gave in and ate, he stripped down to his briefs and stretched out on the mattress beside her. There were other rooms and other beds, but he never left her alone at night. As the only woman among a team of single, testosterone-fueled men, she was grateful he had her back.

Neither she nor Mike selected the men assigned with them. Before this job, they didn't know any of these people. She could count on them to obey orders and earn their wages, but she didn't trust them.

She didn't trust anyone but Mike.

With her dinner eaten and the lights off, she collapsed against him, tucked under a muscled arm with her cheek on his chest. His hand found hers, twining their fingers together.

As much as she didn't want to think about Cole, the instant she closed her eyes, all she saw were his. Huge brown eyes. Disarmingly intelligent.

"How did our prisoner react to his room?" she asked.

"As you would expect."

"He didn't react."

"Nope. No last-ditch attempts to escape. No struggle. Not a twitch behind that beard."

Her chest constricted. "He's smart."

"He's trained. But we've gone up against harder men than him."

"Maybe."

"It's not too late to cut our losses and get *F* out of *H*."

"Are you serious?" She popped up, glaring at

him in the dark. "What the hell, Mike?"

"Calm down. I was just tossing it out there." He gripped a lock of her hair and pulled. "Come here."

She went, returning her head to his chest. "We have to finish this."

"I know."

"No matter what."

His silence rang through the room, his objections deafening. She wriggled closer, resting her brow against his whiskered cheek. His jaw felt like steel, his entire body rigid with tension.

They'd argued about her role in this job, and he wasn't over it.

"I can do this." She ran a hand over his neatly trimmed crew cut, trying to soothe him.

"What if you can't? What if he's as unflappable on the inside as he is on the surface?"

"Everyone has a breaking point. I'll find his."

FIVE

How many days had Cole been in here? Had it been a week? Longer? He hugged his knees to his chest, his body naked and filthy, every inch covered in itchy dust.

No use trying to find a comfortable position on the hard floor. The cell was designed for misery.

Dirty.

Empty.

Pitch-black.

He only saw daylight twice a day when someone opened the door to toss in food and switch out the buckets. A bucket for drinking and a bucket for shitting. Christ, he hoped they didn't mix up the two.

While lying on the cold concrete and living off a repulsive diet of frozen hot dogs, he was forced to listen to the same aggressive, head-pounding, thrash metal song over and over and over. It was a three-minute meth binge on repeat, delivered at a blistering velocity that tried to rip off his fucking face.

He used to love hardcore music, but after a few days of guttural vocals and distorted riffs, the genre was ruined for him. He didn't recognize the song. Not at first. Now he knew every raging word and shredded guitar chord. He hated it. He wanted to stab his goddamn ears with an ice pick.

It was truly painful, digging under his skin and dry-humping at his last nerve.

But that was the point.

Psychological torture.

The only time they shut it off was when they opened the door. He tried not to anticipate those moments, but there was nothing else to do but wait.

And wait.

And wait.

At last, the song fell silent.

He didn't move, didn't lift his head from his bent knees. He could still hear the rampant adrenaline of music, the pounding discord permanently embedded in his eardrums.

Footsteps entered his cell, and three frozen hot dogs landed on the floor beside him, rolling in the dust.

He snatched them up and didn't hesitate to shove the processed meat into his mouth, dirt and all. Eating these things cold made his stomach turn, but he preferred that over lukewarm meat. The ice coating assured him they hadn't been sitting out. They should be safe from contamination and food poisoning.

Swallowing the last bite, he hungered for more. But it was always the same. Three hot dogs per visit. Two visits a day.

As an unarmed man swapped out the buckets, Cole stole a peek at the old factory floor beyond.

Piles of stones, discarded materials, and abandoned machinery lay beneath a coating of dust. Amid the waste material, he identified broken headstones.

It was a clue. But without any knowledge of headstone companies in Texas, it didn't help him determine his location.

Not that he could escape.

A group of men stood just outside the door to his cell. Never less than six in total and always armed. None of them spoke Russian.

He would have to physically overpower them before they fired a weapon.

Impossible.

Any attempt to run would only get him injured, and up until now, they hadn't inflicted so much as a bruise. So he remained motionless during their visits, biding his time.

With the buckets refreshed, the guard stepped out. But today, the door didn't close.

The others moved out of view, their footsteps retreating but not going far. Then a tread of clicking steps approached. A slow, confident gait. Click-clack. Click-clack.

He hadn't heard this one since he'd been thrown in this room, but he knew who it was before she appeared in the doorway.

Cheetah-print pants molded to her sexy figure, and her low-cut white shirt had a skull-and-bones pirate flag across the front.

Her fire-engine red hair was pulled into two high pigtails, leaving wisps of long bangs around her face. Same heavy makeup as the night he'd met her, her fuckable lips shiny with wet gloss.

Leaning a shoulder against the door frame, she raised a rope of red licorice to her mouth and nibbled on the end.

He rested his head back against the wall, watching her with lazy detachment.

"Are you hungry?" She bit off a length of the candy, holding it between her white teeth before slurping it into her mouth. "You look like you could use some sugar."

He would kill for a taste of anything but hot dogs, but he wasn't playing her games.

"You haven't spoken since you arrived." She tapped the licorice against her mouth.

At some point, she would tell him why he was here and what they wanted. Until then, silence was the only control he had over her.

She took a visible breath, straining the fabric of the shirt across her tits. Full, beautifully shaped tits that would more than fill his hands.

Her eyes, dark green in the distance. Her lips, a deadly trap around the candy. Her body, toned with muscle and curved to perfection. Yeah, if he were another man in a different situation, he would fuck the shit out of her.

But he wasn't. He didn't pursue women or harbor sexual fantasies about his enemies.

"You can get out of here." She strolled toward him and crouched at his side, smothering his senses in her soft feminine scent. "You can have all the candy you want, the food you crave, a comfortable bed, and a woman to warm it." She tilted her head, regarding him intently. "Multiple women, if that's your thing."

His lip curled. He couldn't help it. He didn't want anyone in his bed but Danni. His appetite for sex was constant, but wanting and doing were two different things. Celibacy was a choice. His self-punishment. God knew he deserved worse after the torment he'd put

Danni through.

"Do you want a shower?" She reached out and touched his forehead, gently brushing his greasy hair from his eyes. "You want a toothbrush and clean clothes?" Her fingers drifted to his beard, softly stroking. "You can live like a free man. Or you can die like a prisoner on death row."

If revenge was her endgame, she wouldn't be dangling rewards in front of him.

She wanted something from him.

He waited for it, his heart thundering in his chest. What would she demand in exchange for the bullshit she offered?

She glanced down, taking in his nude form. With his knees to his chest and his feet tucked against him, she couldn't see much.

Not that he cared. She could stare all she wanted. She could tease him, touch him, bludgeon him, and cut off his limbs. As long as he had breath in his body, he would not cower to her or her band of merry men.

"I have plans for you, Cole Hartman." She put her face in his, her lips so close he could almost taste the sticky candy on them. "But we have time, and I'm a very patient woman."

She rose and strode toward the door, her spine straight, almost regal, with her pigtails spiraling down her back in tangled glory.

At the threshold, she paused, glancing back. "Think about what I said. We'll talk again in a week or two."

A week or *two*? His molars slammed together, every muscle in his body stiffening to lunge and drag her back. But that was what she wanted. She was baiting him.

He reined in his fear and fought down his anger, blanking his face and maintaining his silence. He gave the bitch nothing, and she gave nothing back.

Except a closed door and inky darkness.

Then the music restarted, striking his ears with a vengeance.

SIX

Days passed. A week. Maybe more. The perpetual isolation wore on Cole, his entire world reduced to hot dogs and the same soul-sucking song on repeat.

He kept his mind and body busy with exercise. Push-ups, sit-ups, lunges, running in place—his options were limited in the confined space. He was losing weight at a rapid pace, and his energy and strength suffered for it.

There were moments when he was convinced that electrocution or dismemberment would've been better. Every minute in the darkness lasted an eternity, every visit from the guards a plaguing disappointment.

He'd never felt so trapped. Restless. Hungry. Unraveling at the seams. They'd kicked open the gates of hell and unleashed a level of torture that left him hopeless and walking the edge of insanity.

Okay, maybe that was the lyrics of the song in his ears, but he felt it. He was fucking living it.

Nevertheless, each time the door opened, he kept his shit together. He didn't beg or reveal a trace of emotion. When the guards taunted him, he met their eyes and showed no response.

It required more self-restraint than he thought he was capable. One of these times, he was going to detonate. He could feel himself slipping, losing his hold on his brittle control.

He wanted to kill them all.

The music shut off again, and the door opened to the man he'd met the first night, the one who'd operated the drone. Fuck, that felt like forever ago.

Did his team disappear like he'd ordered? Or were they still in Texas, searching for him?

Locating people was *his* skill set, not theirs. He was the best at extracting information and siphoning minute details. It took time and patience, but he would eventually elicit what he needed from these assholes and use it to escape. But if they got their hands on his friends, they could manipulate him in ways he didn't want to imagine.

"We haven't officially met," the man said. "My name is Mike."

The fact that he looked like Bruce Willis wasn't comforting. Hopefully, Mike would be easier to take down than the action heroes Bruce often portrayed.

"Get dressed." He tossed a pair of jeans into the cell. "I have a job for you."

Relief warred with distrust, coursing through him with numbing adrenaline. He wanted to ask how long he'd been here, but it wasn't an important question. So he saved the words and woodenly shoved his unwashed legs into the jeans.

"Follow me." Mike ambled toward the factory floor, ignoring the armed guards who stood near the only exit.

Cole followed him out while zipping up his fly. The jeans belonged to him but no longer fit. Even with the button fastened, they sagged, hanging loosely below his hipbones. He'd lost too much weight.

It could be worse. He hadn't lost blood or limbs or his sanity.

Not yet.

He stood in a massive, rectangular warehouse the length of a football field with concrete floors and brick walls. The rafters soared several stories above, and windows lined the upper half, far too high to reach. Grime coated the glass, obscuring the view of the sky. But sunlight filtered through the smudges, bright and hot, burning his eyes.

Up ahead, Mike waited with his arms relaxed at his sides and a lopsided smile tipping his mouth. That smile couldn't be trusted, no matter how friendly it appeared.

Cole pulled up his jeans enough to not trip over the dragging cuffs. Then he made his way toward Mike.

Footsteps sounded behind him. Two guards on his trail.

He could disarm one of them and use the weapon to kill them both. Mike didn't appear to be carrying a gun, so Cole could take him out, too. But what about the three men at the exit? And the other ten beyond the door? Since arriving, he'd counted sixteen altogether, including Lydia. If he started a gunfight, he wouldn't make it out alive.

"We're not going far," Mike said over his shoulder, walking ahead.

Pallets of discarded stones and cracked blocks of granite cluttered the length of the warehouse. Steel siding sealed up the doors at the far end. No way out.

So where the hell were they going?

His nerves frayed, his shoulders twitching with the impulse to turn back.

Then he saw her.

Past a wall of crates, she stood with her back to him.

His gaze caught on the shimmering beauty of red hair, the nip of a tiny waist, and the flashing tease of creamy white legs beneath her dress.

A fucking dress. In a headstone factory. In the middle of the desert.

It cinched at her waist and flared out around her knees. Black fabric with red cherries. Red heels with little red bows. Impractical as fuck. Eye-catching beyond reason.

He couldn't stop staring.

She turned, angling her face into the glow of the windows. Pale shimmers of light accentuated the delicate curves of her profile and illuminated the stunning spirals and brilliant red tones of her hair. Her bangs looped into some sort of pompadour at the front, with the side parts rolling under and down. Strangely vintage. Fashionably retro. Her entire look screamed 1950s.

He'd never seen anything so shockingly exquisite, so uniquely beautiful. Flawless skin, luscious lips, and voluptuous curves. A statuesque woman with the appearance of a goddess, the heart of demoness, and a fashion style all her own.

She touched her chin to her shoulder and gave a slow blink, her unnaturally long lashes fanning over porcelain cheeks. Then her sea-green eyes latched onto his.

Their stares locked for a full second. Long enough

to forget where he was or how he got here. A million things needed to be said, but words didn't exist in the space of their eye contact. Only sensations. Buzzing along the skin. Static in the air. Fire over ice in a heart that couldn't melt.

In that unexpected moment between them, he was a normal man, standing before a woman, with a rush of warmth in his chest. She felt it, too, her lips parting, her gaze losing focus. The world blurred, disorientating, and at the same time, perfectly balanced.

She straightened, turning away, and he released a soundless breath, thunderstruck.

And infuriated.

What the fuck just happened? Did they drug the hot dogs? Or was this a side-effect of prolonged isolation?

He was losing his fucking mind.

Nothing about that woman was real. From her dazzling hair color to her cherry red smile, she wore a false face and a glamorous facade.

Mike prowled over to her and slid a hand around her waist with intimate familiarity. She shifted toward him, and their foreheads came together, touching affectionately. He spoke quietly against her mouth and stroked her hair, her arm, her lower back.

The man's entire manner seemed to transform in her presence, his expression softening, shoulders relaxing, his posture leaning as if sucked in by her orbit.

The pathetic fool loved her.

Hard to tell if she reciprocated the sentiment. She didn't reject his touch. She also didn't look at him in the same way. Not in the breathless, gobsmacked way she'd just looked at Cole.

Mike said a few words near her ear and stepped

away, his demeanor hardening, turning cold as he focused on Cole.

"I mentioned a job." He clasped his hands behind him, his head down and eyes up. "We want you to work for us."

Like hell he would.

If it was a reasonable job, they wouldn't have threatened his friends, forced him here against his will, and locked him in isolation. No, they knew he would never agree to this.

Assuming they knew his range of skills, they probably wanted to recruit him for a heist or infiltration mission to steal something of value—a person, a treasure, or priceless information. Whatever it was, the job would be dangerous, undesirable, and in no way worth his time or risk.

Not that they intended to give him a choice.

He met Mike's eyes, exuding the cagey, reticent persona he'd maintained over the past couple of weeks. They had no idea what was going on in his head, if he was slowly going crazy or completely unaffected by the situation.

A silent man who didn't stand up for himself was often perceived as ignorant and malleable. He needed them to underestimate him and would continue to play that role until they let their guards down.

"Now, I know you're thinking you could never work for us. But I have something you won't be able to resist." Mike moved toward the wall of crates and slid a box into view with his boot. "You want to eat like a king?"

From the box, he removed a can of chicken, a bag of potato chips, and a bottle of beer.

Cole's mouth watered at the sight of the beer.

Fucking Christ, what he wouldn't give for a taste of hops on his tongue.

"Yeah, yeah, I know." Mike chuckled. "It's not really a royal feast, but it's better than the alternative, yeah?"

Better than hot dogs? Damn straight.

"The task is simple." Mike tapped his toe against a pallet of broken granite. "Move these pieces to the pallet over there."

He motioned at the empty platform forty yards away.

The rock pile spanned six-feet high by six-feet wide, and each chunk was wider than his chest. Brutally heavy, no question. His back and feet would bear the brunt of it.

Why did they want debris moved from one platform to another? To test his strength? To torture him psychologically? Maybe they were just bored?

"I want my boots."

"Holy shit, he can talk." Mike pointed at him and arched a brow at Lydia. "After sixteen days of silence, I was starting to wonder."

Sixteen fucking days. He'd guessed it had been that long, but hearing it didn't make it easier to stomach. If they owned this building, which was highly likely, this could go on for months.

Unless the thing they wanted from him had a time limit.

"I know it's lonely in that cell, and you're wondering what the point of all this is." Mike patted him on the shoulder. "Well, we're working up to that. Little steps. Right now, those steps go from this pallet to that pallet. Without your boots. Do a good job and you'll get the food in that box."

He needed the carbohydrates. He desperately wanted the beer. But more than that, it was imperative that he spend as much time as possible outside of that cell. Not only for his mental wellbeing but to observe his captors and do what he did best—listen and learn, make small talk and befriend, all the while subtly extracting information.

So without hesitation, he shouldered past Mike and heaved the first hunk of granite from the pile. His muscles strained beneath the eighty-pound weight.

Sixteen days ago, he would've carried it with no trouble. Today, he felt it in his arms, his back, and his feet as he hauled the load across the warehouse.

Mike stepped away, joining the two guards in conversation. They were too far away for Cole to eavesdrop but close enough to shoot him if he decided to slam a rock into Lydia's head.

She perched on a crate beside the full pallet, watching him drop off his burden and walk back. He took his time. No reason to hurry. The longer it took him to move the pile, the longer he was out of the head-banging cell.

Except that bottle of beer was waiting. An effective incentive.

"Your jeans are falling." She crossed one leg over the other and propped an elbow on her knee.

He paused before her, fully aware that his waistband hung obscenely low, exposing the patch of hair above the root of his cock. Her eyes went there, lingering, before lifting to his.

"Such a shame." She sniffed. "You had a beautiful physique when I met you." Her gaze darted toward Mike and the guards and returned to him, her accent lowering. "Do what you're told, and you'll gain back those muscles."

He glanced down at his torso, trying to see what she saw. Was he skinnier? Yeah. But he still had definition. He was still physically stronger than her and could overpower her tiny body if he got her alone.

Hell, if he got her alone, he would wrench that dress over her head and drive his fist between her legs. He would tear up her cunt and fuck her ass until both holes were permanently stretched open, gaping and waiting to receive his cock again.

He didn't have to like her to imagine her wet pussy slurping around his thrusts. In fact, his hatred for her made the fantasy all the more filthy.

"You know what I want?" He lowered his voice, deliberately rumbling the words.

Her eyes dilated, her breaths quickening. "What?"

"*Palimi* with sour cream and caviar."

She flinched, her brows knitting together.

"Russian pancakes." He cocked his head. "Don't you know what that is?"

"Of course, I know. My grandma made them for me." She narrowed her eyes. "You only moved one stone. Are you tired already?"

"Tired of eating processed shit." He leaned down, exhaling in her face. "I want a toothbrush and toothpaste, and right now, I imagine you want me to have those things."

"Finish the job, and I'll think about it." She didn't shift away, but the scrunch of her nose confessed the state of his breath.

Good.

While his whole body needed a thorough cleaning, the fur on his teeth bothered him the most.

He stepped back and dragged another rock off the pile. As he towed it across the warehouse, he felt her gaze on his ass, knowing the top half of his crack hung above the sagging jeans.

Didn't matter how badly he reeked or how much muscle he'd lost. She liked looking at him as much as he liked looking at her. His was an unwanted attraction. Maybe hers was, too.

Or maybe she put on that dress and made up her hair because she wanted him to notice her.

Was she after information in his head? Or was this a ploy to use him and his skill set to acquire something for them?

They had no idea who they were dealing with.

If she intended to seduce him into cooperating, she should start by washing that shit off her face. But even then, she didn't have a chance in hell.

He hoped she planned to use sex to get to him so that it could backfire on her with deadly consequences.

SEVEN

Lydia couldn't ignore the thudding in her ears or the heat swimming in her belly. It produced a terrible glow inside her, giving rise to a complicated question.

What if?

Two simple words, known to spark monumental theories and discoveries. They could also lead to disastrous mistakes.

She wasn't the only one asking the question. It took two to engage in eye contact, and when she and Cole stared at each other, both of them sizzling in the charged air, she saw her reaction on his face. She saw her shock, her curiosity, her *what if?*

Under no circumstances was she expecting his gaze to grab her and twist her up like it did. She wasn't expecting the sheer intensity in his eyes as they imprisoned hers, seeing her as something other than an enemy.

Deep down, beneath the scars of loss and the vitriol that had led her here, she was a woman like any other, with longings and vulnerabilities and dreams that had nothing to do with violence and death.

She'd done well enough to bury that softer side over the past eleven years, and in one goddamn look, Cole Hartman brought it to life.

She blamed the dimples.

And his mysterious confidence.

Not to mention his alluring sex appeal, the rugged build of his powerful body, the sculpted flex of his ass, and the untamed beard that should smell disgusting in its unwashed state but instead only added to his masculine potency.

Damn him for being so devilishly, unfairly handsome.

And damn him for putting these foolish musings in her head.

Watching him heave stone after stone wasn't helping her concentration. She shouldn't be affected. This was a job. If she started warming to him, years of training and sacrifice would be forfeited.

She couldn't afford to lose all the progress she'd made just because the job happened to be a sexy son of a bitch.

She. Could. Not. Fail.

No more what-ifs. No spontaneous explorations of possibilities. Any deviation from the plan was bad for her and this operation. Because one thing was certain. Cole was precisely the type of man who would use her and leave her for dead when he finished.

As he trudged between the pallets, his teeth clenched with exertion. He'd lost muscle mass, but he'd started out with so much. Far more than the average man.

He still had a decent amount of brawn flexing through his frame. And a golden complexion. Pillowy lips. A chiseled face. His expression, when at rest, wore a natural smile. Flirtatious without even trying. Dangerous to the core. He was a gorgeous, tattooed beast.

If she had a type, it was Cole Hartman. She imagined he was every woman's type. Including the one he let go.

Danni Savoy.

The pretty dancer was inked on his forearm amid a collage of unrelated designs and symbols. She glimpsed a motorcycle, an inverted cross, several suns, a leaf, chains, a spider web, and dozens of other illustrations too small to make out at this distance.

The artwork sleeved both arms and half of his chest. And though she hadn't stolen a glimpse of him naked, Mike had mentioned there was a large black snake coiled around his thigh.

This wasn't a guy who put fortuitous ink on his skin. Every piece told a story, a secret, and she wanted to learn them all. Starting with the dancer.

She knew very little about Danni aside from his relationship with her. They'd dated for ten months. Got engaged. Then he took a job that separated them for three years. That job was the reason he lost her to his best friend.

It was also the reason he was here.

Danni was his greatest weakness. She was also untouchable. Married to an obscenely wealthy casino owner, she was surrounded by a team of bodyguards at all times and hadn't left the security of the casino since Lydia's team started watching her.

Cole must've alerted her husband of possible danger. Not that it mattered. Lydia had what she needed to coax Cole into compliance.

If he thought his time in that cell had been unbearable, he had no idea what she was saving him from. She was the only thing standing in the way of his unspeakable suffering.

But if she failed to hold up her end of the bargain, he was a dead man.

Keeping him in the dark—literally and figuratively—was for his own good. And hers. She needed him alive.

Strangely, though, he wasn't demanding answers about why he was here and what they wanted. Wasn't he wondering why she used isolation and thrash metal over common methods of torture? Maybe his silence was some sort of tactic.

Hard to tell what he was thinking. Right now, he appeared fully engrossed in his task. A task that had been designed to test his cooperation. He was smart enough to realize that. But there were so many things he didn't know.

Halfway through the pallet, he took a break, standing beside her and breathing heavily. As he licked his lips, she couldn't look away from that diabolical mouth.

His gaze raked down her body and lingered on her legs. Then it made a return trip, stroking her like fire. A fire she intended to play with.

He met her eyes. "Why are you dressed like that?"

"To keep you guessing." She handed him a bottle of water.

"Here's my guess." He drained the bottle in one long gulp and tossed it aside. "You're an attention whore."

"Do you think I'm a whore because I have your

attention? Or do I have your attention because you think I'm a whore?"

"I think you're trying too hard. You'd get a lot further with me if you spoke clearly, dropped the act, and washed that shit off your face."

Ouch. He didn't like her makeup? Or her accent?

"Oh, Cole." She rose to her feet, the heels putting her at eye-level with his lips. "I want you to accept me for who I pretend to be."

"You're a fucking freak," he said in a deep, resonant voice. No judgment. All heat. "That much is real."

"Yes, and you like it. You like it so much you want to ride it. See where it takes you. But here's a spoiler." She pressed closer, letting her chest brush against his. "It's a ride you won't ever get off."

"Is that what happened to Mike? He hopped on the ride and lost his balls?"

She glanced over his shoulder and found Mike's hard eyes tracking her like a hawk. His scowl conveyed his displeasure, but he wouldn't intervene unless she was in trouble.

"Mike is my partner."

"Do all your partners love you?"

Nope. Just one.

She rested a palm on the warm, hard ridge of his pec. "I have that effect on people."

"Not on me, darlin'." He bent in, his breath hot against her mouth. "If you want to turn me into a boy toy, if that's your big plan, you need a new one."

Slowly, he edged closer, deleting the space between their lips. His hand slid beneath her hair and around her nape. Warm fingers. Calloused and strong. His beard tickled her chin. Scratchy. Musky. All man.

The heat of his mouth blanketed hers. Taunting. Not quite touching.

Her throat went dry, and uncertainty dipped in her gut as she waited, dreading, anticipating. It was the longest second of her life.

But he didn't kiss her. Instead, he scraped his teeth against her upper lip, biting at the flesh above. Then he surprised her again by stepping back, his gaze strangely vacant.

Her skin tingled where his teeth had been. She reached up to touch beneath her nose and… "The fuck?"

The piercing was gone. He'd bitten the jewelry right out of her lip.

He angled toward the pallet and spat the tiny stone stud into the rock debris.

"How?" She trailed her tongue along the inside of her lip, seeking the tiny hole. "There was a back on it."

"Not anymore." He gave her a smile that he'd borrowed from Satan himself. A beautiful smile. Cruel. And far too smug for her liking.

She wanted to smack it off his face. So she did. With an open palm, she slapped him hard, sending an echoing *whack* through the warehouse.

It only made his smirk widen, lighting up his eyes. He didn't even flinch.

"Mighty arrogant," she said, "for a guy who's looking at another two weeks in isolation."

"You won't put me in there that long again." He turned away, grabbed a rock from the pile, and trucked it toward the other pallet.

"Why is that?"

"You'll miss me." He chucked the stone, landing it perfectly onto the platform and saving himself a few steps.

Miss him? She didn't even know him. That was the problem.

She knew he was allied with the Colombian cartel, was in love with a married woman who lived in St. Louis, had a team of criminals whose identities couldn't be traced. And he had information. Extremely valuable information that she needed.

Unfortunately, this wasn't a job she could just aim a gun at and demand compliance. It required discretion, delicate handling, and perfect timing.

She met Mike's narrowed gaze across the warehouse. He looked angry. And concerned. He didn't think she could pull this off, but she didn't have a choice.

Cole lumbered back and forth between the pallets, hauling rocks, working muscles, silent and watchful. His eyes were always watching, studying everything and everyone around him.

As he neared the bottom of the pile, he bent to snatch a large chunk of granite. A sharp hiss sounded beneath his breath, and he jerked back, empty-handed.

The piece he'd attempted to lift had a wicked sharp edge, and now, it was stained in blood.

For a moment, he just stood there, his brown eyes fixated on his hand. Beads of crimson welled from a deep gash on his palm and trickled down his fingers, dripping from the tips.

Momentary shock held her immobile, her pulse propelling through her veins. He didn't move, either, probably stunned by the pain.

The gush of blood didn't slow. Rivers of it collected in a growing puddle on the floor between them.

"Put pressure on it." She glanced around for something to stanch the flow.

There was nothing soft or clean in the vicinity. It was a stone factory, for fuck's sake. All hard surfaces and layers of dust.

"Shall I use my filthy hand to put pressure on it?" He cocked his head, chillingly calm. "Or some other part of my unwashed body?"

There was a first-aid kit somewhere in the private quarters. She shrugged.

"You didn't throw me in that room for sixteen days to let an infection take me." His gaze lowered, scrutinizing the material of her dress.

She stepped back, gripping the skirt. "I'm not destroying my clothes to bandage your hand."

"Give me your underwear."

Her head jerked back, her mind running at top speed. But once she got over the shock of his command, she saw it as an opportunity to negotiate.

"There's a rumor going around." She toyed with a lock of her hair. "They say you won't touch a woman."

His jaw twitched, his expression otherwise blank.

"Is it because of her?" She directed her eyes to the dancer tattooed on his arm. "I know you still love Danni. But it's been seven years. You let her go and yet, you're still faithful to her?"

That prompted a reaction. His nostrils pulsed. His shoulders tightened, his whole body fighting to rein in his temper.

"That's right, Cole. I know her name. I know what she means to you, and I know she lives in the penthouse of The Regal Arch Casino and Hotel in St. Louis."

He squeezed his hands into fists, wringing a torrent of blood onto the floor.

"I'll give you my panties if you give me something in return." She winged up a brow.

His eyes fired menacingly, his mouth a slash of unholy objection.

"Calm down." She softened her accent. "This is easy. Just tell me the last time you had sex."

He drew in a long breath through his nose, released it, and said nothing.

"Be reasonable," she said. "You're so close to eating a decent meal. Just give me an honest answer. Then you can wrap up that hand and finish the last few stones."

He straightened his spine and took a step forward. She held her ground, gazes locked.

His heat enveloped her, his scent ripe with sweat and dark masculinity as he put his mouth near her cheek.

"Seven years." His head tipped, his eyes sharp, confident, and oh-so-close. "The panties. Now."

EIGHT

Seven years.

Holy.

Fuck.

Her heart galloped at his proximity, the authority in his voice, and the implication of his words.

Seven years ago, Cole ended his relationship with the woman he loved. Yet he'd remained faithful to her all this time?

Whatever the reason, his answer filled Lydia's chest with giddy warmth. Too much. Damn her, but she respected his self-restraint at a depth that had nothing to do with the job.

There was something so very appealing and admirable about a man who didn't fuck everything in a skirt. And let's be clear. He absolutely could. With a crook of his finger, he could have any woman—single, married, or cloistered in a convent—on her back and moaning beneath him. The man was virile. Sexually charged. A deadly ladykiller.

And celibate.

How rare was that? It told her that sex meant something to him. It also confessed an inhuman degree of self-control. She couldn't abstain like that. She'd never even tried.

Christ, what would it be like with him? Seven years of pent-up intensity? The hunger and urgency? The explosiveness? She couldn't fathom it.

She would soon find out. Except it wouldn't be real. The only relationship she could entertain with him was a false one, steeped in lies and coercion.

Even so, she never backed out of a promise.

Without breaking eye contact, she reached beneath the dress and dragged down her panties. He didn't give her space, not an inch, as she carefully worked the silk past her hips without flashing the room.

In the bent position, her gaze went straight to his fly. It was right there, clinging precariously to the bulge beneath and exposing a trim patch of hair. Amid the short brown curls lay the base of his cock, thick and angled down, trapped by the sagging waistband. Even in his flaccid state, the root was substantial, promising the rest of him would be more than satisfying.

She wanted it. The dirtiness. The wrongness of it. She wanted *him*.

But this wasn't about her.

"I'm waiting." He yanked up his jeans, covering himself and breaking the spell.

She swallowed and let the underwear drop to her ankles. Then she straightened and met his eyes.

If he wanted the panties, he would have to get them himself.

He didn't waver.

Lowering to a crouch, he touched his uninjured hand to the back of her heel. She lifted it just enough to allow the garment to slip free. He moved to her other leg, repeating the action. Only this time, his hand lingered.

She stared straight ahead, trying not to react, even as every molecule in her body homed in on his touch.

Four fingertips, like four low-burning flames, ghosted up her ankle. The pressure was so subtle she wondered if she imagined it. But the goosebumps… Dear lord, she was shivering, burning up, unable to rein in her breathing.

The pads of his fingers traveled up her calf and teased the back of her knee. Her legs liquefied, her thighs aching to part, causing her heels to totter ever-so-slightly. He noticed and closed his hand around her leg, steadying her.

Her cheeks caught fire, her palms hot and clammy. She lifted her foot, stepping out of the panties and away from his torturous touch.

Slowly, he rose to his feet, all six feet and then some soaring over her. Her heart beat uncontrollably. Her lungs panted, her entire body flushed and overheated. And he looked aloof. Unfazed. Disinterested.

Cold as ice.

His indifference didn't thaw as he lowered his attention to the red silk in his hand. With a clinical efficiency, he wrapped the material around his injury, staring directly at her as he used his teeth to tie it off.

She didn't move. She couldn't. The man was fucking potent.

Then, as if nothing had happened, he returned to the pallet and resumed his task.

Really, nothing had happened. Nothing had

changed.

Except the entire atmosphere had changed. It felt heavy and loud, buzzing along her skin and choking her lungs. Fucking hell, she needed to get out of here and breathe in some fresh air.

But the masochist in her waited.

She waited until he finished. Then she waited as he sat on the floor and tucked into his hard-earned meal. She couldn't detach her gaze from his strong throat as he drank deep swigs of beer. The pleasure on his face was glorious, breathtaking, and inconceivably mesmerizing.

He didn't speak while he ate, but his eyes stayed with her, watching her while he chewed, contemplating her while he finished off the beer with relish.

The muffled conversation between Mike and the guards drifted from across the warehouse. They'd remained within eyeshot, but she barely noticed them.

When Cole swallowed the last bite, he set the empty containers aside and stared at the red silk around his hand. Moments passed before he met her eyes and asked the question she'd been waiting to hear.

"Why am I here?"

"You have something I need." At his silence, she sighed. "Eleven years ago, information of political value fell into the hands of a bad actor."

His stare was steady, unflinching. "Was it stolen from the U.S. government?"

"Something like that."

"Digital property?"

"Yes."

"Who stole it?"

"Marie Merivale." She pursed her lips. "You caught her and put her in prison for life, but the digital property is still missing. I need you to tell me who bought it from her."

He made a low whistling sound and leaned back against the crate behind him. "Who do you think I am?"

Retired military? Undercover operative? Secret agent? The sexiest James Bond in real-life and fantasy? Who the fuck knew?

All she had to go on were rumors. His name was whispered in the shadows of the underground criminal world from Bucharest to Bogota. Too much talk from the women about his sex life—or lack thereof. Not enough talk from the men about his business dealings—no one really knew. But the gossip about his alliance with the Restrepo Cartel had proved true.

As far as she could discern, he once worked for a U.S. agency. But now, he reported to no one and operated outside the boundaries of the law.

"It doesn't matter who you are, Cole. I'm only interested in what you know. I need the name of the entity who bought that stolen property."

"And I need a toothbrush."

"I told you I would think about it."

"Who do you work for?" He drew up a knee and dangled his injured hand over it, regarding her with lazy detachment. "You're not secret intelligence. Definitely not U.S. government."

She smiled. "Does the accent give it away?"

"No, your lack of knowledge does."

She tried not to be offended, but he hit the mark. She'd been trained by a battle-hardened spy, but she didn't work for the NSA or any other agency. She wasn't in the know about domestic or foreign affairs.

She was completely out of her league.

"Why would stolen intel from eleven years ago

have any relevance today?" he asked.

That got her attention. If he'd known anything about the information she sought, he wouldn't have asked that question.

"How do you not know?" She searched his eyes, her mind spinning. "You took down the defector who sold the intel, but you didn't know what that intel was?"

He just stared at her.

Well, this was unexpected, but it changed nothing. If anything, it gave her more leverage. He didn't care about the missing property. His only stake in this was his survival.

"How do you know about Thurney Bridge?" he asked.

What? She searched her memory and came up blank. She had no idea what he was talking about.

Hiding her confusion, she tucked away his question to investigate later. "Tell me who bought the stolen intel."

"I don't know."

His tone held conviction, his gaze unblinking. She almost believed him. Almost.

A lot of money, time, and risk had been put into Cole Hartman's capture because he was the only one close to Marie Merivale. He might not have known what she was selling, but he knew every person involved, including the buyer.

Lydia's team had made numerous attempts to interrogate Marie. Fruitless attempts. Federal prison was the safest, most inaccessible place for her to be. Any threats to her life were impossible. She had no family or friends to use against her. She was a dead end.

"If Marie wasn't in a high-security prison," she

said, "we would've taken her instead of you. Think about that, Cole. If you would've just let her go and returned to your fiancée, you wouldn't be in this dilemma. And maybe your girl wouldn't have fucked your best friend."

His jaw set, and a vein bulged in his forehead.

Shit. She didn't mean to piss him off. That wasn't her goal.

"I shouldn't have said that. For what it's worth." She lowered onto the crate beside him and fidgeted with the hem of her dress. "No matter how perfect you think she was for you, there's always someone better."

He barked a humorless laugh. "You don't believe in love? Or fate?"

"In our line of work, there is only war, and that, *tigryenok,* is always fueled by hate."

"There's a quote—I think it's G.K. Chesterton—that goes something like, *A soldier fights not because he hates what's in front of him, but because he loves what's behind him.*" He lowered his voice, his cadence thoughtful as he rubbed his forehead. "We all have something valuable behind us, compelling us to fight. You already know mine. My friends, the people you threatened, they're my family."

That was the most personal thing he'd ever revealed, and she was so taken with the unguarded nature of his words that she didn't move, didn't dare interrupt.

"I'll be honest," he said, "when you showed me the video of the drone, it scared the shit out of me. Those people are irreplaceable. Not because they're perfect. They're not. But because they're *mine.* Mine to protect. Mine to fight for."

"Like Danni?"

"Yes, including Danni. So here I am, protecting them, fighting for them, not out of hate, but out of love. Because that's what people do." He dropped his head and raised his eyes, peering at her through his thick lashes. "Don't kid yourself, Lydia. There's more to this, to *you*, than hate. What are you fighting for? What do you love?"

An unwanted flutter thrummed in her belly. Everything he said gripped her deeply, his questions stroking hidden nerves. And those bottomless brown eyes… Jesus, they seemed to understand her. She wanted him to see more, to hear and feel her reasons.

She opened her mouth to answer him. And snapped it shut.

It was a trap. A damn good one. If she weren't so jaded, she would've fallen for it.

"I know what you're doing." She sat taller, meeting him stare for stare.

"Enlighten me."

"Maybe you're used to charming the pants off women before they even stop to wonder why, but…" Her breath caught, her eyes narrowing on the panties wrapped around his hand.

The panties, she realized with dawning horror, that she'd handed over without questioning the real reason he wanted them.

"You were saying?" His thumb roved over the silk on his palm, his expression stony.

Heat bloomed across her skin, her anger rising and something else, something stirring low in her belly. She hated him for this. For tricking her, and at the same time, turning her on.

She could be a petty bitch about it and take back the damn underwear. But no, that wasn't her. Instead, she shook it off and gave credit where credit was due.

"I don't know how you did it." She rose to her feet and smiled down at him. "I don't know how you talked me out of my underwear, but well done."

"You wanted me to have them."

Did she? God, maybe she did. "I won't fall for it next time."

"I look forward to it." He leaned his head back against the crate and closed his eyes. "Until next time, Lydia."

She stood there, bewildered and captivated.

Did he just dismiss her?

He was fucking playing her. She didn't know how exactly, but she felt it in her gut.

She didn't know his skill set, his training, or his background, but if the last few hours taught her anything, it was that she faced an opponent who wouldn't be easily defeated.

Without another glance, she strode toward Mike, who waited with an expectant look.

"Return him to his cell." She dipped her voice to a whisper. "Don't trust a word he says. Search him for weapons and watch your back." She scanned the warehouse. "I'm going to double the number of guards on him."

"What happened?"

Cole was too confident, too smart, and sneaky as fuck. She wouldn't be surprised if he'd stolen away a sharp rock or piece of glass when she wasn't looking. But it was his mouth that worried her the most. He knew how to manipulate people.

"Just following my gut." She squeezed Mike's hand. "We'll talk later."

She left the factory floor and strode down the

corridor, her mind replaying every word and interaction she'd just shared with Cole. Had she unknowingly revealed something important? What if she'd said too much?

Lost in her thoughts, she turned the corner and collided with a hard body.

"Shit!" She looked up, coming face to face with Alec.

"In a hurry?" His smirk made her skin crawl.

"It's been a day." She side-stepped him only to be blocked again. "Move."

"Not so fast." He held out a phone. "You have a call."

The screen showed an unknown caller, but it could only be one person. Vincent Barrington. If he'd been waiting on the other end for any length of time, he wasn't going to be pleasant. Not that he knew the meaning of the word.

Drawing in a deep breath, she snatched the phone from Alec's hand and glared at him until he finally shifted to the side. She exited the building through a side door and took a short sidewalk that led to nothing but desert sand and a postcard-view of the sunset.

"Privet i trakhat' tebya," she said sweetly into the phone.

"Speak English, or I'll replace you with someone who will." Vincent had a high-pitched vocal range with the twang of small-town Georgia. When he was angry, it could shatter glass. Like now. She held the phone away from her ear as he screamed, "When I call, do not keep me waiting!"

She made him wait two full seconds before responding in a monotone. "I was working."

"I don't give a fuck. I want an update."

He'd given her until the end of the year to complete the job. She still had two months. Plenty of time. But he had control issues, a severe lack of patience, and far more at stake in this operation than she did.

"As expected," she said, "he's not talking yet. But he will."

"But he vill," he echoed, mocking her accent. "I want to know *when.*"

"When he realizes it's his only option." Slipping off her heels, she stepped into the warm desert sand. "He asked me how I knew about Thurney Bridge. What is he talking about?"

"I find it concerning that you're interrogating me instead of him."

"I find it concerning," she spat, her voice rising, "that you hired me for a job without giving me all the details to complete it."

"Careful, little girl. You're walking on very thin ice."

She pulled in a calming breath and moved on. "He doesn't know what's on the stolen hard drive."

"Of course, he doesn't. His only job was to uncover who sold the information, just like your only job is to uncover who bought it. Anything else is on a need-to-know, and neither of you needs…to…know."

He drawled out the last part in a condescending tone as if she were stupid for even mentioning it. Little did he know, when she finished this job, he would be the bigger fool.

"Anything else?" She paused, listening, and realized he'd already disconnected. "Good talk, Vincent. You heartless cunt."

He hadn't called to get an update from her. He received those from Alec.

The door opened behind her, followed by the tread of footsteps. A lighter flicked. A cloud of cigarette smoke billowed over her shoulder. She knew it was Alec before he spoke.

"Vincent's getting impatient."

"Vincent was born impatient." She turned to face him, holding the phone in one hand and the heels in the other while wearing a smile that veiled her distrust.

"Step out of the way, and I'll get Cole Hartman to sing."

"What do you know about him?"

He puffed on the cigarette, watching her through the smoke. "Give me an hour with him, and I'll know everything."

"Have you ever tortured a man? How about one who was trained to endure months of unspeakable pain?"

The idiot shrugged.

"The only thing you know is how to run your mouth about shit you don't know." She tossed the phone at him. "Until you have something useful to offer, shut the fuck up."

She strode toward the door, knowing full well he wouldn't let her have the last word.

Sure enough, his footfalls followed. Her muscles tightened, and she adjusted her grip on her heels, holding one in each hand.

As she reached the door, his palm slammed against it above her head, preventing her from opening it. Out of the corner of her eye, his cigarette skipped into the desert.

Over the past few months, her position on this

team had been challenged repeatedly. Some of the men didn't like taking orders from a woman. A few thought because they were bigger than her or because she dressed the way she did that it was an invitation to take whatever they wanted.

They all tried. And failed.

She'd been waiting for Alec to make a move. Of course, just like the others, he chose to jump her when she was alone.

Fucking pussy.

"I have something useful to offer." He pressed his weight against her back and ground his hips. "Lift that dress, and I'll show you."

"Oh, yeah?" She turned her face toward him, resting her chin on her shoulder.

As if caught by an invisible string, his lips crept toward hers, closer, closer, close enough.

She bent her knees and dropped just enough to twist around and hook the heel of her shoe into the corner of his mouth. He yelped, ensnared, as she used the three-inch spike to wrench his head toward the ground.

His hands grappled to dislodge the shoe. But she had control of his head, and where the head went, the body followed. The technique forced him into a large step, opening up an easy takedown. Wobbly balance, a slight turn in his spine, and just like that, his mobility was fucked.

In the next breath, she had him in the sand, his mouth fish-hooked by one heel, and the other pressed into the inner corner of his bulging eye.

"I'm a twitch away," she said in a bored tone, "from slamming this into your tiny brain. Give me a reason, Alec."

His throat jogged with a hard swallow, his mouth gaping like a dying fish on a hook.

"Your job is to follow orders. My orders and Vincent's." She batted her eyelashes. "That's not so hard, is it?"

He tried to shake his head.

"Just so we're clear." She put her face in his, adding slight pressure on the spike against his eye. "Don't ever touch me again."

A sound of agreement coughed from the back of his mouth.

Good enough.

She rose to her feet and brushed off her dress. Without sparing him a glance, she entered the building, confident he wouldn't follow.

He didn't.

NINE

The next day, Cole received the usual ration of hot dogs, two fresh buckets, and some things he didn't expect. With a menacing scowl, the guard tossed in a toothbrush, toothpaste, and a box of medical supplies. None of it would help him escape, but it revealed a great deal about his captors.

One in particular.

Sitting naked in the dark with thrash metal music banging against his skull, he brushed his teeth, blindly patched up his hand, and thought about Lydia.

She wasn't who she pretended to be. She'd said as much during their conversation, but it was what she didn't say that gave her away.

During the few hours he'd spent with her yesterday, he'd put together a rudimentary profile on her. But he needed more time, a few more interactions to formulate a comprehensive outline of her identity, her mental and moral qualities, and most importantly, her motivation.

Once he understood her stakes, he could

manipulate her from that angle.

She appeared to be the one in charge here, but this job was only one piece of a bigger operation. An operation that was controlled and funded by someone else. He'd figured out that much when he asked her about Thurney Bridge. She didn't have a clue what he was talking about.

That meant someone else had hired the hitman who attacked Rylee. Someone else was responsible for killing Rylee's neighbor and two motel clerks. Lydia hadn't been involved.

He shouldn't have felt so relieved, but dammit, he couldn't ignore the lightness in his chest. The hope. Irrational fucking hope that Lydia was more than just a criminal for hire, that maybe she had a forgivable reason for threatening his friends with a hellfire missile.

Dangerous thoughts.

He couldn't get attached. His only priority was survival, and if it came down to it, he would choose his life over hers.

He would choose Danni's life over everyone and everything.

They knew where she lived. But he couldn't dwell on that. He trusted Trace to protect her. There was no one on the planet who would keep her safer than her husband.

Resting his head against the wall, he drummed his fingers on the box of supplies. Lydia had given into his demand for a toothbrush, and the guards weren't happy about it. She hadn't stabbed needles under his fingernails or waterboarded him to death, and the guards didn't appear to be happy about that, either.

Other than her obvious relationship with Mike, she wasn't in sync with the rest of her team. They wanted to torture him for the information while she seemed to have a different agenda.

When she looked at him, he didn't see his demise shining in her eyes. Quite the opposite. The flush in her cheeks, the quiver in her legs, the blatant sexual attraction that radiated from her pores—she wanted him.

But it could all be part of the act.

Sexpionage was a common practice among intelligence services all over the world, especially in Russia. It was a filthy tactic to elicit information, executed by trained ravens and swallows who had little left of their humanity.

Lydia had a red swallow inked on her chest. Was it a clue? It seemed too obvious, but if she was a hired swallow, she had only one objective here—to compromise him sexually. She certainly dressed the part, and it would explain why she hadn't tortured him. Her beauty alone would bring a weaker man to his knees.

But beneath the evocative cleavage and overdone makeup, he detected something softer, something akin to…kindness. An unfeeling sex spy wouldn't give her target a toothbrush and medical supplies. Unless that was part of her act? A ploy to seduce him into trusting her?

He pressed his fingers to his brow, his head pounding with the music and the weariness of his thoughts.

What a goddamn mindfuck.

The kicker was he could give them what they wanted right now. He could bang on the door and tell them who bought the stolen hard drive from Marie Merivale. But the moment he gave it up, he was a dead man.

They had no intention of letting him walk out of here. The only thing keeping him alive was the information in his head.

He had to escape.

So he remained silent, biding his time, waiting for an opportunity to make his move.

That opportunity lay with Lydia.

If she intended to fuck him into compliance, he would be the one doing the fucking.

He would fuck her until she sobbed his name, surrendered to his will, and begged him for more.

TEN

Over the next two weeks, the guards dragged Cole out of the dark, tossed the same pair of unwashed jeans at him, and forced him to move the rock pile from one pallet to the other. Back and forth, every day, he hauled granite, strained muscles, and slowly lost his mind.

A meal waited for him at the end of each godforsaken chore—canned tuna, microwaved burritos, a hodgepodge of processed crap. Anything was better than hot dogs, and he needed the calories.

Each day, he gained weight and rebuilt his strength, but the tedious labor wore on him, putting him on edge and stoking his temper.

The guards fed on that, pushing him when he walked, taunting him when he stumbled, and growing meaner by the hour. Their numbers had doubled, at least ten of them present at all times, while Lydia's appearances dwindled to nothing.

In the beginning, she showed up while he ate, dressed in her tantalizing rockabilly fashion and flanked by half a dozen armed men. It was always the same. The same demand in the same detached tone. "Tell me who bought the stolen intel."

He maintained his silence, which seemed to infuriate her to the point that she stopped coming. He hadn't seen her in days.

By the end of two weeks, he had enough.

His patience waned as the guards shoved him toward the waiting pallet of rock. His blood boiled as a boot connected with his spine, hurrying him along. He staggered, righted his balance, barely remaining vertical. His teeth clenched.

If he attacked, it would give them an excuse to retaliate. The motherfuckers wanted a fight, their hunger for blood burning in their eyes. They baited him endlessly for it.

He could take down any one of them without breaking a sweat. But not ten of them at once. He was outnumbered, and they were armed. Challenging them would be a fool's quest.

Mike stood off to the side, arms crossed over his chest, watching. Always present, he never participated in the harassment. He never stopped them, either.

Where the fuck was Lydia? Was she watching from a hidden corner of the warehouse, delighting in his misery? He thought he would have more time with her, to analyze and manipulate her. That plan went to hell when she stopped showing up.

He was running out of options, out of patience. Inch by inch, he lost his self-control. He felt harried, wired, crackling like a lit fuse, burning down to detonation. It was only a matter of time.

Dragging in a deep breath, he resumed walking. Something had to change. He couldn't, *wouldn't,* spend another goddamn day hauling rocks.

He was done.

Just like that, a switch flipped inside him. His feet stopped moving, planted shoulder-width apart, his arms hanging at his sides. He didn't tense, but he braced for it, ready, waiting with fire seething in his veins.

"Move." Someone shoved his back.

He didn't budge.

When the next shove came, he ducked, spun, and slammed his knuckles into the face behind him, willfully initiating an explosive chain reaction of violence and fury.

He hammered his fists, connecting with flesh, but no amount of skill or training could defeat their numbers. Within seconds, his back hit the concrete, his ribs taking the brunt of the blows as men fell upon him, weapons aimed, and mouths grinning through the blood.

They didn't want to shoot him. They wanted to beat him to a pulp.

Manic energy surged through him, clouding his vision. Octane pumped his heart. Blood and sweat slicked his face. His knuckles throbbed, and his eyes burned from the impact of raining fists. Still, he kept punching, fighting, and roaring through the bone-crunching agony of their strikes.

Until the report of gunfire shuddered the air. A single shot, fired from across the warehouse. Everyone froze.

His pulse thundered, and his lungs crashed together. Then, one by one, the weight of ten men lifted off his body.

He lay on his back, staring at the rafters through blood-soaked eyelashes. Everything hurt, and he relished it—the madness of the pain, the rush of adrenaline, and the utter freedom in unleashing his temper. He savored it almost as much as the sound of her clicking heels heading toward him.

Fucking finally.

"Tie him up." She handed off her rifle to a guard while motioning at the rest of them. "Put him on that pallet."

Christ, she was a vision. He wiped the blood from his eyes to steal a better look, and holy fuck, he couldn't stop looking.

Black combat boots, a tiny skirt checked in white and black, fishnet stockings to her thighs, silk-ribbon garters over skin like fine china, tits spilling from a black corset, and that hair. God, that hair. It hung in rippling waves of fire, as bright as the red swallow tattooed on her chest.

Pressure tightened between his legs, swelling against his zipper. She glared, and he grinned, no doubt resembling a feral, blood-spattered animal.

"I'm gone for five days, and all hell breaks loose." She held her spine ramrod straight, her little hands clenching in fists at her sides. "Goddamn children. The whole lot of you!"

The men, smeared in their own share of blood, shot death looks in her direction. Some of them pressed their lips tight as if biting back scathing retorts. If she wasn't careful, she might have an insurrection among them.

But for now, they followed her orders without argument. Hands fell upon him, hauling him up and dragging him across the factory floor.

They dumped his ass on a stack of wood pallets. Another stack leaned on its side between the wall and his back. Rope bound the platforms together, forming a makeshift *L*-shaped chair, perfect for restraining a crazed man.

He gave them hell, struggling and spitting as they tied his arms, neck, and waist to the pallets at his back. But much like the fight he'd just lost, one against many proved to be a wasted effort.

Thirty yards away, Lydia stood close to Mike, their heads bowed together, talking, touching, paying no attention to his useless thrashing.

When the guards finished trussing him to the platform, her voice snapped through the room. "Everyone out."

She didn't spare the room a glance, her gaze still fixed on Mike as she returned to their conversation.

The factory floor echoed with the tread of retreating footfalls. Mike vanished with the guards, and when the door slammed shut, only Lydia remained.

A thrill ran through him. At last, he would have some time with her, and he needed to make every second count.

She turned to him, her gaze as vibrant as the colorful ink on her arms. An abundance of cleavage decorated her corset, the view goddamn distracting as she pulled in a long breath and slowly released it.

Fucking hell, she was killing him. More painful than a fist, more lethal than a bullet, more formidable than an army of men, she brandished beauty like a mythical weapon, gaining the advantage by merely standing before him, looking like *that*.

Soft auburn brows arched above eyes that sparkled with the luster of polished emeralds. Supple red lips gracefully curved downward, unreasonably sensual. Deadly. Like cherries soaked in poison.

He knew she wasn't real. The hair, the garters, the heat in her gaze—all of it was a honey trap to lure him under her spell. He knew this, and yet, he wanted to risk it. He wanted to risk his whole goddamn existence for a taste.

His body burned for her, restrained as it was beneath the rope, his zipper, and the plight of his circumstances. He would be lying to himself if he thought he could fight the intensity swarming through his system.

There was sexual attraction. Then there was *this.* He had nothing to compare it to. Not his relationship with Danni. Not the countless women who had come before her. He'd never felt this hungry, this captivated, this fucking petrified of his own lust.

Maybe regular sexual activity over the past seven years would've diluted the voraciousness of his appetite. Maybe if he hadn't been sitting naked in a dark cell for the past month with nothing to do but fantasize about his redheaded captor, maybe then he wouldn't…

Fuck.

That was it. That was her plan.

Spending time with her would've worked to his advantage. He would've identified her weaknesses, her flaws, and seen her for who she really was. But spending a month alone? With only random glimpses of her to fuel his hungry imagination? That worked to *her* advantage.

Absence makes the heart grow fonder.

Or, in his case, absence made his lust burn hotter. She'd managed to keep her distance while staying ever-present in his mind. She wore a shroud of mystery that he couldn't peel away, leaving him to obsess over the only thing she let him see.

Her extraordinary beauty.

Once she finally let him in, there would be nothing left of his resolve.

It was fucking brilliant.

He tracked her with his whole body as she strode past him, seemingly ignoring his presence. Pretending. It was what she did best.

A few feet away, she grabbed a rubber hose and twisted a spigot on the wall, turning on the flow of water.

Twitchy, he yanked at the restraints. With his hands bound on either side of his head and more rope tethered around his neck and waist, he couldn't move his upper half. Physically defenseless.

She pulled the hose toward him, grabbed an empty bucket, and tossed a bottle of body wash onto the pallet beside him.

Given the collection of soap, shampoo, and towels along the wall, this was where the team showered. They'd been living here for at least a month, probably longer, and a stone factory wouldn't be equipped with a room for bathing.

"Are you going to bathe me?" He arranged his face into a smile despite the unease simmering inside him.

He hadn't felt the touch of a woman in seven years, and he knew, he fucking *knew* this woman's touch would be his undoing. But he tamped it down, didn't give her a hint of the turmoil rolling in his gut.

She stood before him and squeezed the handle on the hose, shooting a blast of frigid water at his chest. His breath caught, and his muscles tensed. But once the shock wore off, he threw back his head and hooted with maniacal laughter.

After a month without a shower, it felt fucking refreshing. Cold water saturated his filthy beard and crusty jeans, seeping into the creases of his body and rinsing away layers of sand and dirt.

Nothing restrained his legs. So he stretched them out, spreading them wide and soaking up the spray, all the while whooping with unrestrained laughter.

Until she aimed the spray at his face.

He coughed, choking on water. Then he laughed harder.

She shut off the hose. "You're deranged."

"Turn it back on."

"Tell me who bought the stolen intel."

"If I tell you, will you let me go?"

"I won't return you to the cell."

"Ah." He chuckled. "Is my grave already dug?"

Her dainty nostrils stiffened with a sharp inhale. "I won't kill you."

"No, you're too soft to kill an innocent man. You'll make one of your goons do it."

Without breaking eye contact, she fired a burst of water at his groin. The denim added some protection, but fuck, the jet hit hard. And cold. His balls receded up inside him, his laughter effectively cut off.

She shifted the hose away and filled the bucket.

He relaxed, watching her. "Where did you go for five days?"

"Out."

"Out of town?"

"Out of state."

"Why?"

"Why? Yeah, let's start there." She heaved the full bucket onto the pallet beside him, set her hands on his thighs, and leaned into his personal space, surrounding him with the cherry scent of her hair. "Why did you provoke the guards? What the fuck were you thinking?"

"Your concern is touching." He tilted his head. "Does this mean we're friends?"

"What?" She jerked back, eyebrows pinching.

"I'll be honest." He tugged on the rope. "This doesn't feel very friendly. Unless you're into this sort of thing. Which I am. But only when I'm the one playing with the rope."

"Mm-hmm." She narrowed her eyes, her accent laced with sarcasm. "We both know how many times you've played over the past seven years." Holding her hand up between them, she made her fingers and thumb form the shape of a zero.

"You want to be the one." He wet his lips, his mouth inches from hers. "The one I break my celibacy with."

"No," she said too quickly. "You're…just…" She made a sound of frustration. "You're smarter than this, Cole. Smart enough to know the guards were baiting you."

"Smart enough to know *you* are baiting me."

"Sometimes, I wonder…" Her gaze dipped to his lips and returned to his eyes. "Who's baiting who?"

ELEVEN

Intelligent sea-green eyes stared out of the face of a Gothic angel. Enraptured, Cole stared back, knowing eye contact with this cursed creature was treacherous. Lydia didn't just look at him. She looked *into* him as if she knew his darkest desires.

But that was impossible. While he couldn't resist his attraction to her, he made damn sure he didn't show it. He'd been trained to disguise emotion, a skill that had served him well throughout his career.

Without averting her gaze, she reached for the bottle of soap beside him and squirted a cold glob on his chest. She edged closer, pushing into the *V* of his legs, and boldly perched on his knee.

With her featherlight weight on his lap came the smooth touch of her hands on his flesh, fingers splayed, just the right balance of caution and assertion as she spread the gel to his shoulders and throat.

He sank into the warmth of her caress, fixated on her unreadable expression. What sort of woman was she? Heartless? Tender? Promiscuous? Complicated?

He didn't know enough about her to make a judgment. But goddamn, she knew how to touch a man.

Her fingers swept across every inch of his upper body, rubbing gently, working in the lather, unselfish with the soap. With the bucket, she rinsed away the grime, leaving no part of his exposed skin unwashed.

When she reached his hair, her fingernails dug in, scraping his scalp and combing him clean.

He fucking groaned.

It felt surreal, like a day at the damn spa. Not that he would know. He'd never been to a spa, never been pampered or massaged into a pleasure-drunk coma.

He didn't trust the feelings it evoked. She had an agenda. A nasty one. But he let himself, just for a moment, indulge in the sublime ecstasy of her hands on his body.

She spent a lot of time on his facial hair, scrubbing and soaping with rapt concentration. Christ, how he must've reeked. The hair had grown too long, venturing into lumberjack territory. He preferred a quarter-inch military beard.

With his head tipped back, he stared down the length of his nose. "Have you found any creatures crawling in it?"

"No." Her luscious lips crooked up at the corner, amusement glowing in her delicate features. "I'm trying to imagine what you look like without it."

"I've shaved it off many times over the years. I'm sure you've seen photos."

Images of him didn't exist on the Internet or dark web. He made sure of that. But he pretended otherwise as a way to fish for clues and subtly nudge her into giving something away.

"No photos." Her hands moved on to the upper

part of his face, cleaning around the contusions he'd incurred during the fight. "I didn't know what you looked like until the night I met you in the desert."

Shock jolted through him, but he maintained a bored expression. "You met me that night because I allowed it. Because I deliberately activated your bug."

She pressed closer, lathering soap around his eyes and cheeks. "Your breath smells good. Minty. You've been using the gifts I sent."

If she wanted a *thank you,* she could eat a dick.

Biting her lip, she stared at his mouth. "I planted those bugs in Rylee Sutton's house, knowing you would take them and eventually lure me to your location. You met me that night in the desert because *I* allowed it."

"They're not just bugs. You planted customized tech, designed for the NSA."

"Now we're getting somewhere." She slid a hand into his hair and pulled, yanking his head back. "The only way you would recognize that tech is if you worked for them."

Or if he worked for something deeper, darker, and more clandestine. But he wasn't about to tell her that. "What does Rylee Sutton have to do with this?"

"A few months ago, you showed up in Texas, stalking her." She released his hair and leaned to the side, her attention on his hand.

With his arms fastened to the pallet on either side of his head, he opened his fingers and let her look at his palm. The gash from the rock had healed cleanly over the past two weeks, thanks to the supplies she'd provided.

She gently washed the area around the wound and moved to his other hand. "After vanishing off the map for seven years, here you were, riding into the desert on your motorcycle. You went straight to El Paso, then Eldorado, monitoring Rylee's old and current residences. She was your only focus, seemingly the only reason you came out of hiding. So naturally, she became a target for your pursuers."

"I wasn't in hiding, and I didn't realize I had admirers."

"Pursuers."

"Same thing. I see the way you look at me."

"I see the way you look when I mention your pretty dancer."

He didn't blink. Not a twitch.

Danni had never been involved in his affairs. He'd always kept her in the dark, completely separated from his career. Now, she lived a safe, happy life, doing what she loved. Dancing. She married the man she loved. A powerful businessman and billionaire, who had the resources and unparalleled desire to protect her.

Her photos were out there, her personal information available to anyone who wanted to investigate her. That didn't matter since she was no longer connected to Cole.

It wouldn't have mattered if an eleven-year-old assignment hadn't come back to haunt him.

"You're still in love with Danni," she said, her accent straining. "But you came to Texas to stalk Rylee. Who is she to you?"

"Since *you* were stalking *me,* you should know this."

"I think, initially, she was a threat to your friends. While you were digging into her background, she was off in the desert with Tomas, getting stabbed with a hot dog."

"Stabbed with a hot dog," he deadpanned.

"His hot dog. It's a fitting analogy, given your diet over the past month."

"You're a twisted bitch." His nonchalant tone made her smile.

"I'm right about Rylee. Whatever her connection was to you and your friends, it was personal. You wouldn't have returned to the states, otherwise."

She wasn't wrong, but he kept his face unexpressive.

"You haven't been in the country for seven years." She raised a brow.

Not true. He'd visited on three different occasions. Day trips, in and out. Evidently, they weren't watching him closely enough.

Her thumb trailed along his bottom lip, her eyes locked on the movement. "Where have you been all this time?"

"Enjoying retirement."

"You might've retired from a legitimate career, but I know you're working with the Colombian cartel. You've made a name for yourself, Cole Hartman. How does it feel to be notorious in the criminal underworld?"

That was the intel she had on him? The gossip of crime lords and traffickers? He'd put most of those rumors out there himself. All smoke and mirrors to embellish the truth, incite fear, and mislead enemies away from what he was actually doing.

She had no idea he was part of a vigilante group or that his earlier career was in an organization that no one knew existed. That meant she didn't have connections in the intelligence sectors. So how did she have access to those high-tech bugs?

"Who do you work for?" He nipped at her finger

on his lip.

She yanked her hand back. "Tell me who bought—"

"No. I'm not going to tell you what you want to know, and you're not going to let me go. We're at an impasse, Lydia." He flexed his thigh beneath her pert ass. "How long have I been here?"

"Thirty-one days."

"How much time do you have left to complete the assignment?"

"Enough."

"There's always a deadline." He made a tsking sound. "Something has to give."

"You." Her lashes lowered, fanning over porcelain cheekbones before lifting to expose the force of her magnetic glare. "*You* have to give."

"When I don't, you'll take. Am I right?" He glanced at his restraints, his vulnerable position. "How much are you willing to take? How far down this dark hole are you willing to go?"

How evil are you, Lydia?

"All the way." She slid off his lap and opened the button on his jeans. Then the zipper. Her eyes found his, and she yanked on the wet denim.

His stomach coiled. His skin grew hot, and his pulse took off at a sprint.

Enduring the soapy caress of her hands below his waist would be the absolute best and worst thing that could happen. It needed to happen. They needed to get personal and intimate and fucking filthy together, so he could break her open and fuck the stubbornness out of her.

At the same time, he had to remember that she was using the same strategy on him. She intended to ply him with her body, and all the while, he would let her believe she was the one in control.

Remaining aloof, he gave her no reaction as she wrestled with the heavy wet fabric. Her tits rose with shallow inhalations, the gorgeous swells testing the confines of her corset, testing *him.*

He didn't move or lift his weight to help, but that didn't stop her tenacious hands. Keeping a firm hold on his waistband, she wrenched the jeans down his legs and off, exposing the hardening evidence of his arousal.

Yeah, his fucking cock was excited.

Seven years of built-up excitement.

Physically, he was ready and raring to go.

Emotionally, he would never be up for it. He missed his girl. He just…

Christ, he deeply, unendurably missed her.

He shoved down all thoughts of Danni, concealing them behind a mask of indifference. But he couldn't hide the erection. It jutted upward like a damn flagpole, begging for soft hands, a hot mouth, and a wet-ass pussy.

She didn't spare him a glance and instead directed her attention to his largest and oldest tattoo. The black snake wrapped around his thigh from knee to hip, its head angled toward his foot with shimmering scales inked in meticulous detail.

"What's the story on this?" She traced a finger along the curve of the serpent's spine, making him harder, hotter.

"I'll tell you about the snake if you tell me about the swallow."

Her hand went to her chest and dropped just as quickly, her expression empty.

He was convinced now, more than ever, that she

wasn't a trained sex spy. While she excelled at putting on an act, she hadn't mastered the unresponsive austerity of a swallow. She reacted emotionally on impulse. It was subtle, but he caught the little twitches and nuances before she blanked her face.

Maybe she was pretending to be a swallow? But for what reason? The same reason she left him in the dark to fantasize about her for a month?

Because she was fucking with him. Or trying to.

He relaxed against the pallet, curious to see what she would do next.

She washed him. Starting at his feet, she worked her way up his legs. When he halfheartedly tried to kick her, she gripped his knee to hold him down and slid her fingers along his inner thigh.

Heat swept through him as her hands roamed where Danni's had gone before. In rigid silence, he watched her clean his cock and learn the shape of him, her fingers traveling the same path Danni's mouth had been so many times, so long ago.

He fought down the noises that tried to crawl from his throat. Noises of objection. And consent. And reprehensible guilt.

His molars clenched tight, his breaths snapping past his teeth in choppy bursts. Pleasure fused with torment, his body warring with his mind. He wanted it. He didn't want it.

He needed to focus before he fucking lost it.

The ends of her hair brushed his skin, tickling his legs as she lathered and laved. There was no seduction in her touch, the scrubbing efficient and impersonal. Coldly detached.

She wasn't trying to tease him. This was a bath, nothing more. Yet, it was everything.

He throbbed, burning for her. He thought he might die if he didn't get inside her. At the same time, he didn't want her. She was the wrong woman. She wasn't his girl.

Christ, he needed to man the fuck up and get over that. Right now.

Logic over emotion, his mind was in control.

He was going to survive. And to do that, he had to do *her*.

TWELVE

It was just sex.

If Cole remained in control, if he kept himself detached, he could use it as a weapon.

Not an easy undertaking with Lydia's warmth bearing down upon him, so achingly close, shocking his system. Her sweet cherry scent drugged his inhales. Her beauty, even smothered in makeup, drew him in like a supernatural spell.

She washed every inch of his rigid cock, his balls, and farther back, into the recesses of his crack, her fingers like tiny knives slicing their way through his dignity.

Then she took away her touch, her intoxicating heat, and stepped back. With the hose in hand, she sprayed him off like an animal, her stance and expression matching the blast of the water. Cold, aggressive, merciless.

Something felt off about her. She was normally closed-off, but this was different. She suddenly looked way too wooden, her gaze too unfocused, as if she'd retreated into her head. Either she was trying to put herself in a zone, or she was having second thoughts about seducing him.

By the time she shut off the water, she'd completely killed his erection.

The hose dangled from her hand, her gaze fixed over his shoulder, staring at nothing.

"Lydia."

She blinked. Her brow creased, and her eyes went to his mouth, then lower, taking a winding trip from his chest to his soft dick. "I don't want to do this."

Yes, she did. But not for the reason in which she'd been hired.

"Just give me a name, a location, *something*." She glared at him, her jaw flexing. "You don't give a fuck about that hard drive. Tell me where it is."

"Tell me what's on it."

"If I do, will you give me—?"

"No."

She pulled in a breath, standing taller, her posture vibrating with indignation. Then she tossed the hose, turned on her heel, and strode toward the door.

She was leaving.

Dread slammed into him, exploding his pulse. He couldn't spend another month in the dark. Goddammit, he couldn't lose this opportunity with her.

"You're scared," he said to her retreating backside.

She stopped, her spine stiff as she cast a scowl over her shoulder. "Excuse me?"

"You scrubbed me clean because you intended to seduce me. Because you have it in your head that if you wrap that hot little cunt around my dick, my brain will fry, and I'll tell you everything I know. The problem with that plan is you *want* me. Not just to milk me for information. You want to milk my cock because you're wet for it. You've been wet for me since the day I tied the soaked crotch of your underwear around my hand."

She slowly pivoted, facing him with flames in her eyes. "I am *not*—"

"It scares you, this reckless infatuation you have with me. It scares you so much you're running."

As expected, she gasped, mouth gaping and features twisted in fury. "You arrogant son of a—"

"Don't worry, sweetheart. I'm going to fuck you. I'll fuck you so completely that shit on your face will smear and drip off. You'll lose the fake eyelashes like the piercing in your lip. I'm going to fuck you until there are holes in your stockings, tangles in your hair, and bite marks marring those creamy tits. I'm going to ravage you, ruin you, and I'll do it all while my hands are still bound in rope."

She sucked in sharply, nostrils flaring, and smoothed her palms down her short skirt.

Oh, yeah, she was pissed and trying so hard to keep it in check.

Hiding his smile, he waited for it, for her wrath, her passion, and the complete erosion of her composure.

She didn't disappoint.

"You really think because you're a strong, virile man…" She charged toward him, sauntering in her exquisite rage. "That I must surely be dripping down my legs? And that because I'm a woman, I must be quivering in fear of my sexual desires? That this is about me stifling my urges rather than taking matters into my own hands? *That's* the conclusion you're drawing?"

Blood surged to his cock, his balls tightening with every seething word, every assertive step she made in his direction. He held still, his chin tilted up. But he couldn't school his breathing. His lungs danced, heaving enthusiastically in the hellfire of her unholy glare.

"And that because you're a man..." She climbed onto his naked lap, straddling him with her weight on her knees. "It must be *you* who does the *fucking*?"

That word, rasped on her tongue, made him outrageously, painfully hard. He would have to tread with care if he were to last until the end of this.

"You think I should swallow my perceived fear and beg you to ravage me?" She reached between them, wrapped a hand around his cock, and viciously, angrily stroked him. "Do I look scared to you, Cole? Do I look infatuated with your superior manliness? Hmm?"

She yanked hard on his cock, wrenching a grunt from his throat. Her vicious tugging grew meaner, rougher, aggressively working him into a lather.

He pressed his lips together to trap his groans, unleashing ragged exhales through his nose. His muscles contracted, hardening and heating as he fought the onslaught of pleasure and pain.

Her eyes stayed with him, blazing with censure as she lowered herself, lower, closer, until the wet silk between her legs pushed against the crown of his erection, still held cruelly in her fist.

Trapped in the restraints, he couldn't stop her. Not that he would. With a few taunting words, he'd deliberately goaded her into running back and finishing this.

But the position made him uncomfortable, his need for dominance burning violently through his body. He craved control and fought the compulsion to aim himself and quest about until he impaled her.

He had to let her do this, let her believe she held the reins. If she suspected otherwise, he would be back in that cell at once.

She regarded him as if searching for subterfuge. Of course, she knew it was there. But she would ignore it. She wanted this too badly.

Do it, he commanded with his eyes.

Her fingers drove under the barrier of her underwear, shoving the crotch aside. He couldn't see beneath the skirt, but he felt her spreading the soft flesh of her cunt. While her hand was moving, she lifted a knee, squatting over him in a more dominant position, and met his eyes.

He held his breath. She seemed to be holding hers. Then she pounded down hard, plunging the full length of him into soaking wet paradise.

Scalding hot.

Inconceivably tight.

Blinding rapture.

Holy God in heaven, he was inside her, inside a woman for the first time in seven years. He didn't move, couldn't breathe.

He'd forgotten what it felt like. Over the years, he'd recalled the sensations, the incomparable ecstasy of a pussy sucking and gripping his cock. But his recollections paled by comparison. Nothing in memory had ever felt this goddamn magnificent.

Then she moved, ripping the air from his lungs. Her hips caught a diabolical rhythm, circling, grinding, and flattening him to the pallets. Her hands anchored against his palms, pressing his tethered arms to the wood slats on either side of his head.

He squeezed her clenched fists, and a scalding noise rose from her chest. He couldn't help it. He groaned with her, throwing his head back while watching her from beneath heavy eyelids.

She was the most wickedly erotic creature he had ever encountered, her thick, spiral-curling red hair tangling around a voluptuous rack and clinging to a heart-shaped face dominated by the scornful eyes of a *femme fatale.*

Her cheeks flushed with the exertion of her thrusts, her complexion smooth and pale as cream. She was as petite and light as a flower, but there was nothing fragile about her. She slammed down on his shaft with venom, every ram of her hips meant to punish not reward, her fingers stabbing into his hands, her face streaked with contempt.

She used him like a piston, burying his shaft to the hilt, up and down, push and pull, her pace feral, shimmering with hostility. The heavy globes of her tits bounced with aggression until a nipple popped free, the little pink bead hard enough to cut glass.

Perspiration leaked black rivers from her eyes, her lip gloss faded from the swipes of her tongue. Sunlight poked through the smudges of the overhead windows, slanting across her face and rendering her almost immortal, like a dark Fae princess from another world and era. Ethereal. Deceitful. Tragic.

He'd never seen anything more beautiful.

His attraction defied reason. She was everything Danni wasn't. Salty instead of sweet. Calculated instead of free-spirited. Her makeup and tattoos lent her a hard, artificial appearance, not the soft, natural look he preferred. And her heart was cold and closed-off. Not warm. Definitely not attainable.

Or maybe she just wanted him to think that.

Bowing into him, she rode his cock and huffed strangled gasps of air against his mouth. She was so close he wanted to kiss her. Almost as much as he wanted to bite her and make her bleed.

Instead, he lifted into her vigorous need, grunting, ramming his hips, and washing them both with brutal sensations. All else ceased to exist, everything but her body, her breaths, and the intensity of her livid gaze.

Her eyes were like pieces of kryptonite, deep green and luminescent, weakening him by the second. His dick wanted release. His mind wouldn't allow it. He wouldn't give in.

But as they moved together, their tempos syncing and gazes locked, he felt a sliding sensation. Deep in his chest, he felt a tilting, tumbling avalanche that had nothing to do with the earthquaking motion of their bodies.

Before his brain caught up, his mouth was on her, kissing her so thoroughly he damn near exploded inside her.

He didn't pull away. He couldn't. She kissed him back with the same desperation, and the feel of her tongue rubbing and tangling with his was all that mattered.

They melted together, holding each other hostage with their mouths, their thrusts, and harmonious tremors in their bodies. Her hands moved to his face, fingers clamping firmly around his jaw, her lips crashing against his with the force of her passion.

Lost in the throes of frenzied lust, she used him for her pleasure. It was the moment he'd been waiting for, watching her get worked up, feeling his cock sink past her defenses, and knowing her race to completion was no longer about the job and all about the demands of her body.

At that moment, he held the control. He'd mastered her with his hands tied.

Breaking the kiss, he leaned back and admired his handiwork.

She stopped moving, her cheeks flushed, and her snug little pussy clenched spasmodically around his buried cock. She released shallow, rapid-fire breaths and blinked slowly, with great effort, as if struggling to concentrate.

When she realized what she'd done, that she'd lost control of herself, her expression hardened.

Was she angry? Oh, fuck yeah. Ten strangling little expressions of her rage curled around his throat, her blunt nails pressing against his airway in a bid to choke him.

Just as quickly, she regained her composure, released his neck, and shoved his face away.

But she wasn't finished.

Rising on her knees, she pulled off of his cock. He bobbed against her thigh, wanting back in as she reached under her skirt and swept her fingers along the flesh he still hadn't seen.

Her free hand went to his shoulder, holding her upper body steady as she proceeded to rub her cunt. Her knuckles brushed against his unspent cock, teasing him as she chased her release. She shook with the effort, moaning, muscles straining, lashes fluttering, her eyes smoldering with animosity.

A sound of feral relief stole from her throat, and she screamed, groaning, trembling, and coming undone.

Fucking glorious. Hotter than hell. Had he been inside her, he might've shot his load, which was precisely what he didn't want to do. He refused to give her that.

And to think, she intended to deny him.

It's a ride you won't ever get off.

She thought she could torture him with orgasm denial. Little did she know, he had the discipline of a monk.

Climbing to her feet, she swiped her soaked fingers across his mouth. He licked his lips, tasting her, while holding her blistering glare.

Her teeth clenched. "Tell me who bought the hard drive, and I'll relieve that ache between your legs."

"No, thanks. I'll relieve it myself."

"You're going to jerk off in that filthy cell? Where you can't hear yourself think?"

"Yep." He stretched out his legs, delighting in the way her hungry eyes caressed his swollen cock. "I'm a dirty…dirty…dirty man."

"I could shackle you while you're in there."

"You don't want to do that because you like thinking about me touching myself. But when I do, it won't be *you* I'm thinking about. My heart lies elsewhere."

A flicker of hurt crossed her expression, and she looked away, pretending indifference by straightening her clothes and tucking in her tits.

"You, on the other hand, will not get off without me."

Her head shot up at that, eyes wide. "What did you say?"

"Nothing touches that pussy but me. Not Mike. Not your men. Not your fingers. Your body belongs to me."

She made a sound of disbelief that morphed into a sneer of disgust. Then she spun away and stormed to the exit without looking back.

Later, she would think back and relive every thrust, every grunt, every intimate second of eye contact, and she would think about his command.

She would attempt to touch herself because she wanted to hate him. But she wouldn't go through with it because she wanted him. And that want would bring her back for more.

He might not survive it, but he would be ready for her.

THIRTEEN

Three days later, Lydia stood over Cole's nude body, fighting an inner battle between duty and decency.

For as long as she could remember, duty had always won out. She'd lied, cheated, stolen, kidnapped, and sold her soul to the devil in the name of duty.

Her purpose was greater than Cole's life, her own, and that of anyone who tried to stop her. She was prepared to do anything and everything to finish this.

Or so she thought.

As she took in the rope that secured his powerful frame to the factory floor, her stomach churned with an unexpected sense of wrongness. What she was doing to him was unacceptable. Indecent. *Unforgivable.*

Was she developing a goddamn conscience after all these years? Or was it worse? Was she developing feelings for her prisoner?

Lima Syndrome, the inverse of Stockholm syndrome. She knew it could happen. She just didn't think it could happen to her.

It needed to stop.

The moment she met Cole, she knew this wouldn't be easy. Mike had known long before, which was why he'd fought so hard against this plan.

Cole belonged on a motorcycle with a rifle on his back, flying down a lone highway on some hell-raising mission. He didn't belong in restraints, stripped of his clothes and his freedom, and forced to endure another rape.

Because that was what this was. No matter how hard his dick grew in her hands. He wasn't a willing participant. He was a prisoner, and in the last three days, she'd raped him three times, each time finishing herself off while denying him a completion.

The first time, she convinced herself he was right there with her, fucking her as passionately as she fucked him. She thought, when he was seconds from climax, that he was too injured to come. He'd just fought off the raging blows of ten men, his face swollen and covered in blood. But he hadn't flinched when she'd washed his wounds. It was as if he didn't even feel the pain.

The second day, she orgasmed too quickly. With the memory of his feverish, toe-curling kiss still fresh in her mind, she was on the brink of coming before she even got his cock inside her. When her orgasm hit, she collapsed in a boneless puddle against his chest, gasping and so lost in the pleasure she'd forgotten to deny him a release. And yet, he didn't come. As if he were deliberately holding it back.

By the third day, she started questioning who was controlling whom. Just like the times before, she bathed him, teased him, and made him hard as a rock. Then she sat on his lap and rode him to the cusp of orgasm. He grunted vehement sounds with his teeth clamped tight. His eyes blazed. His sinews flexed, and she pushed him harder, faster, testing the limits of his self-restraint.

Instead of denying him a release, she teased him toward it.

She teased and teased until she wore herself out.

Still, he didn't come.

How in the fresh hell was that possible?

Desperate to beat him at his game, she'd ordered the guards to shackle him during his time in the cell, preventing him from touching himself. His only relief would come with her, and much to her despair, that went both ways.

She slept beside Mike every night without a moment of privacy. It was for the best. She wasn't here to engage in self-pleasure. Except, whenever she closed her eyes, Cole's gorgeous face was waiting. His smirking lips. That bottomless brown gaze, searing into her thoughts.

Too often, she caught herself daydreaming, recreating the delicious sensation of his tongue in her mouth, the scratch of his beard on her cheeks, the sultry sounds of his breaths, and the intensity of his strokes.

Didn't matter how tightly the rope cinched around him, he was incapable of holding still while inside her. He fucked her from the bottom, with his cock, his mouth, and the dominance in his dark glare. Every single time.

And he didn't come.

Today, when the men dragged him from the cell, she had him arranged on the floor, arms stretched above him, his gorgeous physique on full display.

After he'd lost so much weight in the beginning, she started feeding him high-calorie, high-protein meals. Then there was the rock hauling, the workouts in his cell, and the sex—all the thrusting and grunting and flexing. He'd regained his strength and then some.

With his back to the floor and the rise and dips of his musculature so round and defined, there were only a few points of contact where his body touched the concrete.

No man should have that many curves. God help her, she'd traced every sinuous muscle with her own hands and knew how outrageously hard and masculine he was, as if each sinew and tendon had been carved with an artist's chisel and stacked together to form a dangerously arousing masterpiece.

The granite bricks of his ass drew his lower spine into a sexy arch, leaving a shadowed tunnel beneath. The circumference of his biceps exceeded that of her thighs, and his shoulder blades, sculpted like marble wings, supported the weight of his upper body on the floor.

His powerful legs—wide at the calves and thighs—were in remarkable proportion to the pillar of his heavy, thick cock. Striae of muscle flanked his eight-pack abdomen, the terrain of his torso like a rippling sheet of metal, hard and flat enough to bounce quarters.

Zero-percent body fat. Not an inch of softness anywhere. Utter perfection through and through.

She might've felt like a despicable pervert, ogling him the way she did. But his gaze, as sharp as a freshly honed blade, violated her just as rudely.

His eyes especially enjoyed the tops of her breasts as they expanded and contracted with her breath. She wore a dress he'd seen before—the black one with red cherries. Yet he stared at it as if it were the first time, feasting upon every stitch and lingering where hemlines met skin until she felt stripped and just as naked as him.

He liked what he saw, if his engorged cock were anything to go by. He never had trouble getting hard.

Each time she came to him, he didn't fight against the rope or make demands. He didn't gnash his teeth or shout at her.

In fact, he hadn't spoken to her at all today.

He never said a word to the guards. Other than the fistfight three days ago, he tolerated their taunting, shoving, kicking. His endurance of pain and hardship without any display of feeling didn't seem human.

How could a man sit in a pitch-black cell, shit in a bucket, and never voice a single protest? How could he listen to the same song on repeat for over a month and never complain? He didn't grumble or whine or express any sign of dissatisfaction.

She'd offered him better accommodations, better food, a warm bed, sex with multiple women, anything in exchange for the location of the hard drive.

Anything but his freedom. She couldn't give him that, and he knew it.

Any other man would've surrendered by now. No one had this much stoicism. Even she was starting to lose her nerve.

So what was his deal? He had the patient self-control of a robot, like an upgraded model of the Terminator.

Except when he looked at her, when it was just the two of them, she saw a human man beneath the steel. A confident, lusty, hotblooded man with so much heat in his eyes she caught fire.

Like now.

He stared at her like he wanted to eat her alive.

Like she was the only thing that existed. But she wasn't. He loved the dancer.

Maybe that was how he maintained such ironclad discipline over his orgasms. His heart wasn't in this. Of course, it wasn't. Nothing they did together was consensual.

Even if it was consensual, would it have changed anything? The man had been celibate for seven years because no one was good enough for him. No one but Danni Savoy.

It only made Lydia want him more, and that was fucking dangerous.

She lowered onto the floor beside him and slid her palm beneath the rope across his chest, soaking in the warmth of his skin. He was so well-built, his pectorals smooth and hairless, the crevice between them deep and inviting. She wanted him to touch her, to be free with her body as she was with his. But if she untied him, he would hurt her. Possibly kill her. She'd given him no choice but to hate her.

"Do you want to end this today?" she asked. "All I need is a name."

One brow, higher than the other, twitched with the force of his stare.

With a sigh, she focused her attention on bathing him. But as her fingers and palms delighted in his texture, firm shape, wiry beard, soft hair, all she wanted of his hands was that they would touch her with the same burning passion as his gaze.

When she finished the final rinse, his gravelly voice broke the silence.

"It's just the two of us. Wash off the makeup. Remove the clothes. Let me see you."

She couldn't do that. The persona she wore was a

safeguard. It protected her identity.

"No." She looked down at his swelling erection. "How you can be so patient is beyond me. Doesn't it hurt?"

"Watching you stare at it is my favorite part." His hands flexed above his head, straining the rope that bound his sinewy forearms. "Your eyes get this disturbing jolt of light, like you want to tear your teeth into me." His voice dropped, rasping with dark sensuality. "There's something deranged and alluring about watching a woman devour what she wants with rabid intent." His eyes hooded. "Go ahead, Lydia. Wrap those filthy lips around me and eat."

Heat bloomed between her legs, pulsing angrily. "I'll use my teeth."

"I'll be disappointed if you don't."

"And you called *me* a freak."

"Takes one to know one." His cock nodded in agreement.

Happy to oblige, she positioned herself over him, straddling one of his restrained legs. Then she lowered her head.

With the flat part of her tongue, she teased the tip of him. He didn't move. She sucked on the plump head, tasting him in languorous strokes. He didn't breathe.

Her lips stretched around his thickness as she slowly drew him in, deeper, harder, opening her airway, until her mouth reached the soft hair at his base.

She fought her gag reflex, breathing through the fullness in her throat as a series of twitches rippled across his abs. His leg trembled between the clinch of her thighs, and his addictive male scent flooded her senses.

As she made her way back up, she found him

watching her, his lids half-mast and lips parted, breathless. Christ, that look on his gorgeous face, the sheer intensity in his eyes, awakened her pulse and spread fire through her circulation.

Without averting her gaze, she sucked him with vigor. The heavy hardness of him pressed down on her tongue, leaking salty beads of arousal from the tip. She lapped it up and felt her own moisture trickling down her thighs.

Since the hem of the dress fell to her knees, she'd gone without panties. Ideal for her position with his leg locked between hers. She rested her pussy against his thigh and let him feel the wetness, rubbing against his hard muscles and soaking his skin.

His groan of pleasure was the greatest reward, spurring her to grind harder as she took him deep into her throat. Her fingers gently kneaded and tugged at the soft heavy bag below his shaft. She hummed around his girth, swallowing a gush of pre-cum and savoring his clean, salty flavor.

She'd performed this act countless times with dozens of men in her adult life, none of which had left a lasting impression. But she would never forget this one. Not his taste, nor his velvety texture, nor the molten desire in his sexy brown eyes.

The man was fucking hot, and the more she pushed and pulled and licked, the more he failed to conceal his reactions. Muscles contracted on top of muscles. His feet scraped and dug against the floor. His exhales chased his inhales, his jaw tipping up, straining with the tautness of his body.

She added her teeth, scratching up and down his silky, turgid flesh, and his groaning turned to growls. His erection grew impossibly harder, and his spine bowed with the force of his need.

Her mouth was beginning to take its toll.

She pushed on, devouring him with slobbery, teeth-cutting, vulgar strokes. There was nothing clean or sweet about the way she sucked cock. But this kinky bastard didn't care. He liked it sick and depraved. The dirtier, the better. Same as her.

With a hand clenched around his sac, she squeezed his dense balls while pressing a fingertip against the tight, silken entrance of his rectum.

"Fuck." He gasped, shaking and flexing, his eyes wild as he stared down the length of his body. "What are you doing?"

"You like your ass fingered." She stroked the little clenching knot of flesh.

"Help me out here because I'm getting mixed signals." His chest heaved, and a twitch kicked up the corner of his lips. "Are you trying to deny orgasms? Or force them?"

Damn him and that lopsided smirk.

She flicked her tongue against the head of his cock and licked deep into the tiny slit, earning another trickle of salty fluid. "Depends."

"On?" He struggled to push the word past his choking breaths.

"You."

Beautiful, strapping, rugged, seductive, iron-willed Cole Hartman. She had eleven years of patience and planning riding on his willingness to cooperate.

It was hopeless.

This man wasn't going to help her in exchange for an orgasm. He was stronger than his baser needs. Smarter.

And he didn't want her.

She knew it weeks ago. But she had to try.

So she renewed her efforts, worshiping every inch of his gorgeous cock. She sucked him with everything she had, working her fist along his length, applying just the right balance of tongue and teeth.

His hips snapped upward, desperately trying to ram himself into the back of her throat, and his groans ran away from him. He was an ensnared beast, seething and bucking in the tethers of his restraints, testing the strength of the rope.

"What do you want from me, woman?" he snarled.

A loaded question. One she could only half-answer. "You know what I want."

He halted abruptly but for the flexing of his need in her mouth. His jaw hardened, and the air changed, growing colder, thinner. His gaze fell flat, and his muscles loosened beneath her.

She continued sucking him, but he wasn't feeling it.

Neither was she.

His erection didn't deflate, but the energy between them all but dissipated, the moment gone.

"Hurry along with your games, Lydia," he said in a cruel tone. "I'm growing bored."

Her stomach sank.

He didn't want her. No amount of seduction would change that.

She'd wasted a month trying to force a different outcome. Because she knew that the suffering he'd endured at her hands was a whole lot better than the brutality that would come from Vincent Barrington's men.

But she'd failed. White torture, psychological

manipulation, isolation, blow jobs—he was immune to it all.

Disappointment constricted her chest. She needed more from him. Far more than the hard drive's location.

She needed him to help her *retrieve* it. But she couldn't tell him that. Not until she trusted him. Until he trusted her. And that would never happen.

Because he despised her.

He despised the way she looked, the way she spoke, the things she did. Could she blame him? She'd threatened his friends, captured him, and raped him. She was a horrible person.

With her heart in her throat, she sat back on her heels and admitted defeat. She only had one option left, and if that didn't work, Vincent would get rid of her and let the team slice, dice, break, and ultimately kill Cole for the information in his head.

She couldn't allow that. Not while there was still blood in her body.

FOURTEEN

Determination chased away the trembling in Lydia's legs as she strode to the bag she'd left nearby.

The guards were never in the warehouse during her sessions with Cole. But Mike was. Always. He remained close, out of view, armed, and ready to step in if Cole managed to overpower her or escape his restraints.

Knowing Mike listened to her having sex with another man was upsetting. But they shared an unusual bond with a complicated background. They would survive this like they'd survived everything else over the past eleven years. *Together.*

She glanced in the direction of the exit, unable to see his position around the corner. But he was there. She bet her life on it.

From the bag, she removed a laptop, launched a recorded video, and set it on the floor beside Cole's head.

He glared at the rafters, refusing to look at the screen. The same reaction he had the night she showed him the footage of the drone. He wasn't stupid. He knew that whatever she intended to show him would hurt. It would hurt worse than anything he'd endured so far.

She pressed play on the video and stepped back, detaching herself from his impending pain. God, how she'd tried to avoid this. Tried and failed.

Because the way to Cole Hartman wasn't through his stomach or his dick.

It was through his heart.

The video began, streaming sultry music through the warehouse. His entire body turned to stone.

Slowly, his neck twisted, his eyes shifting toward the screen. His expression, starkly blank, gave nothing away. He lifted his head, straining to see around the bulge of his bicep. She couldn't see the video, but she knew it well.

The glittery costume, sensual hip rotations, long golden hair, and room full of admirers were but a backdrop to the main attraction.

Danni Savoy was stunning. With huge gray eyes, flawless skin, and a body that dripped sex, she wasn't just a gorgeous woman. She was a gorgeous belly dancer. Dear God, the woman stood on that stage and danced like no one was watching—shameless and serene, self-possessed and sinfully, enchantingly talented. And everyone was watching.

The video captured ten minutes of her performance, focusing on the gyration of her hips, her pretty face, and most importantly, the vulnerability of her position. She wasn't locked away in hiding. She was dancing in public for all to see.

Lydia didn't have to voice the threat to Cole. The footage spoke for itself.

"This is where you went for five days," he said in an eerily calm tone.

"Yes." She'd driven seventeen hours to St. Louis to locate Cole Hartman's heart. "Your dancer is extraordinary. Painfully beautiful. If I were into women, I would be obsessed with her, too."

"I'm not obsessed with her." His dark gaze snapped to hers, stony and unbreakable. "*She* doesn't belong to me, Lydia. *You* do."

His erection, which had lost some of its life, hardened anew. With his magnificent body laid out like an erotic buffet, rigid and vibrating, he exuded an animal magnetism that made her feel things, *want* things that she couldn't freeze out.

It was impossible not to desire him. Any woman with a pulse would throw herself at his feet. So to hear him say that she belonged to him? It satisfied an ache she didn't even know she had.

It also distracted her from the job.

He continued to stare, watching her with a brooding intensity in his eyes, the video seemingly forgotten. Why wasn't he freaking out and asking about Danni's safety?

Because this was Cole, always in control and one step ahead.

"She might not belong to you." She crossed her arms, her pulse thudding. "But you belong to her."

"My position says otherwise. You have me, Lydia." He eased up on the rope, relaxing his limbs, unabashedly sprawled and fully erect. "Come here, and I'll show you."

It had to be a trap, but she was already moving toward it, kicking off her heels as she went.

The music on the video changed, increasing in

crescendo. Danni's hips would be kicking and shimmying along with the beat, but he didn't glance at the screen, didn't remove his eyes from Lydia.

As she reached him, she lowered to her knees and slid over his sculpted body, her hands and lips roaming everywhere, trembling and conflicted. But all the doubts in her mind couldn't stop her from crawling up his chest and touching his beard, his rugged face, those chiseled lips.

"Closer." Panting, he lifted his head and offered his mouth. "Give me your lips."

As if yanked by a fist attached to her throat, she fell into him, kissing him with reckless abandon.

He growled, pushing his tongue into her mouth and taking over. Her insides turned molten as she ground down on him, rubbing her pussy against his flexing abs.

Then she broke the kiss, shocked by how wet she'd become. She was leaking all over him and rocking mindlessly, frantically, desperate to be filled.

Rope bound his arms, chest, and legs, but his hips had freedom to move, and holy sweet Jesus, did they move. He bucked beneath her, twisting and angling as if trying to reposition her, as if dead set on taking her this way.

Maybe it was a trick. Or maybe he really did want her. The video started over, blaring its music, but he never looked at it. His gaze never left her mouth.

She grabbed his face and kissed him again. He groaned, thrusting his tongue, bruising her lips, his muscles contracting and writhing beneath her.

Reaching between them, she gripped his cock and stroked him mercilessly. His entire body went rigid, his breathing choppy and urgent, as slippery strings of pre-cum coated her hand. She increased the pressure, ringing him with her thumb and forefinger until he was groaning, thrusting, panting.

"Goddamn, Lydia. Oh, fuck." He grunted, his sinews straining and creaking the rope. "Put me inside. Right now."

Sharp longing spilled through her, shaking, building, and hurtling her toward delirium. But it wasn't enough.

She needed him.

Shifting backward, she clamped her thighs around his waist and brought her tender flesh against the underside of his cock. He was so fucking hard, so insanely turned on he couldn't catch his breath.

What had sparked it? The glimpse of his dancer on the video?

With more force than was necessary, she smacked the laptop shut and shoved it away. Then she gripped his length between her legs and slammed down on him.

"Ah, God. Fuck yeah, that's incredible." His voice scraped, thick with desire. "Now just sit there like a good girl and let me do the fucking."

Excitement and pleasure shimmered in her blood, heating her breasts and racing her pulse. He arched against the restraints, plowing into her, digging his cock deep, deeper, ramming into the back of her cunt.

Blissfully, maddeningly, she moaned. It felt so good it hurt, building too quickly, too viciously. He stabbed into her harder, faster, his hipbones driving into her buttocks and circling, dragging his length at new depths and angles, and shattering every nerve ending inside her.

Her fingers slid from his face to his flat nipple, her nails burying into muscle and pinning her need against his thrusts. Her other hand clung to his broad shoulder as she leaned toward his mouth, seeking.

He caught her lips, kissing her deep, then deeper with each brutal stroke of his cock. Her hands sought, and his body shook with exertion and pleasure. Somewhere in the recesses of her awareness, she knew she shouldn't enjoy this. But his kiss generated a craving in her neglected heart. As arousing as it was terrifying, she couldn't separate her emotions. She could not stop.

She needed more. More of his hunger. More of his kisses. More of his hot, hard maleness sliding and flexing against her.

And he gave it to her, deeper, harder, fucking her mouth as passionately as he fucked between her legs. They were sweat and spit, feral lust and smacking flesh. Together, they were explosive. Unstoppable. Dangerous as hell.

He thrust again and again, the heat so fierce, the sensations so shockingly uninhibited, she burned. Melting from the inside out, she clutched at the rigid muscles of his arms and sank into his strokes.

His aggressive kisses held their mouths together. She opened to him, her lips and thighs, welcoming the invasion, inviting him to take and touch as he wished.

She wanted his hands on her, groping and bruising. She needed his arms around her, wrenching her closer. But he was still restrained. He couldn't touch her, couldn't hold her, and she resented that.

His teeth caught her lips, biting wildly, the kiss breaking and reconnecting with the frenzy of their hunger.

"I have a weakness," he grunted against her mouth.

"Only one?"

"Right now, it's the only one that matters." His hands balled into fists above his head, his eyes locked on hers. "Give me your ass."

"You want to fuck my ass?" Her breath fled. "That's your weakness?"

"You have no idea." A shudder ran through him. "You're so goddamn hot, so unbelievably slick and greedy. The tight fist of your cunt…" He snapped his hips, hammering into her. "Fuck, you make me crazy. I can't even imagine what your little asshole would do to me."

A gaping, throbbing sensation ignited between her legs, dripping, swelling, aching to be punished.

"Jesus." He gasped. "I can feel you clenching. You want it. Christ, I knew you wouldn't pass up a dick in your ass."

"You're so fucking kinky." She stretched over him, chest to chest, mouth to mouth, with her hands braced on his restrained arms. "I want *your* dick in my ass."

"Then spread your cheeks, woman. Don't make me wait."

She was far from an inexperienced newcomer to anal. When she was younger, she had a regular lover who preferred her ass over all else.

Relaxation, arousal, and lube were crucial in making it enjoyable, and holy hell, she had all of that working for her right now. She'd never been so turned on, so utterly loose and ready for it. And wet. So goddamn wet her fluids were everywhere, leaking into her crack and running all over his thighs.

She rose on her knees, disconnecting them. He grunted at the abrupt loss of contact, his body stiff and waiting. The folds of her dress kept her covered as she reached behind her and angled his erection between her flexing cheeks.

The head of him sluiced through her slippery crevice until he notched against her back entrance, pushing against the tight outer ring. She breathed in, out, and slowly lowered, pushing down, down, all the way to the root.

So much pressure, the fullness, the overwhelming stimulation… Her body gushed in response, and his echoed her every spasm. He wasn't breathing, his mouth hanging open, his eyes wide and glazed.

Then she lifted, stretching around him and crying out before sinking again.

He choked on a groan and started pumping away, harder, faster. "I'm going to come."

"Wait." Her hand skidded down his abs to his hip, holding him fast, while she fumbled beneath the dress to rub her clit.

He didn't wait. His muscles went taut. His spine arched, and he roared, thrusting feverishly, erratically, and jetting a torrent of hot liquid warmth into her ass.

He came.

At last, he fucking surrendered.

Despite not finding her own release, she couldn't help but savor the victory.

"Wipe that look off your face." His voice cut through her like a whip, shockingly cold and mean. "Get off me."

She flinched, frozen, with him still buried in her rectum.

"Get up!" He punched his hips, dislodging her, his eyes blazing with fury. "Get the fuck away from me."

FIFTEEN

Stunned and teetering, Lydia fell off Cole's lap and landed on the floor beside him.

"What the fuck is wrong with you?" She shoved to her feet, shaking with her fists at her sides.

"Are you fucking kidding me? You've been forcing yourself on me for days, and you have the nerve to ask what's wrong with *me?*"

Footsteps pounded behind her, sounding Mike's approach. When he reached her side, she shivered at anger rolling off him. But neither she nor Cole spared him a glance, their gazes locked.

"Orgasm denial doesn't work on a man who doesn't want to come." Cole laughed cruelly. "He has to be interested."

"You just came—"

"I *literally* fucked you in the ass, Lydia. With my hands tied. Let that sink in for a second."

It sank, and it sank *hard*, caving in her chest and leaving a trail of ice.

After a long, heart-pounding pause, Cole went in

for the kill. "The only pleasure I derived from that orgasm was knowing that while you're coming to terms with how fantastically you've been manipulated, you get to feel my payback dribbling from your filthy asshole."

Bile hit her throat. She was going to throw up.

Mike lunged forward with his pistol drawn, his expression murderous.

She swung out an arm and caught him across the chest, halting him. She needed to hear this. No matter how badly it hurt.

With a growl, he snatched Cole's jeans from the floor and tossed them over Cole's soft cock.

Grateful to not have to see that part of him, she moved to the hose and twisted it on. She could, in fact, feel him dripping down her legs. An irritation that would soon be remedied.

Cole and Mike watched as she lifted the hem of the dress and sprayed off the slime between her thighs. She kept herself covered, but it wasn't her finest moment.

Her humiliation was absolute, but she hid it beneath a mien of rancor, which she directed at Cole, shouting with her eyes. *Fuck you.*

The corners of his mouth twisted up, defiling his gorgeous face. So antagonistic, that smirk.

"Danni is surrounded by bodyguards, right?" He glanced at the laptop and returned to her. "You can't touch her. If you could, she would be here with a gun aimed at her head. The casino has top-notch security, so you couldn't even plant bugs. You had to wear a camera on your clothes and sit in the restaurant with all the other patrons just to capture a recording of her."

Her throat closed.

He'd known all along. That explained why the video hadn't upset him.

Everything they just did together had been deliberately contrived. None of it had been real. How hypocritical of her to think otherwise. She'd been coercing him all along.

Except that wasn't entirely true. She was using him and at the same time, saving him. She wanted him to survive. And for a fleeting moment, when they were together, she wanted him simply because she wanted to be with him.

"The video was only good as a scare tactic. A hollow threat," he said, his voice rumbling, crawling beneath her skin. "You're desperate. That tells me you searched for my friends and couldn't find them. Danni was your only option."

Mike stiffened beside her, his finger twitching against the trigger on the pistol. He wouldn't shoot unless he had to. He wasn't that impulsive.

She'd tried to track Cole's friends. But while she was getting him settled in his cell, his friends had fled the states. They were nowhere to be found.

"Why are you telling me this?" She turned off the hose and dried her legs with a towel. "Why not just tell me where the hard drive is?"

"We both know I'm not walking out of here. You're not going to kill me. But there are fifteen men, including your boyfriend here, who are gunning to rip me apart."

She ground her teeth, feeling pretty fucking homicidal. "You don't know me or what I'm capable of."

"No, but I've learned a lot over the past month. Enough to know you're too soft to torture me."

"I wasn't too soft to fuck you, was I?"

"You convinced yourself I was into it, but you feel guilt. Puts a new light on the walk of shame."

Her cheeks heated, and a ringing sound blared in her ears. She hated him for this. Hated how easily he dissected her.

"You don't have the stomach for torture, and you're not cold enough to be a Russian swallow." His jaw tightened, twitching his beard. "You're not even Russian."

The blood drained from her face, chilling her skin. Oh God, how did he know?

She didn't dare speak, too afraid she would give away more than she already had.

"During the first week, you had a good handle on the accent." Furrows formed between his brows. "It was stiff, but convincing. Then it started to slip. The more comfortable you were around me, the more your inflection relaxed. Especially when you're aroused. That's when I hear the Midwestern drawl. Chicago, I think."

"She's lived in the states for years." Mike shook his head, refusing to give up her ruse. "Of course, she picked up an American accent."

"That's what I thought until she made a glaring mistake." Cole met her eyes. "The day I told you I wanted *palimi* with sour cream and caviar, you didn't correct me. You played it off like you knew what I was saying. But you don't. *Blini* is a pancake. A Russian staple for breakfast. *Palimi* isn't even a word."

Her lungs collapsed, and her hands slicked with sweat. She'd fucked up, and if Cole saw through her disguise, who else had? If Vincent Barrington was half as smart as Cole, she was dead.

Mike stepped forward, and she recognized the look in his eyes. He was ready to end this with a bullet in Cole's head.

Cole knew too much. He couldn't live, and given the *fuck-it* vibes radiating from him, he'd already accepted his fate.

"Mike." She set a hand on his forearm and dropped the accent. "This isn't finished."

He glanced behind them, confirming they were alone. Then he gave a nod.

"Why Chicago?" she asked Cole.

"Your *th* sounds get lazy. Instead of *zis,* you slip into *dis. Da* hard drive, instead of *za* hard drive. You've used *fer* instead of *for,* among a dozen other little tells." Cole switched to Russian, speaking each word with flawless articulation. "You use Midwestern slang that doesn't make sense to native Russians."

He was right. Goddammit, she knew it happened sometimes and tried to cover it. But nothing slipped past him.

She blew it. The gig was up, and she had no idea what to do.

Pacing, she grasped at strings, desperate to fix this. "Tell me who bought the hard drive, and I'll let you go. Right now. Just give me a name, and you're free."

Mike went still, his gaze cutting to her. This wasn't part of the plan, and he didn't like it. If Cole went free, he would hunt her down. After everything she did to him, she expected nothing less.

"You won't let me go." He twisted his arms in the rope. "Even if you tried, you won't succeed. You're not in charge."

"What are you talking about? I'm leading this—"

"Thurney Bridge."

Her neck went taut. He'd mentioned that before, and she'd looked into it. There was a bridge in France by that name, but she found nothing else. Nothing related to Cole Hartman.

"Five months ago," he said, "a hitman killed Rylee Sutton's neighbor, two motel clerks, and when he attempted to kill Rylee, he mentioned Thurney Bridge."

Vincent Barrington. That corrupt son of a bitch. Putting hits on innocent people? What else was he doing behind her back?

"That wasn't me." Her heart pounded. "I don't know anything about that."

"Your boss was behind it."

"He's not my boss."

"He."

Shit. She'd just given way another detail. For the love of God, she needed to keep her mouth shut.

"Your boss knows the connection between me, Thurney Bridge, Marie Merivale, and the hard drive," he said. "That suggests he has access to classified information."

She pressed her lips together, refusing to confirm or deny.

"So how do you fit in?" He slowly released a breath through his nose. "You posed as a Russian swallow to get hired for this job. Your boss sent you here to capture me and seduce me into talking. Not an uncommon tactic, but complicated. Physical torture would've been simpler."

She shared a look with Mike. Trusting Cole was out of the question, but if she disclosed their strategy, there might still be a way to use him.

"I wasn't just hired to seduce you into talking."

She met Cole's steady gaze. "I was hired to seduce the person in possession of the hard drive."

"So you can steal it."

"Yes. My employer doesn't give a fuck how I get it, just as long as it's in his hands by the end of the year."

Cole nodded, his expression pensive. "You kept me alive, with all my limbs, because you need me to help you steal it."

"That would make things easier."

"I don't do retrievals of that nature." He relaxed into the floor, his chest glistening with sweat and scratches from her nails. "I'm not a goddamn thief."

"I know. That's why you're in this position."

"What do you know about me?"

"For the past seven years, you've accepted jobs that involved finding missing persons and information. Information such as secret trafficking routes and criminal headquarters, which often puts you deep in the bowels of cartels and organized crime syndicates. But you've never taken a job related to politics or government intelligence. I assume you're bound by loyalty to your country or some sort of legality related to the job you held in the government. How am I doing so far?"

"Not bad. Your boss gave you this intel?"

"Yes."

Vincent knew a lot about Cole, but he'd only given her the bare minimum. Without Vincent, she wouldn't have connected Cole to the hard drive. She wouldn't have even known he existed.

"You deceived your boss about who and what you are." Cole inclined his head, eyes tapered. "He believes he hired a sex spy when in reality, you're here with your own agenda. You don't intend to deliver the hard drive to him. You want it for yourself."

A chill swept down her spine, and her neck twisted impulsively toward the exit, her eyes scanning every shadow and nook in the warehouse. If Vincent or his men knew the truth, it was game over.

Vincent thought she didn't know what was on that hard drive. He believed she and Mike were just here for a paycheck.

"He's going to kill you," Cole said, reading her mind.

"Not if I kill him first. Listen to me." She crouched beside his hip and set a hand on his thigh.

He flinched and bared his teeth, looking for all the world like he wanted to rip her to shreds.

"You hate me. Fine." Her heart in knots, she removed her touch. "But if we work together, we can survive this."

"Burn in hell."

"I'll pay you. Name your price." She was talking out of her ass. She had no money. "I'll pay you whatever you want for your cooperation."

"What was your exit strategy, Lydia? You seduce me and learn the hard drive's location. Then what? How were you going to sneak out of here, with me, without giving your boss the information he wants?"

She lowered her gaze to his body, taking in his strength, his sheer muscle mass.

"I see." Disappointment roughened his voice. "You thought I'd be so blinded by your pussy that I'd lead you out like fucking G.I. Joe, maybe take some bullets for you in the process. And if I survived, I'd be useful in infiltrating the next target."

"You have powerful friends. Once we get out of

here—"

"You want my friends to help you? The same friends you targeted with hellfire?"

"The drone wasn't armed."

"Lydia," Mike growled.

"You were bluffing?" Cole barked out a laugh. "Fucking awesome." In the next breath, he sobered, his eyes hard as steel. "Give me the name of the motherfucker who's funding this shit show."

"He's—"

In a blur, Mike pounced, swinging the pistol and whipping it across Cole's head. The smack echoed through the warehouse, leaving Cole knocked out cold.

She gasped. "Why did you do that?"

He turned his furious gaze on her. "You said too much. If you tell him who's involved, he'll go after the hard drive himself."

"That's what we want." She grabbed a towel and a bucket of water and knelt beside Cole's head.

"We want it in the right hands. You know how valuable it is." He raked his fingers through his hair, yanking at the roots. "Jesus, Lydia. You can't trust him. You don't know anything about him."

She bent down and wiped the wet rag along the gash near Cole's temple. A trickle of blood fell from the cut, but it would heal cleanly without stitches. Mike knew how to strike with minimal damage.

"I don't trust him." She applied pressure to the wound and let her fingers trail down his sculpted face.

Mike's expression clouded as he watched her. "You trusted him with your ass."

She sucked in a sharp breath, hurt by the disgust in his tone. "Don't you dare shame me for that."

"Lydia." Sighing, he closed his eyes and pinched

the bridge of his nose. "I'm not…" He dropped his hand and stared at her with bloodshot eyes. "Look, I get why you did it. Why you let him…" His stance widened, shifting with the weight of his frustration. "Just tell me you're not falling for him."

"What?" She blinked. Then choked out a laugh. "No. God. This is bigger than me, Mike. It's bigger than *us*."

"I know." His eyes narrowed on her hands in Cole's hair.

"Good grief." She tossed the towel in the bucket and stood, staring down at Cole's limp body. "He beat me at my own game. I seduced him. He seduced me. He won. That's all this is. I don't know the extent of his skill set, but I can tell you this. He's a master at reading people. He knew how to strip me down and make me talk before I had a clue what was happening. But he doesn't know everything. We can let him go. Let him live."

"Lydia."

"We're a lot of things, but we're not murderers. If we leave him here, he's dead." Her chest squeezed. "He's never going to talk. He'll let them kill him first."

"This is so fucked." He paced away with his hands clasped behind his neck. "We're not giving up."

"Never." Her pulse quickened, her voice breathless.

"All right. Go back to the room." He squatted beside Cole and reached for the jeans. "I'll dress him and return him to the cell."

"What if he tries to talk to the guards? If he tells them what he knows…?"

He flashed a menacing smile. "I'll gladly knock his ass out again."

SIXTEEN

Lydia dozed off. She hadn't meant to close her eyes, but when she opened them, a rude buzzing crashed through her grogginess.

"Fuck!" She scrambled off the mattress and stumbled through the room, hunting the vibrating sounds of her phone.

Where the hell was Mike? He should've returned by now.

She spotted the buzzing device on the table amid the clutter of cosmetics. Snatching it up, she gasped at the time. Jesus, she'd slept for two hours?

Because…Cole. He'd put her body through the wringer and mangled her emotions. But she couldn't think about that now. The unknown caller wasn't going to be happy about waiting through five rings. Six.

"Yes?" She hacked the greeting from the back of her throat, overly conscious about her fake accent. "You need something?"

"Change of plans." Vincent's high-pitched drawl set her teeth on edge. "I'm moving up the deadline."

"You can't do that." She tightened her hand around the phone, making it creak. "We had a deal."

"It's already done. The team is extracting the information now, and once they have it, they'll pass it along to you. Then you will retrieve the package. Maybe your cunt will be more effective on the next target."

Her blood pressure hit the roof, and she reached out a hand, catching herself on the table, attempting to steady her legs and quash the panic in her voice.

"Whatever," she said with as much boredom as she could summon. "The payment doesn't change."

"You'll get your money. Just don't fuck this up."

"I'm very good at my job."

"You keep saying that. Yet you've produced nothing."

"I delivered him here."

"Yeah, all right, I'll give you that." He hardened his tone, which succeeded only in making him sound whiny. "You will stay out of the way until the others get the information you need. Then you will finish this. Understood?"

He expected her to sit here while they butchered and killed Cole.

Yeah, whatever you say, boss.

She swallowed down her rising fury. "Yes."

He disconnected.

She'd never met him in person, and maybe she never would. But as she tossed the phone and dragged on a pair of black jeans, she vowed that, before she surrendered her last breath, she would witness the glorious annihilation of Vincent Barrington.

Quickly, she pulled on a white t-shirt, combat boots, and checked her appearance in the mirror. The false eyelashes barely hung on. Black eyeliner melted down her cheeks and smeared into her blush. Bright red lipstick slanted over her chin as if streaked by a river of drool.

She looked like a redheaded Harley Quinn, freshly fucked, one-hundred-percent psychotic, and ready to party.

Yeah, her makeup was utterly ruined—*thank you, Cole*—but it still did its job. It hid her true face.

On her way out, she grabbed a handgun, slid in a full magazine, and clipped a spare mag on her hip. Then she took off down the hall.

Passing the break room, she counted four guys gathered around the table eating and drinking beer. She slipped by unnoticed and turned the corner, pausing at the bathroom. Two men inside. She intersected two more farther down the corridor.

One of them stopped her. "Where are you going?"

"I need a shower." She gave him a look. "That's not an invite."

He held up his hands and backed away, smirking as his eyes drifted down her body.

"The warehouse is all yours, honey." He turned and paced off in the opposite direction.

Had he just come from there? God, she hoped Cole was still in his cell, and Mike was keeping guard.

As she measured her steps, trying to appear calm, Vincent's words coiled in her belly.

The team is extracting the information now.

That could mean anything, but her mind conjured knives cutting through flesh, extracting bones, organs, and any part of Cole that would bring out the answer.

By the time she burst into the warehouse, she was

sweating and out of breath.

Silence surrounded her, thrashing in her ears. No one was here. She spun toward Cole's cell.

The door stood open. He was gone.

Oh fuck, oh fuck, oh fuck. Where the hell was he?

Where was Mike? Was he in trouble? If Vincent's men overheard her conversation with him, if they were hurting him…

Horror glued her boots to the floor. Terror pulled through her gut. A helpless void resonated in her chest.

The loading dock.

It was the only place they could be. Unless Cole and Mike were taken somewhere. Somewhere she would never find them.

She raced out of the warehouse, down the eerily quiet corridor, toward the dock.

What if it was a trap? Were they waiting for her to come running? Had they figured out why she was here?

Her eyes darted behind her, expecting one of the doors to open and hands to shoot out.

Paranoia pushed her harder, and dread dug in its claws. She wrestled with it, fighting it down, burying it deep enough to control her breathing. Then she forced herself to holster the weapon in her waistband. She couldn't burst in with guns blazing. Not without giving herself away.

At the entrance to the loading dock, she pulled in another calming breath and opened the door.

Voices drew her attention to the far side. She flattened her back to the wall, remaining out of view. Then she peered around the corner.

Alec stood beside a massive machine, his attention on the cast-iron bridge that rose overhead, twenty feet in length, with steel pillars supporting each end. She didn't know anything about the tools required for cutting stone into grave markers, but it didn't take a genius to understand how this one worked.

Suspended from the center of its bridge was a circular saw, at least six feet in diameter. Rusty, broken teeth fringed the outer edge. It was large enough to cut blocks of granite into narrow slabs.

Or human bodies into little messy slivers.

She worked her throat against a knot of fear.

The machine didn't function. None of the junk left behind was operational. Unless someone had fixed it? Was there a mechanic on the team?

"What's it going to be?" Alec folded his arms across his chest. "Your hands? Or your feet? Or you can keep your extremities and tell us the location of the hard drive."

Her shoulders bunched to her ears, and her heart landed somewhere in the vicinity of her stomach. She silenced her breathing and leaned forward, straining for a better look.

Five men stood around the machine, including Alec. *And Mike.*

A vein of relief swept through her.

Angled slightly away from her position, Mike rested his hands in his pockets, exuding the appearance of cool indifference. But she knew him.

She knew his shoulders held too much stiffness. His neck elongated with the tensing of muscles, and trenches rutted his hair from his fingers repeatedly pushing through it. He was anything but relaxed.

He was also the only man not armed.

Alec and the others must've taken him by surprise, and now he was pretending to go along with this to avoid raising alarms. *This* being the torture of Cole Hartman.

Cole lay on the platform beneath the giant circular saw, his body restrained to the steel structure. He didn't move, didn't make a sound.

"We'll start with your hands, then." Alec flicked a lever on the machine.

An ear-splitting screech cracked the air, springing the rusty saw to life and making her jump.

No, no, no!

She stared in horror as Alec hit another switch and lowered the enormous whirring blade. Cole's arm lay two feet beneath it, trapped in rope. He didn't struggle or twitch a muscle. The fucking asshole was just going to lie there and let that saw take his hand.

Mike's shadowed eyes flicked back and forth, lingering on the men's holstered guns. He was going to attempt something. Something stupid like swiping one of their weapons. Dammit, he was going to get himself shot.

Perspiration formed on her spine.

At the speed in which the blade lowered, she only had seconds.

A huge breath filled her lungs as she drew her weapon. Then she bolted forward, the sound of her approach swallowed by the chest-rattling squeal of the machine.

Alec spotted her first, his brows leaping to his hairline. Twenty-feet away, she fired.

Missed.

Fucking shit! She sprinted forward. He reached for his gun.

Fifteen-feet. She shot again and hit him in the chest. He dropped instantly.

The need to gasp set her lungs on fire, but she couldn't draw air. Adrenaline spiked her blood as she set her sights on the remaining three.

Their guns, already drawn, turned toward her as the spinning blade continued its descent, the toothy edge blurring inches from Cole's arm.

All at once, Mike grabbed one of the men, and a bullet fired, whizzing past her ear as she squeezed the trigger.

Over and over, she shot off rounds, charging forward and blowing through the magazine until the only man left standing was Mike.

Without taking a breath, she fell upon the machine and smacked the lever. Her heart stopped, waiting in agony as the motor ground to a soundless halt, freezing the circular saw.

The blade sat against Cole's sinewy forearm, drawing a bead of blood around the serrated, rust-colored edge. So goddamn close, and he never struggled. Never moved a muscle.

Her pulse pounded as she dragged her eyes over the rest of him. Boots, dirty jeans, powerful legs, shredded abs, tattooed chest and arms, and a scraggly beard that only enhanced his intimidating, masculine appearance.

No visible injuries.

"Other than the cut," she said, quickly flipping the switch to lift the blade, "you're not harmed?"

His silence pulled her gaze to his, and lord have mercy, those molten brown eyes imprisoned her, suffocated her, and refused to let go. He was so beautiful, so utterly unruffled and fearless, just watching her, breathing calmly, *alive.*

As she met his stare head-on, she swore she saw

that look again, the one from before when she thought she felt something forging between them. Something real and not of this cold, ugly world.

Tingling sparked through her arms and fingers, and she gulped a breath.

"In less than a minute, we're going to be under fire." Mike scuttered back and forth behind her, collecting weapons. "Time to go."

The moment she'd shot the first bullet, the report had alerted the rest of the team of trouble. Any second, ten men would explode through that door with more firepower than she and Mike could defend.

"Hurry." He slapped a knife onto the platform beside Cole and sprinted across the ramp toward the parked vehicles.

Two motorcycles sat out there somewhere among the cars and trucks, with the keys in the ignitions.

"We'll take the bikes," she shouted after Mike and cut one of Cole's arms free.

Then she set the blade in his hand so that he could remove the rest. As he calmly sawed his way through the rope, she replaced the magazine in her gun and stepped back, keeping the weapon trained on him.

Outside, Mike darted from one parked vehicle to the next, slashing all the tires. All but the two bikes they would leave with.

"Have you ever killed a man?" Cole freed his arm and moved to his legs, regarding her from beneath his dark brows.

"N—" Her voice cracked, and she cleared her throat. "No."

"You did good. Most people hesitate the first time." The corner of his mouth quirked up as he glanced at the gash on his arm. "You didn't."

"I made a choice." She held the gun with both hands, her fingers clammy and ribcage wrapped in rubber bands. "Don't make me regret it."

He cut through the final restraint and shoved to his feet, his gaze instantly falling on the dead bodies, scanning their clothes. She knew what he was looking for, but Mike had already taken the weapons.

She might've sabotaged the entire fucking mission to save Cole's life. But that didn't mean she and Mike trusted him with a gun. If he was the revengeful sort, she wasn't safe.

She would never be safe again.

An ache swelled in her chest.

Walk away, Lydia.

He stared at her, expressionless, and she stared back, miserable and heartbroken. There was so much to say. If things had been different, if she were a gentler person with better circumstances…

There was no time.

"Go." She stepped forward, aiming the gun at his handsome face. "You're free. Take the second bike and get out of here."

"Lydia!" Mike yelled from outside as the engine of a motorcycle rumbled to life.

Cole's dark gaze lifted toward the door thirty yards behind her, and his eyebrows pinched. In the next heartbeat, the door crashed open.

"Run!" She raced toward the ramp and found Mike waiting at the far end on the motorcycle.

Shots fired, pelting the ground behind her and whistling past her head. The spare bike sat twenty-some yards in the other direction. But rather than darting for it, Cole remained at her back, breathing down her neck.

"Get out of here!" She pointed at his ride. "That

way!"

The volley of bullets multiplied as more men poured onto the loading dock. A couple of them were closing in, gaining on her. She couldn't outrun the spray of lead.

As she started to turn and fire back, a hand gripped her arm.

Everything happened so fast, the chaos of gunfire ricocheting in her ears, disorienting her as Cole yanked her off the ramp.

Her back hit the ground, and he fell atop of her, dodging bullets with laughter in his eyes.

What the fuck? Her heart thundered so violently she thought her ribs were cracking. And he was laughing?

"First gunfight?" He grinned down at her, his shirtless chest smothering her in heat.

Yes. But before she could answer, he plucked the pistol from her grip, extended his arm, and returned fire.

Pinned beneath him, she craned her neck and watched the men scatter. Two of them dropped, hit by Cole's bullets. At least six more took cover.

On the other side of the ramp, Mike sped forward on the motorcycle, firing his gun at the shooters on the loading dock.

Cole used the diversion to wrap his arms around her and roll them across the ground, seeking cover. He found it beneath a nearby box truck, where he yanked her up and dragged her around to the other side, shoving her behind it, shielding her from gunfire.

Buying them time.

A moment.

With her back pressed to the vehicle, he leaned in

and flattened a hand on the steel above her head. Her breathing tumbled into asthmatic hysteria while his remained normal, controlled, unnervingly composed.

But his eyes told a different story, the dark depths pulsing with the hungry fires of hell.

This wasn't the man who fucked her ass and knocked her away with a nasty sneer. This devil was far more deadly, possessive, protective, deeply passionate, and complicated. She stared into the soul of a man she could fall in love with.

The longing that gripped her was enormous, the pull toward him more than she could bear.

"Go." She shoved at his chest.

Gunfire boomed just beyond the truck, growing closer. Amid the mayhem, she heard the motorcycle, the engine revving, speeding toward her.

"Leave." She slammed her palms against his shoulders and pushed harder. "You're free!"

He stepped back, swaying with her shove. Then he was on her again, cupping her head with both hands. With the gun in his grip, the length of it lay against her cheek as he held her, forcing her to look at him.

"Darius Skutnik." His thumb tenderly stroked across her cheekbone.

"What?"

"The *nașu* of the Romanian mafia. The godfather." He brought their foreheads together and breathed against her lips. "He has the hard drive."

Shock and elation stole through her, weakening her legs and her voice. But she didn't need either as he lifted her up his body and kissed her hard on the mouth. His tongue knifed past her lips. His beard scratched her face, and his fingers dug into the backs of her thighs.

She grabbed his shoulders to pull. No, to push. It was too much. *He* was too much.

He wrenched his mouth away and turned just as Mike rolled up on the motorcycle.

"Let her go." He trained the gun on Cole. "They're coming."

Cole shifted and set her on the seat behind Mike. As he pulled back, her heart tore. Another retreating step, and her trembling hands slid off his shoulders, down his biceps, her fingers curling, hanging on.

He slipped free, and her palm came away wet. Soaked in blood.

"Oh my God." Her eyes darted to the hole in his arm, her bloody hand reaching for him. "You were shot?"

Footsteps stampeded toward the truck.

Cole's gaze stayed with her for another second before he tore it away, spun, and fired the pistol.

"Hold on!" Mike opened the throttle, and the motorcycle lurched forward. She wrapped her arms around him and twisted, watching as Cole shot into the fray and sprinted toward the second bike.

Her hair whipped around her face, obstructing her view as Mike put more and more separation between them and the gunfight. She didn't breathe until she heard the roar of another engine. She didn't straighten her neck until Cole appeared off in the distance, bent low over the bike as he sped through the desert in the opposite direction.

Twilight approached, streaking the horizon in ribbons of orange and violet. Within seconds, the swirling shadows swallowed his form. He was safe.

Gone.

A painful clot amassed deep inside her, and a

terrible burn bubbled from her chest, forming a lump in her throat and searing the backs of her eyes. Everything she felt was irrational and wrong, but it was real.

What she felt for him was real and raw and unbearable.

She screwed her eyes shut and rested her cheek against Mike's strong back, her arms holding him tight.

They survived. All three of them. And Cole had given her a name. Now she knew the location of the hard drive.

This wasn't over.

Not the job.

And not this other thing…this unresolved connection.

She knew at gut level she hadn't seen the last of Cole Hartman.

SEVENTEEN

Drenched in sweat and trammeled by exhaustion, Cole stood at the bathroom sink in Tomas' vacant house and patched up the gunshot wound.

It was a clean shot through his bicep, with an entry and exit point. It would hurt like a bitch for a while and fuck with his muscle movement. But it could've been worse.

He could be lying beneath the stonecutter in a hundred sliced-up pieces.

Once he finished treating the injury, he slumped onto the couch and contemplated who to call first.

Maybe because the image of red hair was heavy on his mind, he dialed the only ginger he knew.

Luke answered with a heavy exhale of relief. "Holy shit, you're alive."

"Thanks for the vote of confidence."

"The doubt was real."

"I'm safe, in case you're wondering."

"Where are you?"

"Making a pit stop at the house in the desert."

He couldn't stay here. Lydia knew about this place, which meant the person she'd just betrayed knew about it, too. He just needed to grab some gear. Shit, shower, and shave. Then he would be on his way.

"You've been missing for a goddamn month," Luke growled. "Where have you been?"

Despite the overload of fatigue and unease, Cole managed a smile. It was nice to have people who cared enough to worry about him.

"Calm down." He chuckled. "I made it out with all my parts intact."

"We thought you were dead."

"No, you didn't."

"We had a funeral service and everything. Van cried. Huge crocodile tears. It made everyone uncomfortable."

"Fuck off."

"Seriously, man." Luke's voice sobered. "We've been freaked the fuck out. What happened?"

"I spent a month in a pitch-black cell, eating hot dogs and listening to thrash metal music."

"Are you fucking with me?"

"Wish I was."

"What about the freaky Russian pin-up girl? Did she do that to you?"

"She isn't Russian." His heart drummed at the mention of her, his thoughts a conflicting jumble of anger and desire. "She restrained me, fucked me, and saved my life."

A stretch of silence ensued, followed by Luke's exhale. "I can't tell by your tone if you participated or if it was torture, so I'm just going to come out and ask. Were you raped?"

Coming from Luke, it was an earnest question.

He'd been raped by Van, and most recently, by a strap-on worn by a crazy bitch in La Rocha Cartel.

"Dubious," Cole said. "In the end, I fucked her in the ass."

He gave Luke a rundown of the events, walking through the details, and answering one-hundred-and-one questions.

Once Luke was up to speed, Cole asked, "Is everyone back in Colombia?"

"Yeah, we're all here. We stayed in Texas for a few weeks. When we couldn't find you, we assumed you'd been transported out of the state. Or out of the country. We didn't know. So we returned home where we could regroup in a safe place and wait for you to make contact, per your orders."

"You did good."

"Now what? There's a lot you don't know about these people. What are you going to do?"

"I can leave the country and join you guys in Colombia. If they're hunting me, they won't be able to find me there."

"You're talking about hiding." Luke made a huffing sound. "We both know you won't do that. You're going to go after her."

"I'm going to *track* her. Whatever she's involved in is big. Bigger than she can handle. She's in way over her head."

"You want to help this woman?"

"No. I don't want anything to do with this shit. But I need to know. *Fuck.*" He scrubbed a hand over his head, on edge and needing sleep. "I need to know who she is and what she's trying to achieve."

He would stay in the shadows and remain unseen. No contact with her. No exceptions. Whoever she betrayed today wasn't going to let her live. That hard drive held something valuable. Valuable enough to orchestrate an elaborate plan that involved a fifteen-man team, a Russian swallow, and the capture of a retired operative from the *activity.*

A shit storm was brewing. He felt it in his bones.

"How can we help?" Luke asked.

"I need to follow her every movement without being seen by her or whoever might be hunting her."

"You need Romero."

"Yep."

Romero was the computer whiz kid who had been instrumental in helping Luke and Vera escape La Rocha Cartel earlier this year. The kid had designed and maintained the proprietary technology that secured the cartel compound, but his range of tech skills went far beyond that.

"I'm heading through the halls to look for him now." Luke's breathing picked up, confirming he was on the move. "He can hack into security systems and run facial recognition software on the camera footage, but he'll need information. Names, aliases, physical descriptions, whatever you have."

"I can give him hair color, eye color, height, weight, a detailed description of every tattoo on her body, what she was wearing when she left the desert, how she dresses, which direction she headed, and so on."

"Okay, cool. I'll call you back in a bit. In the meantime, you need to get out of that house."

"On it."

It took him ten minutes to pack all the clothes, weapons, tech gear, and travel documents he would need for an extended mission. More time was doled to showering and shaving off his beard, as well as all the hair on his head. He grabbed Danni's engagement ring and secured the chain around his neck. Then he devoured a can of chili.

When Luke called back, he put Romero on the phone, and Cole gave the kid every detail he had on Lydia and Mike. It was probably more information than Romero would need. The tattoos alone would make Lydia stand out like a beacon.

"Give me a few hours," Romero said. "Should I contact you at this number?"

"Yeah, it's a secure phone. Thanks, Romero."

"You bet."

Six hours later, Cole was sitting on a bench outside Dallas Fort Worth International Airport when his phone buzzed.

Concealed behind sunglasses and the bill of a baseball hat, he lifted the device to his ear. "What do you have for me?"

"Two hours ago," Romero said, "a woman and man matching your description bought airline tickets at George Bush Intercontinental Airport in Houston. They're traveling under the names Lydia and Micheál Johnson."

His pulse kicked up. "Excellent work, kid."

He'd gone to the airport in Dallas on a hunch that they would fly somewhere. But he didn't need to be in the same airport to follow them to their destination.

"Their flight leaves in three hours," Romero said. "Headed to London. You want the flight info?"

"Nah. I just need to know where they go after they land. Can you track them overseas?"

"Now that I have the names they're using and digital images of their faces, I can track them anywhere."

"They probably travel under multiple aliases."

"I won't lose them," Romero said with excitement in his voice.

"I know you won't." He stood and grabbed his bag. "I'll call you when I land."

"I'll be here."

As he strode into the airport to buy a ticket to London, a voice in the back of his head told him to forget this quest. He had no stakes in it. Nothing to offset the risks he would be taking.

Except the woman.

In seven years, no one had come close to capturing his interest. He was officially, certifiably enthralled, and until he understood why, he wasn't walking away from this.

EIGHTEEN

Rome, Italy
Six months later

Lydia's hand grew hot and sticky in Mike's unbending grip as he led her through the exclusive nightclub. Prolonged exhaustion and stress lived in her bones, the weeks blurring into months until she'd lost track of where she was and how much time she had left.

But she didn't lose track of faces. She memorized every detail of every person she passed, knowing any one of them could be connected to her.

Her shoulder blades twitched, her spine tingling with the feeling of exposure. Not just from the backless dress, but from the constant sensation of being watched.

She and Mike weren't just hunting. They were being hunted.

Her neck tightened with the impulse to look over her shoulder. But she kept her eyes directed at Mike's broad back and reached out her senses, probing the shadows around them.

Her short blonde bob and skintight sequin dress blended in with this crowd. The wig hid her hair, and heavy makeup covered the tattoos on her arms and chest and completely altered the contours of her face.

She looked like a drag queen, and Mike played the role of her gay lover. He'd grown out his brown hair and dyed the shaggy mop black. His fashionable linen suit, yellow bowtie, and lopsided Bruce Willis grin underscored the facade. Who knew he could look so adorable?

Every week brought a different city and a different disguise. Through Romania, Italy, Spain, England, France, and Moldova, they tracked the highest-ranking made members of the Romanian crime family, all the while staying one step ahead of the threat on their heels.

Vincent Barrington's men.

She'd already killed two of his assassins since leaving the states. More would follow. Vincent needed that hard drive. His livelihood depended on it, and his only means to find it was through her, Mike, or Cole.

Since she'd betrayed Vincent and escaped with Mike and Cole, Vincent's objective would be to kill them all—and hope to get the hard drive's location from one of them before they died.

She assumed Cole was faring better than her. He had money, powerful friends, and wasn't out in public, stalking the Romanian mafia. He'd disappeared that day in the desert, and she hadn't seen or heard from him since.

Sometimes, she thought she sensed him. When the hairs on her nape prickled, when a flutter stirred in her belly, when the shadows of an alley or dark corner of a pub seemed darker, more intense, she *felt* him. But she never saw him.

She needed to forget all about those bottomless brown eyes, the sinful slide of his tongue, the guttural sounds of his groans when he fucked. God, she needed to stop torturing herself.

Not that she had the time or resources to look for him. Every second that she wasn't running reconnaissance and surveilling the Romanian mob, she was trying to outrun Vincent's men.

Tonight, she was doing both.

The discotheque sat on the Tiber River with a stunning view of Rome. The mirrored decor was grungy, vintage, the space almost exclusively black. The rafters vibrated with the electronic beats of techno, funk, and dance tracks. But she wasn't here for the music.

She'd heard this was the place to spot a Romanian mercenary or two. To penetrate Darius Skutnik and steal the hard drive, she needed more than her body. The job required stealth, and she had a particular sort of criminal in mind. A technically trained criminal with a passion for cybercrime.

But first, she had to deal with whoever was following her.

Bodies swayed, gyrating and grinding and bumping against her as she followed Mike deeper into the horde. Amid flawlessly dressed ladies and trendy, aftershave-scented men, he stopped walking, pivoted around, and brought her chest and hips flush with his.

"Hi." She smiled and slid her hands up his strong neck.

"Hey." His lips crooked up, and his body caught the thumping rhythm.

She rolled with him. Or *tried*. He was a much better dancer, his movements natural and loose as he pulled her tight and placed his mouth at her ear.

"Black shirt, black tie. Crooked nose." He splayed a hand over her tail bone, the other curling around her waist. "At your seven o'clock."

Spinning slowly with the music, he turned them in a full rotation so that she could cast her gaze about the room without appearing obvious. She spotted the man Mike noticed, recognizing him immediately.

He leaned against a high-top table off to the side, pretending to stare at something behind her.

Mike shifted her away, letting the throng of dancers sweep them into the undulating wave of heat and sex.

"He was in Paris last week." She hooked her arms around his neck and rested her cheek against the clean-shaved curve of his jaw as her hips reeled and plunged with his. "In the train station, when we were leaving."

"And in London the week before that."

"He's our guy."

One of Vincent's. They had to kill him. Once they did, it would buy them a few months to infiltrate the Romanian mafia before Vincent deployed more hired guns.

It was a fine line they walked, trying to get close to the mafia without Vincent figuring out *who* they were tracking. If he learned the location of the hard drive, all would be lost.

"The veranda out back is ideal." She stretched on her toes to speak in his ear. "Last I checked, no one was out there."

All the smokers congregated on the huge veranda in front with a full bar.

"I'll go." It was easier for her to do it since she could employ her feminine wiles—give the man a look, flash a little cleavage, lead him into a dark corner, and slide a steel blade between his ribs.

"No, you did the last two. I want this one." He squeezed her hip, his breath against her neck. "I'll have a smoke on the veranda and wait for him. Stay here in the crowd. Keep an eye out. Don't fucking wander off."

They were both armed. She wore a stiletto strapped to her garters on her inner thigh. He had multiple blades concealed beneath his suit, as well as two pistols.

The guns were for emergency. The last thing they needed was a showdown with the *polizia*.

"Do it *quietly.*" She narrowed her eyes then danced off into the fray.

The gunman wouldn't engage her in a crowd. Vincent didn't pay his employees enough for them to risk getting arrested. The last two had been run-of-the-mill street thugs, looking for quick money. They'd waited until she was alone, where there were no witnesses, before they attacked.

Sidling up to a group of laughing women, she danced with them while watching the man out of the corner of her eye. His gaze discreetly tracked Mike through the nightclub. He took a sip from his cocktail, watching over the rim of the glass long after Mike vanished beyond the doors of the veranda.

Mike was alone in a poorly lit area. An easy target. Why wasn't the man going after him?

Maybe she and Mike hadn't been marked after all. They'd changed disguises since Paris and London. Was she just being paranoid?

No, it was too coincidental. Of all the nightclubs

in all the cities, why would this guy come to this one, if not for her and Mike?

People bounced and whirled around her, blocking and unblocking her view. Her heart rate quickened as she repositioned, trying to keep an eye on the threat while remaining inconspicuous.

In her periphery, he finished his drink and set it on the table. Then he stood.

She held her breath, her hips twitching, barely dancing.

He didn't turn toward the veranda. Without looking in her direction, he prowled directly toward her.

Goddammit!

What was he going to do? Drag her off the dance floor? Shoot her in front of all these people?

Mike wasn't here. She was alone among strangers. Maybe that was the only incentive this guy needed?

The din of clinking bottles, pouring liquor, shouting, chatter, laughter, drunken revelry—it all melded together and swirled around her as she held her position. Running would be the absolute worst thing to do. She needed the cover and protection of the crowd.

He wove around the dancers, never making eye contact with her. But he was undeniably headed for her. Twenty feet away. Fifteen.

She moved deeper into the crowd of writhing, sweaty bodies, shoulder to shoulder, bouncing in sync. Hands and hips, heat and breaths, men and women—strangers rubbed up against her and slid away, only to be replaced by another and another.

A friendly pair of arms came around her from behind, hugging her waist. A solid chest pressed against her back, bringing with it the scent of leather from the jacket he wore. Or maybe it was his skin? He was all around her, the flex of lean masculine muscle grinding intimately, brazenly, with her body.

Ten feet away, her pursuer paused, looking everywhere but at her. Then he veered off to the left, fading into the throng.

She relaxed against the stranger's tall frame behind her, letting him guide her into a sensual dance. If she stayed with this guy long enough, maybe her pursuer would go after Mike.

Christ, the guy knew how to move his body. The rock of his pelvis controlled the pace of hers, and his hands wandered with bold, confident strokes down her hips, molding around the fronts of her thighs, and slipping aggressive fingers beneath the short hem of her dress.

Whoa! Down boy.

Rough breaths pushed past her lips, and her insides melted into lava. So erotic, his touch. So dominating. Possessive.

Dangerous.

She gripped his forearms, pushing them away, but they were too strong. Unmoving.

Familiar.

With a gasp, she tried to turn toward him.

He stopped her in the cage of his arms, tugging her in close and dragging his hard, whiskered jaw along her neck. "You're a terrible dancer."

That voice, the gravelly rumble, the dark, silken cadence.

Cole Hartman.

Her entire body went rigid, and her lungs went up in smoke.

"Don't go stiff on me. Relax your hips." His palms ran down the outsides of her thighs, charging her blood with seductive energy. "Your stalker is watching."

Evidently, she had more than one stalker, and this one wanted far more than a quick paycheck.

His mission was personal.

NINETEEN

As months of paranoia hardened into reality, Lydia's heartbeat exploded, ramming against her chest.

She'd wronged Cole unforgivably. Of course, he would come after her. She should've trusted her instinct.

He wanted revenge, but not here. He wouldn't kill her in public. Too messy. Too many witnesses.

Until she figured out his plan, all she could do was play along.

Wiping the shock and fear off her face, she leaned back against his chest and angled her mouth toward his bent head. "How did you find me?"

"I never lost you." He twisted her around, dragging her pussy right up against his muscled thigh.

Stunned by his words, his proximity, and his unrecognizable appearance, she could only stare. "You never had me."

"Oh, I've had you." With his leg between hers and his hands on her waist, he drove their hips together, flexing and thrusting in the delicious rolling movements of sex. "I've had every hole in this body."

She didn't need the reminder. Most nights, she sneaked away from Mike and pleasured herself in the bathroom to the memory. Cole had been an unforgettable experience, no matter how tainted the circumstances. She'd forced herself on him, and he'd fucked her right back. Tit for tat.

He kept her moving with the grind of his body, maintaining the ruse of a flirtatious stranger. God help her, he looked like one.

A tattered *Misfits* t-shirt peeked out from beneath a black motorcycle jacket. Black boots. Dark jeans. Clean, spiked hair. No beard. Just a shadow of stubble. And dimples.

Treacherous dimples. Deep, sexy, ensnaring little dips of deception. They made him look boyish, harmless, and so goddamn gorgeous her hands shook with the effort not to touch his sculpted face.

"What have you done to yourself?" She gave into the compulsion and set her fingers on his scratchy cheek, trying to reconcile her memory of him with the image before her.

He leaned forward, bending her and putting a sexy roll into movement before yanking her back up. "You prefer the beard?"

"Can't decide."

The beard shouted male dominance, maturity, and sexual virility. The five o'clock shadow attempted to affect the same rugged masculinity with deliberate untidiness while not actually being unkempt.

He probably smelled different. Cleaner. Less musky. A disheartening thought. She desperately missed his manly scent. But without all the hair, his dimples dramatically popped.

She needed to stop staring at them.

The song changed, and she forced her gaze around the nightclub, searching for the other stalker.

"He's on his way out." Cole pulled her in close and pivoted, putting the front entrance in her line of sight.

Sure enough, the man with the crooked nose headed to the door and slipped outside.

Had Cole been watching Vincent's man watch her? Had he not planned on revealing himself to her? He seemed only to pop in because Vincent's goon was approaching.

How long would Mike wait before he gave up and came back inside? Another ten minutes? Long enough for Cole to get what he came for?

"Are you going to kill me?" She dragged her gaze to his, burning in the heat of his twisting, writhing, gloriously ripped body.

"Can't decide."

"I keep thinking I should've let the stonecutter take your dick."

"I haven't stopped thinking about you, either. Your perfect rack. Your sloppy cunt." He palmed her backside, grinding her body against his thigh. "Your tight little asshole clenching around me. Fucking heaven."

With each word and rocking gyration of his hips, he slid closer, hotter, his hands traveling everywhere, feeling her up and down. If there was a lie in that smoldering look, she didn't sense it. The man was a baffling contradiction.

"You said you weren't interested." She pushed at his chest. "You fucked my ass to manipulate me."

"Is that what I did?" He pulled her back in. "Or

what I *said*?"

"You said it. Sure felt like you did it."

Was he fucking with her? Then? Or now?

He touched the blonde tips of her wig, his knuckles brushing against her jaw. "I prefer the red."

Interesting. The wig matched the color of Danni's hair.

"It was fake." She smacked his hand away.

"Was any of it real?"

Her pulse thrummed. "You tell me."

Their gazes locked, and electricity crackled across her skin, resurrecting her fear, for with it rose the flames of reckless longing. Their hips undulated together, and her insides buzzed, sparking with blistering desire.

She never knew sexual tension like this existed. It seethed beneath his touch, growled through his heavy breaths, and dripped down her legs because dammit, she wasn't wearing panties.

Their grinding became so obscenely sexual she knew they were making a scene. But she couldn't shove him away, and he showed no signs of stopping.

Fused at the hips, they connected in rhythm and motion, pushing and pulling, slowing down and speeding up, dancing as one. Not fighting. Not trying to kill each other. They molded together and clung, sinking into the addictive burn. The hunger. The danger.

She shivered, her breaths growing faster with the heavy rush of his. Nothing was sexier or more sinful than grooving up against this man. She wanted to live in his arms and do this for the rest of her life.

But doubt and duty trickled in.

Why was he dancing with her? Touching her? Staring at her like he was into her? Was it another trick?

How many women had he fucked in the past six months? After seven years of celibacy, surely he hadn't gone back to abstaining. He was too sexually charged, too goddamn filthy-minded to go without.

And his dancing? Yeah, he had moves. All the moves. He was by far the best dancer in the discotheque. Maybe in all of Italy. She didn't have to stretch her mind to guess who'd taught him.

So what was he doing with her? With his good looks, sexy confidence, and dirty dancing, he wouldn't be hard up for pussy. He could get it anywhere, anytime.

Even now, every woman in the nightclub was eye-fucking him. The ladies corralled around, shaking their hips, waiting for him to toss away his current distraction and notice them.

If he noticed them, he didn't show it. His dark brown eyes never strayed from her. The longer he held her in his gaze, the more adventurous her hands became. Chiseled pecs, solid shoulders, corded neck, pillowy lips—she touched him everywhere, rubbing, caressing, stroking, and burning up.

She was soaked between her legs, made worse by the blatant need hardening his body. He didn't ram his erection against her, but he couldn't hide it. She was intimately familiar with its shape in every stage of hardness. She knew his girth as he stretched every orifice of her body with dominating force.

She knew it and missed it terribly. She missed *him.*

The scent of him warmed her senses with outdoorsy undertones of leather and earth and masculine pheromones. Yeah, even without the beard, he still smelled deliciously lickable and distinctively him.

He rocked against her, changing up the tempo, bringing her hips in for a slow grind. Then he gripped her nape, bringing her mouth in for a heated exchange of breaths, teasing her with a brush of lips, taunting her with the promise of more.

Every action was sensual and calculated, wildly hungry and terrifyingly confident. Damn, but he knew what he was doing.

He scared the shit out of her.

So when his mouth fully captured hers, she tensed and tried to pull away. He grabbed her head, trapped her waist, and deepened the kiss, chasing her tongue and decimating her resistance.

Controlled by desire, they attacked each other in a frenzy, dancing and moaning to their own music, spinning in their private orbit of touching, kissing, biting, licking, and grabbing. Whatever this was, it was impulsive, carnal, dangerous, and *real*. They weren't capable of stopping. It was too potent, too infectious, taking over and twisting them up.

He kissed her until she melted. Until they were panting together and pulling at each other's clothes. She needed more of his touch, his hands on her skin. Her body had never felt more alive, her breasts heavy, and her breaths shallow and fast.

She was so caught up in it she hadn't realized they'd drifted away from the crowd. With her eyes screwed shut and all five senses wrapped up in Cole, she didn't know he'd danced her into a nearby passageway until her back hit the wall.

Her eyes flew open, and the air evacuated her lungs as he pinned her body with the weight of his. There was no one in view, this part of the club currently unused. It was just her and him and the fingers trailing up the outsides of her thighs.

This was it. He'd separated her from the crowd, pulled her away from witnesses. He was going to fuck her or kill her. Probably both.

She deserved it. She'd let him seduce her *again* and was officially too stupid to live.

"What do you want from me?" She lifted her chin.

"The truth."

Don't trust him. It's another manipulation.

She was prepared to fight, but she wouldn't kill him. She couldn't, and that put her at a severe disadvantage. She blanked her expression.

"Who's Mike?" he asked. "Who is he to you?"

"My partner."

"You're fucking him." A shadow passed over his beautiful face.

"Why do you care?"

"Do you love him? Every night, every city, you share a bed with him."

"You creepy pervert." A chill ran down her spine. "You're watching me?"

"Who are *you* watching? I told you where to find the hard drive. He's in Romania, not in a nightclub in Rome. Why are you here?"

"You told me *where*. I'm working on *how*."

"Explain."

"Are you going to help me?"

Please, help me.

"No." His eyes hardened. "Who's trying to kill you?"

"You?"

"Who else? These men who are hunting

you…they're connected to the team in Texas. But I can't trace their employer. Who is it? Who hired you to seduce me?" At her silence, he asked, "What's on that hard drive?"

"Help me retrieve it, and I'll tell you."

"Tell me how you're connected to it, and I'll think about it."

"What?" Her breath hitched. "You will? You'll help me?"

"No. Fuck." His jaw flexed, and he swiped a hand down his face. "I can't, Lydia. I spent a year embedded in the Romanian mafia, searching for the traitor who sold that hard drive. Darius Skutnik knows me. He knows my face, my disguises, my loyalties. My cover's blown. Bridges burned. And besides, I don't get involved in political or government affairs. Not anymore."

"Then why are you here? Why are you following me?"

His expression clouded.

"Is this about revenge? Do you want an apology?" She cupped his strong jaw, holding his gaze. "I won't give it. I'm not sorry. I'm not sorry for meeting you or fucking you or learning how strong and resilient you are. You scare the bejesus out of me and fascinate me and turn me on like no other. If I were a normal girl with average problems, I would chase you and date you and do all the normal-girl things with you. Because this? You and me? It's *real.*" She lowered her hand. "You wanted the truth. That's *my* truth."

She pressed her tongue against the back of her teeth, immediately regretting her verbal ejaculation. She'd said too much, overexposed herself, and couldn't take it back.

How many times would she stumble and fall over this man?

Maybe this was the last time. Maybe he would try to kill her now, and she would finally learn to keep her guard up around him.

"I'm not interested in normal girls." His finger traced circles on her thigh, invoking goosebumps.

In the span of an eternal moment, her life flashed before her eyes. She lived, and she died, but she didn't regret. He'd woken her from a long, cold dead sleep, and she wouldn't change that for anything.

Slowly, his hand dipped between her legs, going straight to the stiletto like he knew it was strapped there. Of course, he knew. She'd rubbed it up and down his leg while they were dancing.

He made no attempt to take it as his fingers crept upward, seeking something softer, warmer, more welcoming.

A tremor crashed through her, and she rose on her toes, trying to slow the climb of his hand. "What do you want from me?"

"This." He kissed her, deeply, possessively, and sank a finger between her legs. "This greedy pussy's been leaking all over my jeans."

She whimpered, her hands clenching on his shoulders, pulling.

"I want your surrender." His chest pressed against hers, his teeth scraping her gaping mouth as if he were trying to crawl inside her. "Give it to me."

She was already careening toward it before he added another finger, and another, dipping inside and plunging to the knuckles. His tongue knifed through her mouth, assaulting, owning, and twining her fear and need together.

As if he had all the time in the world, he played with her ache, teasing her soaked flesh, and mounting her lust until she clung to him, moaning and panting against his hot lips.

He seduced her with his mouth, his smoldering looks, and oh God, his touch. His fingers unfurled ribbons of heat within her, clenching her inner muscles, and dribbling past flesh that had become far too hungry for him. It was stupid and irresponsible and…

"There." She widened her thighs to deepen the thrust of his fingers. "Please, Cole."

"Good girl."

"We both know I'm not, but I love the way you lie."

He slapped his free hand against the wall above her and bowed in, twisting his fingers between her legs. Then his thumb circled her clit and broke the dam.

Her body split apart in waves of orgasmic pleasure. Shimmery stars seized her vision. Trembling bursts of electricity washed up her legs and rendered her senseless, boneless, until noises she didn't recognize tumbled from her mouth.

He continued to stroke. His fingers. His tongue. Hot and aggressive, he pulled her under and submerged her in the sweetest delirium. Her head tipped back. Her eyes fell shut, and her flesh rippled with unadulterated, carnal bliss.

She shook, stunned and overcome, high on ecstasy and thoroughly mortified.

Mortified, because the voice that broke through her haze didn't belong to Cole.

"Don't move, motherfucker." Mike stood behind Cole, aiming a knife at Cole's stomach and a gun beneath his jaw. "How do you want to die?"

"Buried three-knuckles-deep." Cole had the audacity to wriggle the knuckles still buried inside her.

Mike's lips pulled back, baring his teeth, his eyes blazing with fury.

It was one thing for her to get naked with Cole in Texas when seduction had been part of the mission. Mike had been passionately against it but went along with the plan because there'd been no other way.

But this was a whole other thing. She had no explanation for why she was pressed against him in a dark hallway with her dress shoved to her hips. No explanation would assuage Mike. This had nothing to do with the job. Cole wasn't even supposed to be here.

Mike didn't kill unless it was the only option. But given his current signals—flushed neck, bulging veins, wild eyes, grinding teeth, and not one but two weapons drawn—he saw only one option. Cole's lifeless body.

This wasn't a bluff. Mike was going to kill him.

Heedless, Cole removed his hand from between her legs and held up his soaked fingers, stretching them apart to display the thick, milky strings of her come. "She's a gusher."

"Mike." Pulse racing, she clasped the hand that held the blade against Cole's stomach. "Don't do it. He's baiting you."

"I'm going to fucking kill him." He pushed against her grip.

"No, you're not." Cole slipped a sticky finger between his lips and groaned with satisfaction. "She won't forgive you if you do. You don't want to lose her." He licked another digit, his eyes shutting briefly. "Goddamn, when a woman tastes this good, I imagine you'll do anything to keep her."

He curled his tongue around the next finger, and

the next, slurping with relish.

"Stop antagonizing him." Her hand started to sweat around Mike's grip, battling over control of the knife.

The gun beneath Cole's jaw was less concerning. Mike wouldn't fire it and risk getting them arrested.

"I would've left some for you to taste." Cole flicked a menacing glare over his shoulder at Mike. "But you're dipping into this pussy every night, aren't you? That's why you're itching to gut me. You don't like to share. I get it. I don't share, either."

"Enough." She pushed at Cole's chest, attempting to upset his balance.

He jerked, and they all moved at once. She went for the knife at Cole's stomach. Mike fought her grip, trying not to cut her as Cole swiped the stiletto from between her legs. In a blur of motion, he twisted between her and Mike. His torso tensed, flexing with the snap of his arm as he stabbed the blade toward Mike's shoulder.

She opened her mouth to scream, the sound cutting off as the dagger sank. Blood spurted, not from Mike but from the neck of someone else. A man with black hair.

Her heart stopped. Mike spun away, and Cole stabbed the knife again, cutting through the throat. Blood spilled over his hand. The man dropped to the floor, and she stared down at a face with a crooked nose.

Vincent's man.

Her hands trembled, her pulse thrashing in her ears, sounding out the muffled thump of the music.

Goddammit, she was smarter than this. She didn't get distracted. She didn't let assassins sneak up on her.

"Get out of here." Cole wiped the stiletto on the dead man's pants and handed it to her. "Go!"

The chatter of feminine voices sounded around the corner. People were close. A whole nightclub of people. Anyone could step into view and sound the alarms.

"Come on." She concealed the knife beneath her dress and tugged on Mike's clenching hand. "We need to go."

Cole bent over the body and dragged it into a shadowed corner. She looked up, scanning the ceiling with surging panic.

"There are no cameras." Cole met her eyes, his voice thundering with command. "Get the fuck out of here."

Heart hammering, she held his gaze for a moment longer, and he stared back, forging the connection in fire.

They needed more time, more moments. If only he would agree to help her, if they could find a way to trust each other…

"Let's go." Mike gripped her elbow and led her away.

They walked straight out of the club without stopping or looking back. Outside, the summer night air wrapped around her. She didn't breathe until they reached a less-congested part of the busy street. There, a few blocks from the nightclub, they lingered in the shadows without speaking.

Patrons milled along the stone walkways, flitting in and out of the nearby bars. The alleyways between belched a thousand unbearable stenches caused by calls of nature. She thought she might throw up, not from the rank air but from her unbearable nerves.

Huddled in a dark doorway with Mike's arm around her, she had a direct view of the discotheque's entrance. Her neck grew taut as she waited for the sound of sirens. Her molars clenched painfully as she waited for Cole to step outside.

Ten minutes passed.

Fifteen.

He never emerged, and the *polizia* never came.

"He hid the body and found another exit." Mike clasped her hand and pulled her down the street, getting them out of there. "If he's smart, we'll never see him again."

She didn't want that, did she? Her chest constricted. "He just saved our lives."

"If he hadn't distracted you, you wouldn't have needed saving."

Good point.

Walking alongside him, she twined their fingers together and acknowledged the guilt stabbing her insides. "I'm sorry."

"No, you're not." He glanced at her sidelong, the anger still alive in his eyes. "What did he say to you?"

Lowering her voice, she recapped every word she'd shared with Cole. When she fell quiet, his expression darkened, and he quickened his gait.

She jogged to keep up, wobbling in the heels. "What's wrong?"

"What's wrong?" He stopped abruptly and turned to glare at her. "He followed you across Europe for six months. You haven't just become his mission. You've become his obsession."

TWENTY

London, England
Eight months later

Lydia had become a dangerous obsession.

An obsession that had brought Cole to this tattoo parlor to do something he never fathomed.

Why?

She was an anomaly. A goddamn mystery. He knew so little about her, and that only made him crave and crave and crave. His thirst for knowledge demanded he unravel her.

Who was she? Where had she come from? Why was she always on the move?

Why am I still following her?

It had been fourteen months since she'd saved his life beneath the stonecutter. He'd given her the location of the hard drive, and she wasn't even trying to infiltrate the Romanian mafia.

Instead, she visited strip clubs, nightclubs, fluttering from venue to venue in red-light districts across Europe. *Dancing*. Or attempting to dance. She had terrible coordination.

Still, he loved watching her. Stalking her. He couldn't let go of this infatuation.

She and Mike never used the same last name twice. Their identification documents were forged. They paid for everything in cash, traveled light, and spent little, sleeping on trains and staying in low-rent hostels and dingy hotels.

They must've had a plan, but for the life of him, he couldn't figure it out.

"Almost finished." A twenty-something Englishman wiped a towel along Cole's forearm, admiring the artwork. "You ready to see it?"

He hadn't looked at his arm. Not once in five hours as the tattoo gun stabbed into his skin. He couldn't bear to watch the inked symbol of Danni slowly disappear. He just wanted it gone.

Out with the old obsession, in with the new one.

Breathing deeply, he turned his gaze on the fresh ink.

From wrist to elbow, a deadly snake coiled tightly around his arm, leaving no unmarked skin between the tight spiral of its thick, scaly body.

It was a diamondback rattlesnake, commonly found in the Chihuahuan Desert where he'd met Lydia.

Warmth spread through his chest as he held it up for a closer inspection. Shocking bursts of red poked out from beneath the twisting, winding predator. Red feathers.

He turned his arm, revealing the head of a red swallow peering out of the snake's constricting hold.

His lips twitched with morbid satisfaction. "It's perfect."

"Ace." The tattoo artist grinned. "You got a pet snake, mate?"

"A pet bird."

"Ah." The man's eyes twinkled as if he comprehended the meaning.

He didn't. Cole didn't even understand it.

As the Brit wrapped up his arm, the TV on the wall streamed endless commercials, each one to the tune of a Christmas jingle. It was the first week of December, and the holiday season was choking the life out of the air.

Blinking lights, glittery ribbons, peppermint coffee, swarms of shoppers, singing, and laughing—the spirit of Christmas forced itself on everyone, everywhere. He couldn't escape it. Not even here. Sitting in a dark, grungy tattoo parlor on the outskirts of London, he felt it jabbing under his skin.

He despised this time of year, for it only served to remind him just how goddamn lonely he was.

He'd turned thirty-eight this year. Thirty-eight Christmases, and he'd spent half of those alone. He should've been used to it by now. But he couldn't forget the holidays he'd shared with Trace and one he'd had with Danni. Those were good times. The best.

Maybe that was why he hated Christmas so much.

"Hell of a time to be an American." The tattooist nodded at the TV, which had switched to a world news report about American politics.

It was an election year in the states, and though the election had ended a month ago, the country was in an uproar over who had unofficially won. The President-elect wasn't a politician. He was a business magnate, software developer, and philanthropist.

His presence in the White House promised to shake things up. Maybe that was what the country needed, but Cole didn't hold out hope. He knew too much about the collusion and cronyism that existed within the U.S. political system.

"Can you turn that off?" He flicked a hand at the TV.

"Sure."

Christ, he was in a mood. If he were honest, his head hadn't been in a good place for months.

He needed to see her.

No, he needed more than that. He needed to feel Lydia's warmth under his hands, taste her cherry lips on his tongue, and hear her husky voice whispering his name.

He longed to make contact with her, but he couldn't. He wasn't the only one watching her. Whatever she was involved in, people were hunting her. They would've been tracking him, too, but he kept himself hidden.

Until eight months ago.

In a total lapse of sanity, he'd approached her in that nightclub in Rome. He'd done it to protect her. Mike had left her alone with a damn assassin in the building.

Dancing with her had gone too far. He'd needlessly and recklessly indulged. Holy fuck, he'd indulged in every inch of her luscious body.

He couldn't do that again. He couldn't be seen with her. Couldn't get involved.

He told her he wouldn't help her, and he meant it.

When he finished his transaction at the tattoo parlor, he returned to Central London and walked the streets, soaking in the historical ambiance while evading the Christmas shoppers. He was looking for something, searching for a distraction from his thoughts.

Lydia was somewhere in the city. According to Romero, she'd arrived yesterday by train.

He told himself he wouldn't walk by her hotel this time, that he wouldn't watch her from the shadows. But he knew it was a lie. She was the only reason he'd flown in this morning.

Wandering aimlessly with his hands tucked in his pockets, he kept to the side streets, kept his feet moving, tried to keep his thoughts away from the object of his obsession.

Late into the early morning, the foot traffic died down, the tourists all tucked into their temporary beds.

Was Lydia out dancing in some dodgy nightclub? Or was she in bed, too? With Mike?

His stomach buckled, roiling with acid. The undetermined state of her relationship with Mike twisted him up. He tried not to think about it, but his imagination was a bitch.

So was his jealousy.

It awakened toxic memories. Memories of the months he'd shared Danni with Trace. He wouldn't do that again. Not with any woman. No matter how fucking lonely he was.

His breaths quickened, forming angry white clouds in the chilly air as he strolled across Westminster Bridge. He stopped at the center with no one around and stared down at the inky water of the River Thames.

He needed to give up this pointless quest and return to the states. Better yet, he should go to Colombia and spend the holidays with his friends. His family.

For a moment, he tried to imagine it—sitting around some elaborate Christmas tree at the Restrepo headquarters, drinking, opening presents, and celebrating togetherness. He wanted that, longed for it, right up until everyone paired off and went to bed.

Where would that leave him?

Alone and pining for the love he'd lost.

Fucking pathetic.

He laughed aloud, and the ache in his voice caught on the cold breeze, tumbling toward the river. He sounded insane—in his mind and out loud. Even the voice in his head thought he was nuts.

Maybe he was having a breakdown? Or going through some sort of mid-life crisis?

Or maybe this was what it felt like to finally let go? He'd carried the guilt around for twelve fucking years, and tonight, he'd let some of it go.

He erased her from his skin.

His feelings about it were complicated. He felt a torrent of anger and relief, guilt and redemption, grief and hope, and never-ending loneliness. It was difficult to parse through when all of it twisted up around Lydia.

"This isn't about her," he murmured. "Stop being a goddamn pussy and move on. This is long overdue."

He reached beneath the neckline of his jacket and yanked his necklace free, breaking the chain. Danni's engagement ring sat in his palm, glinting in the moonlight. Such a tiny thing, yet so heavy with broken promises and lies and loss.

He'd carried the weight of this thing for too long. Danni was happy, and he could get there, too, if he stopped punishing himself.

It was time to let go.

His vision blurred, and his eyes burned with sudden, uncontrollable anguish.

Fuck it.

He blinked away the moisture and flung the ring into the river.

Then he closed his eyes and let the tears fall. Silently, lightly, they gathered at the creases of his mouth, and he wiped them away.

He felt numb. Hollow. But so much lighter.

Removing the phone from his pocket, he dialed the number he'd called countless times over the past fourteen months.

"Hello?" Rylee's groggy voice whispered over the line.

"Did I wake you?" He did the time conversion in his head. "It's only eleven at night there."

"No. Yes. It's fine. Hang on."

Sounds of rustling indicated she was crawling out of bed, probably trying not to wake Tomas.

"Okay," she breathed. "You there?"

"I did it."

"What? What did you do, Cole?"

"I inked over the tattoo and threw the ring into the River Thames."

"Oh."

"Oh?" He exhaled and rubbed his pounding head. "I thought you would…I don't know…have something therapeutic to say."

"I'm processing. Give me a minute."

He hadn't seen her or any of the Freedom Fighters since the night he left with Lydia in the desert. That was fifteen months ago. But he talked to all of them regularly, keeping them updated on where he was and what he knew about Lydia and Mike.

"So," Rylee said, "after twelve years of holding onto the symbols of a life you wanted, you let them go. Good for you. What prompted it?"

"I don't know."

"Yes, you do." She sighed. "You finally realized you don't want that life anymore, that maybe you never did."

"I disagree. I would take back Danni if—"

"*Staaaahp.* Do you actually believe you would be content settling down in the suburbs with a wholesome little wife, an unremarkable job, and the same uneventful, unchallenging routine day in and day out for the rest of your boring existence?"

With Danni? He would've made it work. He would've been happy with her.

And miserable in every other aspect of his life.

"Something opened your eyes," Rylee said. "Something or maybe…*someone* with a flair for tattoos, knives, garters, mystery, and danger."

His groin tightened. "She's a threat."

"That's not why you've been stalking her for fourteen months. Do you remember what I said to you when we met?"

"You said a lot of crazy shit."

"A lot of crazy, *smart* shit. You remember."

Yeah, he remembered.

If love comes for you again, it's going to blindside you and knock you on your ass. You'll deny it. You'll fight it with every breath in your body. But having already experienced it once, you know it's a fight you can't win. So maybe, if and when it happens, give yourself a break. Don't fight so hard.

"That's not what this is." He dragged a hand through his hair and started walking toward his rented apartment. "What she did to me is unforgivable. She can't be trusted. Ever. She's a goddamn risk."

"If she consumes your mind, she's a risk worth taking. Take the risk, Cole. Or lose the chance."

"I already did that with Danni. I took the risk *and* lost the chance."

"That's why second chances were invented. It's never too late to begin again, have a dream, and make her yours."

"She already has someone."

"That didn't stop Trace when he went after Danni, and look how that worked out for him."

"Ouch." His jaw flexed. "Direct hit below the waist, Rylee."

"Did it clear your head?"

"No."

"Come home. If you don't feel anything for this woman, bring your ass back to Colombia, spend the holidays with your family, and put some distance between you and this thing you're wrestling with."

"Not yet." His voice cracked, and he cleared his throat. "I can't."

"I didn't think so. When you're ready, we're here. You know that."

"I know."

"Try not to take too much longer. We miss you."

"I miss you, too," he said quietly, uncomfortably. But he meant it.

"Night, Cole."

"Good-night."

An hour later, he lay on a cold mattress in an unfamiliar apartment and thought about Lydia.

He didn't know her natural hair color. She wore it in every shade and style possible, usually wigs, always eye-catching. But he preferred it red, and that was how he imagined it every night when he wrapped a hand around his cock and beat off.

He thought of the thick, silken, blazing red mass of waves tumbling off her shoulders and curling around the pink peaks of her gorgeous tits. He thought of the hair between her legs, imagining it a lighter shade of red and glistening with her arousal as he penetrated her with his tongue, his fingers, and hungry cock. He thought about her rebellious little chin lifting toward him, her lips parting, begging to be kissed as he teased her, worshiped her, and gave her everything she wanted.

Christ, he was hungry. So fucking ravenous for her. He finished too quickly and continued to stroke, milking the final drops, trying to prolong the transient moment of pleasure.

When the sensation passed, and his body grew cold, he lay there in the dark, breathless, empty, and more alone than he'd ever felt in his life.

Dublin, Ireland
Three weeks later

If the idea of Christmas heaven was bundling up under layers of clothes and slushing through wet snow across cobbled streets in an epically festive pub crawl, then Dublin was the place.

Cole didn't mind the cold, and frankly, nothing warmed the blood like a hot Irish whiskey in a cozy Irish inn. So in the dark hours of Christmas Eve, he sat in the quiet corner of a small pub off the beaten path and treated himself to a few of those hot toddies.

Outside, the wind beat against the windows in an icy serenade, forming frozen lace on the glass, delicate and jewel-like. Fire crackled in a nearby hearth, and periodically, the door opened with the draft of snow and incoming Dubliners.

Woolen hats pulled over reddened ears. Scarves wrapped around rosy cheeks. They arrived in pairs, small groups, but never solo as they stamped their boots on the entry mat and made a beeline to the bar.

For this small island of emigrants, Christmas was a time for family and friends. Many returned home to Ireland to spend the season with their loved ones. Others reconnected like the older couple across the room.

With their hands clasped together at shoulder height, they slowly danced in front of the hearth fire, smiling, swaying, locked in eye contact, and lost in their own private world.

Love.

It was the greatest gift they could give each other.

Physical closeness. Emotional warmth. Partners for life. They shared a lasting, soulful kind of love that lifted every part of who and what Cole was.

In that moment, in his dark, solitary corner of the world, all he wished for was another beating heart, one less empty chair, and one more pair of gloves resting on the table beside his.

He'd learned how to fly solo, how to sleep alone, and how to solve his problems unassisted. Over the past twelve years, he'd become a lone wolf, and it had made him a successful, unstoppable force in his job.

But what it left was a form of loneliness that he couldn't mend by himself.

What it left was a sad man who sat alone in a pub on Christmas.

Throwing back his whiskey, he dropped some money on the table and returned to the streets.

The toothy bite of winter wind nipped at his face. Ice crackled underfoot. Carolers crooned in the distance, and shop window displays flickered beneath strings of rainbow-colored lights.

Grafton Street at Christmas was a wonderland, and for anyone who believed, they could pluck the magic right out of the air.

But he wasn't a believer in the spirit of anything. Not in a world where he walked alone.

His teeth chattered as the cold seeped into his gloves, numbing his fingers until they ceased to bend. Burrowing deeper into his leather jacket, he pulled his beanie low on his head and stuffed his hands in his pockets. Then he walked.

He tried to walk off the chill and the direction of his thoughts, all the while keeping constant vigilance on his surroundings, always on the lookout for threats.

Miles later, he took a cab to Dublin 22 and walked some more.

His breath rose in white puffs and faded into the dark, frozen sky. Naked winter trees lined streets that slept peacefully beneath no boots, save his.

The houses around him were home to those in full swing of togetherness, their merriment shining from decorated windows. But out here, he felt only the beat of his heart. A lonely beat, but strong, and growing stronger on the cusp of a decision.

Treading slowly, he kept to the shadows, out of sight, his senses on alert. As if the snow had stopped time and covered all the distractions, he couldn't see anything but what was right in front of him.

He wasn't lost. He knew exactly where he was and what he was doing as he stared up at a three-story, mid-terraced house made of fieldstones and ancient wood.

With neighbors attached on either side, the old, dilapidated property belonged to Micheál and Shannon O'Sullivan.

Micheál O'Sullivan. *Mike.*

Shannon O'Sullivan. *Lydia's real name?*

Were they married? This seemed to be their permanent home. They'd been holed up in there for two weeks, the longest they'd stayed in any one place since leaving Texas.

He shouldn't be here.

The wind whipped sleet into his eyelashes and chafed the exposed skin above his beard. But the freezing chill brought a crispness to his thoughts.

Once he walked up to that door, he was involved in this. Connected to her. Committed.

There were a lot of risks.

She could shoot him. Her husband could shoot him. Those who hunted her could shoot him.

They could try.

Under a black sky of wintry snow, he backed away.

Around the property and along the surrounding streets, he slipped through the shadows and swept the perimeter. There was no one outside. No late-night wanderers. No Santa. No reindeer. No hitmen. No present danger.

Dark windows veneered the O'Sullivan house on both sides, suggesting they were asleep or not home. The thought of catching them in bed together sucked the life from his soul, but he wasn't stopping.

He'd gone as far as he could on this path alone. His next step forward would be with her, and he was prepared to fight.

When he was buried inside her in Texas, she was with him. When he kissed her in Rome, she was with him. Every time he had her body, she gave him her passion, her beautiful desire. And Mike had tolerated it.

Fuck Micheál O'Sullivan, and fuck their relationship.

Keeping to the darkest areas of the walkway, Cole ghosted to the door with a single-minded focus.

The porch creaked beneath his boots, and he paused. A chill crawled over his scalp. Breathless, he glanced back, searching the perimeter for movement. All held still.

As he reached for the handle to check the lock, the wind wiggled the door, cracking it open. It hadn't been latched. What the fuck?

Alarms fired in his head, tensing his muscles. Quickly, he removed his bulky gloves and drew the handgun from the back of his waistband. Holding it up and out, he expelled a soundless breath and pushed open the door.

Dark, deafening silence enveloped him. He slipped out of the doorway and pressed his back to the adjacent wall, staying hidden. The narrow entryway accommodated only a stairwell that rose into more pitch-black darkness. No other doors on this level. No other rooms. Nowhere to go but up.

He kept the gun trained as he stepped toward the bottom stair, steadily, quietly. Until the shadows moved in his periphery.

The darkness beside the staircase dispersed, and Mike prowled forward, blocking the path to the stairs. He wore a heavy coat, no doubt concealing a myriad of weaponry.

"What do you want, Cole?" Mike asked in a heavy, distinctive brogue.

He felt his eyebrows shoot up. "You're Irish?"

"Born and raised in this house, you thick knacker scumbag." Mike folded his arms across his chest, his expression etched in hostility. "Why are you trespassing on my property?"

Blood thrashed in his ears, his fingers aching with tension. "Where's Lydia?"

"Leave."

"Move. Don't make me shoot you."

"You won't." Mike smiled cruelly, repeating Cole's words from Rome. "She won't forgive you if you do."

"Who is she to you, Micheál O'Sullivan? Is her real name Shannon? Your wife?"

"Shannon was my mam. God rest her soul." Mike's mouth tilted down. "And no, Lydia and I haven't tied the knot."

Relief thrummed through him, but it still didn't explain their relationship.

He glanced at the top of the stairs, probing the thick blackness. Was she up there, standing just beyond the reach of his sight? He was seconds from knocking Mike out and scaling those steps.

"Who is she to *you*?" Mike cocked his head, his body rigid and unmoving.

"She's a risk," he said honestly. "A risk I want to take."

"Of course, you want to take her." Mike laughed, his accent thickening. "You're a manky stalker. Following her around for months and months. You have a problem, pal. An obsession."

"Yeah, I have an obsession, one that takes dedication, discipline, and sacrifice." His voice vibrated with a growl. "I'm not walking away from this. Nor will I leave it up to chance or fate. Not this time. I'm taking this risk because, without her, there can only be a lonely goddamn existence."

Mike blinked, his expression cast in shadows. After a long, fraught silence, he opened his mouth, but Lydia's voice cut him off.

"I love you, Micheál," she said from the dark landing above. "More than anything in the world. So I say this with the utmost respect and adoration." Her tone turned to steel. "Get lost."

Cole's breathing quickened, and he wrestled to control it. A swell of heat spread inside him, blooming into a fire so intense it made his pulse spark and flutter.

Cautiously, Mike stepped forward until his chest pushed against the barrel of the gun, which brought a playful smile to his face.

"If you hurt my sister, I'll remove your bollocks with a bloody spoon." Mike clapped him on the shoulder and strolled toward the door. "Merry Christmas, fecker."

Sister.

Not lovers.

The door shut, and he closed his eyes, just for a moment, savoring the pure and utter joy in that revelation.

Siblings.

"Lock the door," she said.

His skin heated with buzzing energy as he stowed the gun in the pocket of his jacket and engaged the outrageous number of locks, bolts, chains, and bars on the house's only entry point. "Mike won't be able to open—"

"He'll be gone all night."

"Where?" He stepped toward the stairs, straining his eyes, trying to see her at the top.

"Wherever there's pussy. He hasn't left my side in…I don't even know. It's been a long time."

"He trusts me with you?" He climbed a step.

"He trusts you'll be here all night and that you'll shoot anything that tries to come through that door." Her voice grew breathy, and she coughed, hardening it. "Did you mean it? What you said? Or are you just here for sex? I know you're not going to kill me. You would've done that by now."

"I meant it." He felt his way up the railing, ascending into the dark. "Where're the lights?"

"No electricity on this level. Old wiring." She shifted, creaking the floor just a few steps away. "You never lost me."

"No." He measured his footfalls, his entire body strumming, attuned to her voice. "I followed you out of the desert and across the Atlantic. I've been following you ever since."

"Four-hundred-and-forty-one days of dedication. Why?"

"Because you were mine, Lydia." Hot anticipation coiled inside him as he reached through the dark and caught her nape. Then he hauled her gasping mouth to his. "You're still mine."

Their lips collided, tongues seeking and connecting. She flung her arms around his neck, and he lifted her, stumbling blindly until her back hit a wall.

The kiss caught fire, desperate and starving, building into a tameless, unholy fever. The aggressive savagery with which she met the strokes of his tongue only made him harder. Jesus Christ, he was so fucking hard for her.

His hands threaded through her hair. Long, silky, heavy waves of hair down her back. He found her delicate neck, her slim shoulders, and continued downward, searching for skin beneath her clothes.

She wore a baggy t-shirt. Nothing on her legs. By the time his fingers reached her pussy and sank deep into her heat, he was ready to explode.

Goosebumps prickled her thighs, and she shivered in the chilly air. He needed to move her to a warm bed, where he could take his time looking at her. He'd never seen her without clothes, and dammit, he needed to *see* her.

With his hands cupping her firm, bare backside, he turned and carried her up the next set of stairs. Her legs circled his waist. His palm pressed against her lower back, and he curled his middle finger deep into her asshole. A placeholder, to let her know he was coming for it.

Her gasp tore their kiss. He bit at her lips, her neck, nipping at her shoulders and marking her flesh with his teeth.

"I own you." His mouth covered hers, claiming her with rough, unbridled hunger.

"I own you." She molded his urgency to her own with a fierce passion.

"You don't have an Irish accent."

"I'm not Irish." She frantically kissed his face, panting. "Mike and I have different mothers."

"You're going to tell me everything."

"Yes."

"I want it all, Lydia. All of *you*."

"Take it."

TWENTY-TWO

A possessive hum resonated in Cole's chest. A wanting wrenched his gut. He ran a shaking thumb across Lydia's lips, unable to stop himself from touching her. Then he kissed her, claiming her with the sweeping, stroking blade of his tongue.

Mouths locked, hands grappling, they bounced off the wall, bumped into the railing, stumbled over the last stair.

The third level greeted him with more darkness. But a sliver of moonlight poked through the curtains, giving shape to furniture and obstacles as he carried her through the space. A modest room with an open kitchen and a couch.

Without breaking the kiss, he headed toward the door that led to the only bedroom. Except he didn't make it past the next wall. He crashed against it, deliberately falling against her, trapping her tight little body beneath his mindlessly grinding, humping, trying to assuage his blistering need.

He tore off his jacket, dropping it. She lowered

her legs and fumbled with his zipper, opening it. His shirt and hat went next. Then his boots, his jeans, until he wore nothing but ink.

She bit her lip, breathing heavily and eyes slitted, trying to see him in the dark.

"Need light." He gripped her waist and looked around.

"Bedroom."

With spiking urgency, he hoisted her legs around his hips and attacked her mouth. She weighed nothing, her body twisting as she wrestled off her shirt.

Her sexy moans and whimpers drove him crazy, vocalizing unspoken wants. He quickened his gait, each step increasing the friction and persistence between them. Her hot mouth fell upon his neck, his shoulder, showering him in a frenzy of kisses as her hands clawed and pulled, scratching his back and tangling in his hair.

"You grew back your beard." She kissed the scruff from one cheek to the other and cupped his face. "You're so handsome, Cole Hartman."

"Lydia." Groaning, he bumped into the bedroom door and slapped a hand along the wall, hunting for a light switch.

"The table."

He knocked over a slew of shit in his path and wiped out everything on the nightstand in his quest to find the bulb. "How do I turn the damn thing on?"

She laughed against his mouth. Then she threw back her head and laughed harder, the musical sound alive with relief and breathy with need.

He tossed her onto the bed and focused on the lamp. There. He caught the chain and yanked.

A dim glow illuminated the small, spartan room. Curtains blacked out the single window. No adjoining bathroom. No pictures on the walls. No knickknacks. Just a bed and the most beautiful woman he'd ever seen sprawled atop it.

Red hair. *Natural* red on her head and between her legs. Porcelain complexion, almost flawless, save for the freckles that speckled her brow and nose. Without the makeup and the wigs and evocative clothing, she looked outrageously innocent and young.

"How old are you?" He feathered his fingers up her calf, shaking with the force of his desire.

She shivered. "Twenty-seven."

"I'm eleven years older than you."

"Afraid you can't keep up with me?" She stared up at him, panting, her sea-green eyes dazed and hooded, and her lips... Sweet hell, those full, fuckable lips pouted as she opened her legs, taunting him. "Let's go, old man."

"Shut the fuck up and let me look." He sat back on his heels and soaked in the sensual lines of her body.

She arched into a sensuous stretch that mounted the pounding in his blood. She was perfect. So painfully, insanely gorgeous.

"You're stunning. Jesus. You're always beautiful, but this face..." He trailed a knuckle along her graceful jawline. "Your real face shines in breathtaking contrast to the one you paint on."

"Cole." She reached out a hand and scissored her legs back and forth, restless, needy.

He caught her fingers, entwining them with his. Until her eyes widened.

"Oh, my God." With a gasp, she sat up, her attention locked on his new tattoo. "You removed her?"

"I didn't belong to her." He met her riveting gaze. "I belong to someone else."

He twisted his arm, showing her the red swallow caught in the serpent's deadly clutch.

Her hand fell to the bird on her chest, and little ruts formed between her brows. "I don't know what to say."

"Do you hate it?"

She shook her head, slowly at first, then faster, harder, her eyes tearing up. "I love it."

His chest lifted, soaring. "Lie back."

As she relaxed into the bed, he followed her down, sliding over her and dwarfing her tiny frame. She hooked her legs around him, and their lips came together.

And their bodies.

For the first time, he felt her skin flush with his, the soft warmth of her nudity rubbing and quivering beneath him.

With a shaky hand, he reached between them, cupping her, watching her eyes. Long, auburn eyelashes fluttered closed. Warm, supple, soaked flesh welcomed his caresses. He traced his fingertips around her opening, evoking short rapid inhalations on her cherry red lips.

Passionate woman.

So easily aroused.

"Cole, please." She lifted her hips, wriggling, demanding.

He swatted her thigh, chastising her for her impatience. But his own was just as bodacious.

Shifting down her body, he pushed the bedding away, freed her legs, and opened her wide. She shuddered, whimpered, and reached for her clit. Such a shameless, wanton creature.

He knocked her touch away. "My hands are no

longer tied, Lydia. I command. You obey."

"Even with your hands restrained, you were always the one in command."

The throbbing stiffness of his cock demanded he do dirty, dirty things. From the moment he'd met her, he fantasized about eating her, front to back, inside and out.

"How many cocks have been here after me?" He speared his thumbs into her pussy and spread apart her needy flesh.

"I've never been one to abstain. I gave away my virginity at a young age and…" She stroked a hand through his hair, blushing. "I just really love sex. But since I met you, I've found something I love more." She shrugged. "I'm in love with love."

He grinned. "That's a pretty drastic leap from *There is only war, and that is always fueled by hate.*"

"I've taken a lot of leaps recently." She slid her fingers down his face. "I'm on birth control, and I haven't been with anyone since you."

The tension in his shoulders loosened. "You're the only woman I've touched in eight years."

"Why?"

"I was waiting for something extraordinary." He glided his thumbs up and down in opposing directions, working her tight little pussy into a sticky, squelching suction of need. "I was waiting for you."

Her breaths punched out in disbelieving rasps as her fingers threaded through his hair. "You're making me really, really fucking hot, Cole. If you don't put something inside me, I'm legit going to die."

Gazes locked, he flashed her a grin. Then he buried his face between her legs.

She cried out. Spasms rippled against his tongue,

drenching her with more heat and saturating his beard. Her heavenly taste flooded his mouth, and he groaned, needing more.

He draped her legs over his shoulders and dragged her pussy hard against his face, really getting in there, tucking into his sweet meal. His beard scraped against her thighs, turning her skin red, and the strokes he inflicted between her legs teased out more of her desperate sounds, painting them in a picture of devotion and greed.

She writhed and thrashed beneath him, her hair splayed across the pillow in luminous waves, trapping the lamplight in metallic shades of red. The texture was softer, fuller, more luminous than he ever imagined it could be.

His starved mouth inched up to her other hair—the short red curls on her mound. He pressed his nose in the patch and inhaled deeply, basking in her pheromones and the sinfully ripe scent of her musk.

"You're smelling my pussy." She half-laughed, half-moaned. "God, you're so filthy."

"Just getting started."

Moving his tongue away from his first conquest, he licked his way backward, along the sexy slit of her body until he reached the next opening.

With his hands locked behind her knees, he pushed her thighs to her chest, angling her tightest channel heavenward. Then he shoved his tongue inside.

She made a scandalized sound and clenched the tight ring of muscle, trying to keep him out as her hands swatted and pushed. "What are you doing?"

"Your ass and my dick are going to spend a lot of time together. I'm talking about regular visits. At least once a day."

"Oh my fuck, you weren't kidding? Anal is your weakness?"

"It's my weakness at a premature-ejaculation level." He gripped himself, collecting the thick, abundant pre-cum from his tip. Then he held up his wet hand. "I'm leaking all over just thinking about it."

She burst out laughing. "You traumatized my brother doing that."

"Oh shit. In Rome."

"Yes, in Rome. Mike and I have been forced into some awkward situations together, but that was the first time my come was shoved in his face."

"I'm not sorry." He stabbed his tongue again, rimming her, violating her, and making her scream.

Once he had her thoroughly loosened up and drenched in both holes, he gripped her hips and dragged her toward his lap, tight against his cock.

The four times they'd had sex, he'd been restrained by rope, unable to move the way he needed with her on top. Not a comfortable position for a man of his nature. So this was going to feel fucking fantastic, having her under him, pinned beneath the drive of his need.

"It was real." She trembled, gripping his arms. "In Texas, when we fucked, every second of it was real. I never faked my desire for you."

"It was real for me, too. That last time, when I took your ass, my cruelty was unforgivable. The things I said afterward were lies. I'm—"

"Don't apologize." She pressed a finger to his mouth. "We're not doing that. We're not going to regret the actions that brought us together, okay?"

"No regrets." Poised between her thighs, hard and thick and pulsing with eagerness, he lined himself up and met her eyes.

In that look, he felt as though he were already inside her, and she was inside him, their connection sparking, twisting, soldering into something brighter, denser, and more profound.

Then he pushed, sinking inside her body, stroking his tongue into her wet mouth, and burying his cock to the hilt.

Jolts of overwhelming sensations coursed back and forth and everywhere. They held themselves motionless, her lips parted around a soundless cry as he attempted to master his breathing and not bust a nut.

Her lissome beauty was intoxicating. Impossible to look away. Not to mention the pleasure that gathered where they were joined. The strangling grip of her pussy brought a flush of sweat across his brow.

He flexed within her. He couldn't help it, and the pulsing sent her chest into motion, rising and falling and thrusting her gorgeous tits upward.

With the dip of his head, he took the taut nipples into his mouth, sucking and biting until she groaned and yanked his hair.

"I'm dying a mini-death here." She pulled his mouth toward hers. "Fuck me already."

He obliged, bruising her lips, attacking with teeth, and shutting her up with the swift, invasive thrusts of his body. He held her gaze as he fucked her. He never looked away as he stretched her and filled her so full and deep she had no time to brace herself when the first orgasm hit. He watched as she exploded around him, and his pleasure rose in dark, swirling torrents, pushing him to join her. But he fought it off, unwilling to surrender so quickly.

Before she caught her breath, he flipped her over

and plowed into her from behind.

Over the next couple of hours, he took his time with her, exploring her body, worshiping her curves, and pumping his seed in all of her holes.

He found his ultimate release in her ass, his cock buried to the root and his eyes jammed shut against the violent, jetting spurts of his climax. Seconds later, she joined him from below, moaning through yet another orgasm. He lost count of how many she'd had.

On hands and knees, she collapsed beneath him. He rolled to his back, his cock throbbing and sore. Deliciously used.

She panted beside him, her hair plastered to her flushed, sweaty face and her eyes aglow with dazed satisfaction. A huff of laughter broke through her gasps for breath. She swallowed, heaving and short-winded, and laughed again.

Happiness looked good on her. Dazzling and magical. She was absolutely extraordinary and so vibrantly, naturally gorgeous. Her beauty was true to life.

"What the ever-loving hell, Cole?" A beaming smile lifted her cheeks as she crawled toward him, climbing up his chest and sliding a lazy kiss across his mouth. "You've been holding back on me."

"Ready for round two?"

"Oh, no, no, no. You just blew through ten rounds. Pretty sure you broke my vagina."

"Let me see." He shoved a hand between her legs.

With a yelp, she stumbled back and off the bed. "I'm going to feed you, you beast." She turned and sashayed toward the door. "Then we're going to talk."

TWENTY-THREE

Contentment sifted through Lydia as she sat at the kitchen table, watching Cole dig into his second bowl of mutton stew. He hummed as he chewed, his eyes hooded with pleasure.

She savored the moment, knowing it wouldn't last. A somber conversation loomed ahead. And the job. She had to finish the job by the twentieth of January. Less than a month. If she didn't, it would be out of her reach.

"I can't believe you're here." She propped her elbow on the table and rested her chin on her hand. "I've never cared much for Christmas presents, but you just gave me a dozen unforgettable ones. I'll never walk the same again."

"I hate this time of year." His eyes twinkled as he stared at her over his spoon. "At least, I *did*. You might've changed my mind."

He slid the bite of stew between his chiseled lips, licking the utensil.

The temperature of her body rose several degrees.

Was he trying to be sexy? Or was it an involuntary reflex, like the salivation happening in her mouth?

Seriously, though. Why was he so beautiful?

His facial hair was thick but not long. Nothing like the beard he wore in Texas. Neatly trimmed, soft, and tidy, the length lay somewhere between stubble and a full-on beard. The scruff took those boyish dimples and made them so manly. She loved it. She really did.

Two small pink scars glowed amid the tattoos on his arm. One in front and one in back, they marked the pathway of the bullet he'd taken in Texas. If he hadn't stayed at her side that day, that bullet might've gone through her.

He wore his jeans with the button unfastened. Nothing underneath. No shirt. A lot of ink. Tousled, just-been-fucked hair. Lethal from head to toe. Sexy as fuck.

The man looked like he'd been playing football his entire life. A linebacker with a solid eight-pack and enough aggression to push back an army. Beneath all that brawn and those adorable dimples was a guy she could have a beer with, or tear up a dance floor with, or run into a gunfight with, or share a dozen orgasms with. He was the most dangerous person she knew, and maybe, just maybe he was the safest.

"Thank you." She smiled softly.

"For the orgasms?"

"For spending Christmas with me."

"I should be thanking *you*. Earlier tonight, I was sitting in a pub alone, feeling woefully sorry for myself." He slurped down another spoonful of stew. "This is our first Christmas together. The first of *forever."*

"Whoa. Forever is a long—"

"Forever." The sharpness in his tone cut through her. "I get all of you, Lydia. Every holiday. Every non-holiday. Every damn thing for the rest of your life."

She straightened, stunned, disturbed, and strangely aroused.

"Having second thoughts? It's too late for that." He pointed the spoon at her. "You opened that door, knowing what you were letting in. You welcomed me into your bed, knowing what kind of lover I was. A celibate one, in fact, until I met you. Because I *don't* do casual sex. I'm a partner for life. A dedicated, faithful, protective, possessive, jealous, obsessive partner. Welcome to my world." He flashed her a wolfish smile, all teeth and somewhat scary, and returned to his bowl. "This is deadly. Seriously, the best stew I've ever eaten. What's in it?"

Whirling, she opened her mouth and tried to untie her tongue. His deranged declaration tangled her up and strung her out. But after several hard swallows and a calming breath, she knew he was right. She knew exactly who and what she was letting into her life when she told Mike to unlock the door.

"Mutton chops," she said. "Potatoes, onions, water, and magic. It's Shannon O'Sullivan's recipe. She always made her homemade stew when it snowed. It warmed us down to our toes, like we were somehow imbibing some of her hardiness, her glow. I think it's because she made it with love. That was her magic ingredient." Her chest warmed with the memory. "I have a lot to tell you, Cole. I don't know where to start."

"Mike is your brother. Let's start there."

"We met twelve years ago. I was fifteen. He was

sixteen." Her shoulders loosened, her love for Mike all-consuming. "My mother was a Russian swallow. I don't remember her. I was two-years-old when she died. I was born in Russia, but my dad raised me in Chicago. He was American."

His gaze dipped to the tattoo on her chest, the symbol of her mother. "You really are Russian."

"My bloodline, yes. But I never lived there. I'm American."

"And Mike?"

"He was raised in this house by his mother, Shannon. He didn't know our dad, never met him. Mike and I didn't know about each other until Dad died."

"How did you find out?"

"My dad named Mike's mother as my legal guardian should something happen to him. I was fifteen when a lawyer showed up at my door and told me that my dad was gone, I had a brother, and this woman I didn't know would be my guardian. I was uprooted from Chicago and sent to Dublin, and man, oh man, I was angry. I was an angry, grieving, rebellious teenager with a penchant for stealing. And suddenly, I was Shannon O'Sullivan's problem. You know what she did?"

"She beat your ass?"

"No." She laughed. "She loved me. That's what she did. She loved me with every breath in her body. And so did her son. A brother I never knew I had. They took me into their humble home, made sure I had everything I needed, and they gave me love."

"Where the hell did you all sleep?" He glanced around at the cramped space, the small kitchen, the couch, the single bedroom.

"Shannon and I slept in the bedroom. And this

was Mike's room." She pointed at the couch. "After Shannon died, I demanded he sleep beside me. When we travel, he sleeps beside me. We have a unique relationship because we didn't grow up together. We're best friends. Siblings, too. But it's our friendship that binds us." She pulled in a guilt-ridden breath. "I know you thought we were fucking, and I let you believe it. It's a ruse he and I employ to ward off unwanted attention."

"Male attention."

"Yes."

"He's protective of you."

"That's an understatement. When I met him, he was the biggest troublemaker in Dublin 22. The leader of the troublemakers. I was a thief when I arrived here, and he made me a better thief. I went from picking pockets to luring powerful businessmen back to their hotel rooms and scraping their phones while they were in the shower."

"Scraping digital information?" His eyes darkened. "Information that, I assume, you sold on the black market?"

"Yep. I saved up a shitload of money from those jobs."

"Did you fuck these men before you robbed them?"

"Sometimes. Look, Mike and I got mixed up in some dirty shit. We needed money. A lot of it. We've been planning our revenge for our father's death for years. So we ran criminal schemes and robbed people to fund it. It was the only way we could afford to do this for as long as we have."

"Why didn't Mike meet your dad?"

"Dad was protecting him and Shannon. He kept

their existence a secret. Something he couldn't do with me because I didn't have a mother."

"Who was he?"

"Richard Pictam."

"That's your real name? Lydia Pictam?"

"Yeah." She looked down at the table and picked at a deep scratch in the wood. "I loved him so much I idolized him. He was my entire world. My protector. He had this rugged rebelliousness about him, an air of danger, but he made me feel safe. Untouchable. Like I could do anything because he would always have my back. My own personal action hero." She sucked in her cheeks. "I wanted to be just like him. So I ran the streets, got into trouble, picked fights, and acquired some bad habits. But he's the one who taught me how to defend myself. Combat training, weaponry, tactical skills—he taught me everything I needed to know to protect myself." She looked up and met Cole's eyes. "He was an NSA agent, part of the Special Collection Service."

"Ah." He sat back and wiped his mouth with the back of his hand. "An intelligence spy."

"Yeah. He worked jointly with the CIA abroad to penetrate foreign communications networks."

"That explains how you got access to those customized bugs. But how the hell did he hook up with a Russian sex spy?"

"No idea. He never talked about my mother. I don't even know how she died." She shrugged. "Shannon O'Sullivan held his heart, and he protected her and Mike until the day he was killed."

"How did he die?"

"That's a critical question." A dull pain pressed behind her breastbone. "With a dangerous answer."

"Come here." He pushed back his chair and

gripped her hand, pulling.

She went into his arms, her heart so swollen with years of grief and anger she didn't know how her ribcage continued to contain it. He slid an arm behind her legs, and in one swift motion, he hoisted her up and onto his lap.

And just like that, her chest felt instantly lighter.

"I used to have a pet snake." He rested his mouth against her head. "My foster family gave it to me."

"Foster?"

"I'm one of those unlucky few who spent eighteen years in foster care. But I always considered myself lucky. I lived with nice families. Good people."

"But none of them were permanent."

"No." He rubbed his hand up and down her arm. "I said I would tell you about the snake tattoo, if you told me about the swallow. You told me about the swallow."

"And now you have two snake tattoos."

"I used to have more on my arms. I had them removed after I faked my death on Thurney Bridge."

"What?" She jerked back.

"A story for another time." His fingers found her hair, absently playing with the tangled strands. "The pet snake I had in high school gave me a dangerous reputation, especially with the girls. It got me laid. A lot."

"Bullshit."

"I swear." He laughed. "What I learned was that snakes represented danger, and having a dangerous reputation earned respect and elicited fear. No one fucked with me. It gave me the confidence to take what I want."

He held out his arm, punctuating his point with

the tattoo of the serpent taking what it wanted. *Her.*

She traced a finger over the ink. "I don't know if I should be honored or scared."

"You're safe with me." He cupped her face and pulled her in for a deep kiss. "Always. I protect what's mine."

"I do, too." She kissed him in turn, tongues entwining, deep and languorous. Then she leaned back and combed her fingers through his unruly brown hair. "Twelve years ago, my dad was involved in an operation with a CIA informant in Russia. I don't know the details, only that it pertained to Russia's interference campaign in U.S. elections. My dad was sent to Russia to meet with someone, to do something. I don't know. It's all classified. But he never came home. He was murdered in a hotel room, and the murder was recorded on a hard drive."

His entire body tensed beneath her. She twisted on his lap and studied his expression, watching as he absorbed and processed her words.

"My dad's colleague and loyal friend in the NSA was there," she said. "He was the tech guy, monitoring from another room. He turned in the hard drive, but it was stolen and sold by Marie Merivale."

"To the Romanian mafia." He narrowed his eyes. "How did you get this intel? It's classified."

"My dad's NSA friend has done a few things for me over the years. He told me about the hard drive, gave me those customized bugs, and erased my identity and Mike's so that we wouldn't be connected to our dad."

"That's why I couldn't find anything about you. Neither of you exists."

"I don't know the identity of my dad's friend and

have no way to contact him. He wishes to remain anonymous and separated from all this. I imagine he's protecting his own family and his career. I get it, and I'm grateful. Without him, I would've never learned the truth about how my dad died."

"Who murdered him?"

"Vincent Barrington."

"What?' He stopped breathing, and his hand clamped down on her leg. "I don't think I heard you correctly."

"Yes, you did."

"Vincent Barrington, the United States President-elect. *That* Vincent Barrington?"

"Yeah."

TWENTY-FOUR

With a thudding heart, Lydia stiffened on Cole's lap, watching his expression morph from shock to confusion to steely resolve.

This was it. She'd given him the single most important secret of her life. He could choose to help her. Or he could fuck her eight ways to Sunday, steal the hard drive, and sell it to Vincent himself.

"Why?" he asked on a heavy exhale.

"Why did Vincent do it? Why was he in that Russian hotel room twelve years ago? Why did he kill my dad? I don't have those answers, but I can confirm that he wants that hard drive as badly as I do."

"It was Vincent who hired you to capture and torture me in Texas?"

"Yes. Fifteen months ago, he hadn't announced his intent to run for U.S. President, but I knew it was coming. Mike and I spent a fucking decade investigating him, watching his every move. All that effort, and we could never get close enough to kill him. He has so much wealth and power. Mike was on his payroll for years as part of his security team, and even then, he couldn't get near the man."

"How did *you* get on his payroll?"

"Through Mike. He suggested using a Russian swallow and offered up my contact information."

"You're the daughter of an NSA agent who was murdered by Vincent Barrington. You should be in protective custody, not *working for him!*" A vein bulged in his forehead, his entire body rigid. "What if he learned your identity? Jesus fuck, Lydia. Do you know how fucking dangerous it was to put yourself on his radar?"

"Yes, Cole." She pushed off his lap and paced through the kitchen, clenching her fists. "That's why I wore all that makeup and dyed my hair and learned Russian. I concealed my identity. Doesn't matter anyway, because he's already sent eight people after me since my stint in Texas, and more will come. He wants me dead."

"Fuck." He leaned over his lap, elbows braced on his knees, and shoved a hand through his hair. *"Fuck!"*

"It's a lot to take in. The President-elect put a hit on your friend, Rylee, and her neighbor. And God knows who else? But he couldn't kill you, because he needed you to surrender the location of that hard drive. If the video goes public…"

"He won't just be impeached. He'll be arrested."

"Instead of living in the White House, he would spend the rest of his life in a 6x9 cell."

"We need that hard drive."

"Now more than ever." Uncertainty buzzed through her, clashing with hope. "Does that mean you'll help me?"

"I'm committed one-hundred-percent. To this. To

you."

"Okay." She released a ragged breath and reached for the kitchen cabinet. From within, she removed a package of Twizzlers. "He's not the President yet. We still have time to expose him before he becomes the most powerful person in the world. This is no longer about revenge for my dad. It's about keeping an extremely dangerous, corrupt man from taking control of the most important position in our country. He won that election with Russia's interference campaign. Imagine what he'll do once he takes office. He'll rip our country apart."

He slowly nodded as if coming to terms with the stakes and the gravity of the situation. "You must have a plan, but I can't for the life of me figure it out. What have you been doing for the past fourteen months? Besides driving me completely insane?"

"You're the one stalking me, Cole Hartman." She bit a rope of licorice out of the package, smiling as she chewed it down. "I couldn't infiltrate the Romanian mafia. I'm not a super-secret spy or government operative or whatever you were. I'm just a girl."

"With a really great rack."

She glanced down at her chest, which was exposed in the wide-open gap of her silk robe. She spread the material wider and cocked her head. "Is it great enough to seduce a high-ranking member of the mafia?"

"Not without getting your ass blistered." His gaze turned to stone, his voice gravelly. "Remember that part about me being jealous and possessive? You don't want to see what happens if you try to seduce anyone but me."

She arched a brow. "Moving on. What does the

mafia want with that hard drive?"

"Profit. They sat on it, waiting for its worth to reach its highest potential."

"Which is now. It incriminates the President-elect. So they'll sell it to the highest bidder?"

"Yes, and the highest bidder would be Vincent Barrington."

"Yet they haven't sold it to him." She rubbed her nape, frustrated. She'd turned this round and round in her head so many times. "Vincent doesn't even know they have it."

"Good point." He drummed his fingers on his knee. "So they must intend to use it as blackmail. To control him once he's in office."

"They'll have a huge goddamn bargaining chip if that's the case. Do you know what the Romanian mafia is known for?"

"ATM-skimmings and cybercrime."

"Yep." She gnawed on her candy, her mind spinning. "That brings me to my plan. Do you want to hear it?"

"I'm on pins and needles," he deadpanned.

"PaulVer."

"What?"

"PaulVer Rize. You haven't heard of him?"

"No, should I?"

"I'm disappointed, Cole. He's only the most notorious hacker in the world. He stole more than 200 million payment card accounts from major retailers in the U.S. He created back doors in several corporate networks and pocketed an estimated 300 million dollars from one company alone." Her pulse accelerated, and her hands fluttered through the air as she talked. She could feel herself getting excited. "He's on fire."

"You want him to hack into the mafia and steal the video file?"

"Yes. They would've made copies as a safeguard and stored them on a server somewhere. I just need PaulVer to hack in, snatch the file, and blast it all over the Internet."

"Wow." He leaned back and clasped his fingers behind his neck, his expression thoughtful. Then his lips curled into a smile. "That's fucking brilliant."

"Thank you." She released a slow breath. "Only problem is no one knows who he is. PaulVer is his hacker name."

"I'll start digging around, see what I can find on him."

"Already did that. For fourteen months, Mike and I have chased him and his hacker friends all over Europe. You know where he spends his time?"

"In strip clubs."

"And nightclubs and anywhere there are dancing girls. No one knows what he looks like, and those who do would never say. There are a lot of rumors about him, but the one that is consistent in every club in every city he visits is that he's drawn to talented female dancers. When he sees one that impresses him, he gives her a painted Easter egg."

He stared at her, incredulous.

"What?" She widened her eyes. "I'm not making this up."

"It's ridiculous."

"I thought so, too. At first. Until I saw one of these Easter eggs with my own eyes. Then I saw more. Mike and I have literally been on an Easter egg hunt for the past year. After bouncing between strip clubs to dance clubs all over Europe, we know which clubs are his favorite and the type of girl he approaches. He targets the most beautiful, most talented dancer in the club, comes up behind her, and slips a painted egg in her hand. By the time she examines the strange object and turns around, he's gone. No one has ever seen him."

"Have you ever witnessed it happening?"

"No. I'm always watching for it. But I never spot an occurrence until after a girl makes a fuss over the egg in her hand and waves it around. Of course, these women have no idea the meaning or that it has anything to do with a notorious hacker. It's not like they're dancing in these clubs to win a painted egg. They just shrug it off. Most of them just leave the egg on a table."

"So that's your plan? Try to catch him handing off an egg and confront him? Then what? Make him an offer to hack the mafia for you?"

"Yes. I've also been trying to draw him to me. With enough glamour and the right dance moves, I was hoping he would put an egg in *my* hand."

He laughed. The mean son of a bitch actually threw his head back and laughed.

"Fuck you." She crossed her arms over her chest and flung him her most venomous glare.

His amusement cut off, and in its place rose a brooding, stony-faced, intimidating man. He stood and prowled toward her, getting right up in her face. "You are undeniably the most gorgeous woman in all of those clubs. But you can't dance."

"Yes, I can." She slammed her fists on her hips and met him stare for stare, noses touching.

"Let me clarify. You can't dance as well as the dancers I've seen in those clubs." He kissed her lips.

"But you can learn."

Her chest hitched. "You like my plan."

"I fucking love your plan. It offers the least amount of risk with the greatest chance of success. If this hacker is as good as you say, he can snatch that video file and transmit it all over the world in one night from the safety of his computer."

"I just need to learn how to dance. You think you can teach me?"

"No. But I know someone who can."

"Danni Savoy." Her stomach clenched beneath a fist of insecurities.

"You good with that?" He narrowed his eyes.

"Will she agree to it?"

"I can convince her."

Why? Did he see this as an opportunity to rekindle old flames?

"Whatever you're thinking, stop." He cupped her face and drew her mouth to his. "She's a solution to a problem. That's all. How badly do you want this hard drive?"

"You know the answer to that."

"Yeah. You wanted it badly enough to capture an innocent man, lock him in the dark for thirty days, and torture him with the worst thrash metal song ever created."

She cringed. "I said I regretted nothing, but I really do regret that. I'm sorry."

"I survived. And I'll take hot dogs and terrible music over that stonecutter any day."

She wrapped her arms around his strong shoulders and rested her forehead against his. "So you'll call Danni?"

"I'll call Trace and have them meet us in

Missouri. I have a safe house there."

"We only have until Inauguration Day. Less than a month."

"Danni will have you dancing like a pro in less than a week. Then you'll get your Easter egg."

Her heart melted, falling, crashing, and breaking open for this man. "Take me to bed."

His eyes made hungry promises as he lifted her. "I'm going to take you on this table first."

TWENTY-FIVE

Hours later, Cole lay in bed, staring into the sleepy, sea-green eyes of Lydia Pictam. Such an exquisite creature. Arresting. Rebellious. Fearless. *Mine.*

He ghosted his fingers along the outer curve of her breast, savoring the soft noises each caress drew from her cherry lips. Every touch reinforced their connection. A connection forged so deeply inside him his bones thrummed with it.

After he took her on the kitchen table, he fucked her again in the shower. Still, he couldn't stop touching her, looking at her. She was a dream. An erotic Christmas angel.

And a remarkably good listener.

He'd spent the last couple of hours talking her ear off. He told her everything, holding nothing back. Thurney Bridge, his fake death, Danni and Trace, his career in the *activity,* and his current endeavors with his vigilante family.

His activities and relationships with the Freedom Fighters fascinated her the most. Her questions were hungry, her attention enraptured. She wanted to meet them, get to know them, and she would.

After their shower, he'd made several phone calls.

The first was to Matias, requesting transportation on the private jet back to the states. He wouldn't risk putting Lydia on a commercial flight. Not with Vincent Barrington gunning for her. Matias gladly agreed to pick them up the day after Christmas and fly them to Missouri.

He called Romero next, inquiring about PaulVer. No surprise that the kid knew of and admired the notorious hacker. Romero validated PaulVer's expertise, saying that if anyone could break into the Romanian mafia, it was the Romanian hacker known as PaulVer Rize.

The final phone call was to Trace, the conversation terse and to the point as always. He checked in with Trace several times a year, but he never asked for anything. So his request had taken his friend by surprise.

"I need a favor."

"Are you in danger?"

"No more than usual. I need you and Danni to go to the lakehouse."

"Are we in danger?"

"No. But this is important. I'll explain everything when I arrive in two days."

"I'm not agreeing to this."

"Yes, you are. This is connected to Thurney Bridge, but bigger. I haven't asked anything of you in eight years. I'm asking for a week of your time. Danni's time, actually. I need her to teach someone how to dance."

"Who?"

"A woman."

"Is she your *woman?"*

"In every way."

"Well, fuck. Now you have my attention."

"Don't be a dick. Just be there."

"We'll be there."

"It's officially Christmas morning." Lydia twisted her fingers in his hair, playing with the messy spikes. "Merry Christmas."

"You need to sleep. We have a lot of planning to do today."

"I'm all hyped up on adrenaline."

"And candy."

"And sex."

He gripped her waist and tucked her in close. "I can fuck you into a coma."

She groaned against his chest. "Definitely need a rain check on that."

His thoughts flitted to the plan with the hacker, sparking a question he was meaning to ask. "Any theories on why he uses Easter eggs as his calling card?"

"Easter is a big holiday in Romania, and they love their hand-painted eggs. They empty the eggs and paint the shells, creating these fragile little artistic masterpieces. It could also have something to do with the Easter eggs used in computing and video games. You know, the hidden messages and secret responses that programmers love to sneak in? It's like this guy wants to leave a mysterious trail, hoping someone will take the time to find him."

"We'll find him. The question is, will he help us? I

assume he's motivated by money? How did you plan on paying him?"

"Is it that obvious that I'm broke?"

"I've been watching you for a long time. I assumed your money was running out."

"Oh, it ran out. That's why we came back to Ireland. We decided to sell this house and use the money to keep going until we finish."

"Don't sell it. I'm funding this venture going forward."

"I can't ask you to do that."

"You didn't, and I'm doing it." He ran his hand through her hair, thinking through the logistics. "How much does a hacker like PaulVer charge for one of these heists?"

"PaulVer doesn't charge anything. He's already filthy rich. If the job interests him, he'll do it pro bono. And trust me, the job will interest him. There's nothing these black-hat hackers love more than sticking it to the man, especially if the man is a greedy, corrupt, self-serving politician."

They talked a little longer about the hacker. Then they drifted into stories about their tattoos, explaining how each one came about and the meaning behind them.

As she fell asleep in his arms, he felt untroubled, clearheaded, and happier than he ever remembered being. She rejuvenated his soul, elevated his spirit, and gave him a new reason to fight. It might be cold and dark in this tiny room, but there was beauty in it, inspiration, and a promising future.

She was all those things, and he was so damn glad he'd taken the risk.

TWENTY-SIX

Cole woke Christmas morning with a hard-on. Nothing unusual about that. What had changed, however, was the soft, warm body rubbing up against it.

Lydia stretched with a lazy, drawn-out hum in her throat. Her colorfully inked arms reached overhead, her sweet ass shimmying and shaking as she extended her body to its full length.

She did all this in the cage of his arms. Then, in one fluid motion, she turned so that she was astride him, wearing nothing but a beaming smile.

"Good morning." He smiled back, spellbound by her beauty.

"Nothing says *good morning* like morning wood." She rocked her hips, teasing her pussy along his rigid length.

Her hair, wildly tangled and gloriously red, tumbled down her chest, inviting him to twine it around his fingers and pull her down for a kiss.

With a nudge of her jaw, she flicked her tongue along the seam of his lips, urging him to play.

He pinched her nipple hard and chased the gasp inside her mouth. Then he chased her hot little tongue. They kissed slowly, languidly, in a greeting of sighs with no expectation beyond the pleasure of closeness.

Leaning up, she took her lower lip between her teeth and dipped her chin to her chest. "Other than my brother, who doesn't count, I've never woken beside a man." She snapped her head up, eyes wide. Then she scrambled out of bed in a sudden burst of energy. "Where is he?"

"Who? Mike?"

"Yeah. He should've called." She yanked the curtain aside, spilling light into the room, and searched the worn carpet. "Where's my phone?"

He followed her out of bed and dragged on his jeans, the quickening of his pulse feeding off hers.

"Here." He spotted it on the floor beside the nightstand, where he must've knocked it off last night.

He tossed it to her, waiting as she unlocked the screen.

"No missed calls. Dammit, Mike." She dialed and held the phone to her ear while sliding on her silk robe. "Voicemail." Her brows knitted together as she left a message. "Come home. You're worrying me." She disconnected and dropped her arms to her sides. "He should've returned by now."

"You said he was getting laid." He yanked on his shirt, keeping his voice calm despite the shiver in his veins.

"I know, but it's Christmas." She turned and faced the window, her hair falling in rampant waves of red down her back.

Gray, watery light washed the sky, illuminating thin patches of ice on the house behind hers.

"I'll go look for him." He pulled on his boots and strode out of the bedroom. "Do you know where he went?"

"No, but he wouldn't have gone far." She followed him into the kitchen. "Somewhere on foot. He doesn't have a car or money for transportation."

He found his jacket and beanie on the floor and pulled them on. The gun sat securely in the coat pocket. He left it there, not wanting to alarm her.

"It's not a good idea for you to walk out of this house in the daylight." She stepped toward the window that faced the street and eased back the curtain. "If Vincent's men are watching…" She gasped, squinting at something outside. "What…is…? Oh, my God, that's blood."

As she tore away from the window and darted for the stairs, he slipped by her and yanked back the curtain. The third-story view showed the pathway to the street. Snow blanketed the trees, the front yard, the pavement, and…

He stopped breathing. That was blood. A dark red trail of it from the street to the front door of her house. Footprints surrounded crimson splatter. Stumbling, falling impressions from shoes.

"Lydia!" He took off down the stairs, hitting the second level to the sounds of sliding locks. "Don't open that door!"

She opened the door.

Then she stumbled, clapped her hands over her mouth, and released a shrilling, keening wail. "Nooooo! Not my brother! Oh, God, please, no! Not him!"

The sounds coming from her made his blood run cold. His muscles went taut, and his pulse skyrocketed as he bolted down the remaining flight of stairs.

Drawing his gun, he watched in horror as she fell to her knees on the porch, making herself a wide-open target for whoever was out there.

Lydia! Inside! Now!" He leaped over the final steps, weapon raised, and hooked an arm around her chest, dragging her back inside.

As she kicked and screamed and tried to claw away from him, he took in the grim scene.

Mike lay face down on the porch, half on, half off the short stoop, with an arm outstretched, reaching toward the door. The dusting of snow on his lifeless body suggested he'd been there a while.

Gunshot wounds were visible on his calf, lower back, and right shoulder. He'd been shot from behind, but it couldn't have happened nearby. They would've heard the report of gunfire.

That meant Mike had run here with those injuries. Given the trail of blood that led down the street and around the corner, it was a miracle he'd made it home.

The shooter was out there somewhere, probably waiting nearby. In Mike's attempt to reach Lydia, he might've inadvertently led the threat right to her door.

She wailed in Cole's arms, her legs buckling and her hands grappling, trying to get to Mike. It fucking hurt—the sounds of her agony, the sight of her brother, the goddamn fucking needlessness of it. His chest burned. His throat closed, and his training took over.

She had a vicious amount of strength as he muscled her backward, fighting to keep her out of view of the doorway. With her back to the wall, he flattened an immovable hand against her chest. His other imprisoned her chin, forcing her shattered gaze to his.

"I need you to push it down," he said sternly.

"Push it way, way down where you don't feel it. It'll be there later, but right now, I need you to bury it, Lydia. Bury it and focus. I need you alive and with me."

She stared at him out of glazed eyes, not seeing him. Not seeing anything but hopelessness.

"He's my rock." Her face collapsed. "My world. He's all I have left." A sob ripped from her throat, followed by an avalanche of mewling convulsive gasps.

Any minute, someone would drive by and see the body on the porch. The saving grace was the overnight snow. It would discourage people from wandering out this morning. And it was Christmas. Most were tucked around their decorated trees, opening presents and listening to holiday music.

"Look at me." He tightened his grip on her jaw until her eyes cleared and locked on his. "You have three minutes to go upstairs and pack what you need. I know you can do this. You can do it because you're strong as fuck, and you want to live."

She shook her head, knocking more tears loose. "Every day at his side was a good day to die hard."

"You know what?" He put his face in hers. "Today is a good day to *live* hard because that's the only way we're going to avenge his death."

That got her attention.

She gripped his wrists and worked her throat, swallowing down the sobs. More tried to rise, overwhelming her breaths. She whimpered, choking, and her gaze started drifting away, toward the door. He was losing her.

"Breathe with me, Lydia. In and out. In and out. Just like this." He inhaled, exhaled, slowly, loudly, forcing her to follow along. "Good girl. Keep breathing. In. Out. Focus on my breaths. There you go."

He held still, watching her power through the anguish until her legs regained strength, firmly holding her up. Her shoulders squared. Her jaw stiffened, and her breathing evened out.

"Christ, you're so fucking strong." He grasped her nape and brought their foreheads together. "You've got this. Three minutes. Go."

He stepped back, and she walked stiffly up the stairs, moving quickly, up and around the corner.

Returning to the doorway, he stayed out of view and scanned the perimeter. No movement. Then he stepped outside and quickly rummaged through Mike's clothes while keeping an eye on the street.

Both of Mike's guns were holstered, suggesting he'd been caught unaware and didn't have time to fire off a shot.

Cole collected the weapons, a wallet, phone, and… He pried open Mike's frozen hand and lifted a small wrapped present.

A Christmas present with a tiny red bow.

"Goddammit, Mike." He pocketed the gift in his jacket, his chest aching. "This is going to fucking hurt her. She's going to mourn you for the rest of her life."

But she wouldn't do it alone. Cole would be with her in whatever capacity she needed.

Once he'd gathered everything he thought she would want to keep, he piled it in the entryway and surveyed the snow-covered surroundings.

His blood heated with the sprint of his pulse, every instinct inside him demanding swift action. They needed to go before someone called the gardai. They needed to disappear, but Lydia didn't have a car, and cabs didn't travel through here.

They would have to flee on foot.

With Mike's murderer on the loose.

He twisted at the sound of her footsteps on the stairs. As he shifted to turn back to the front, a resounding boom cracked the air. The gunshot discharged from the street and splintered the doorframe an inch away from his head.

His lungs emptied. He aimed the pistol and dropped low to the ground, his senses reaching for Lydia.

"Stay down." He thrust a hand behind him, stalling her descent on the stairs. "Lock the door behind me. Do not open it until I return. Understand?"

"Cole—"

"Lock the door!" Adrenalized and laser-focused, he slipped onto the porch, ducking low and shutting the door behind him.

At the sounds of engaging locks, he melted into the shadows of the hedgerow lining the property.

Surrounded by parked cars, icy trees, wheelie bins, and terraced houses, he probed the spaces between, frozen in wait for some sign of movement.

Then he saw it. Across the street between two houses, a man dressed in black stood out in stark contrast against the wintry backdrop. The dark clothing would've aided him last night, but in the daylight, it only helped Cole.

He bolted toward the shooter, weaving in and out of cover while refraining from squeezing the trigger until he had a clear shot.

Then he fired. Missed the target. The man spun around the corner of the house while blindly shooting back, forcing Cole to wait behind a car for breathless seconds until the thug stopped spraying lead.

A moment of silence. Then Cole gave chase.

The gunfight moved through the quiet neighborhood. Bullets pelleted cars and shattered house windows. He didn't aim at homes, conscious of civilian casualties. But his adversary didn't give a fuck. The bastard ran down the street, heedlessly swinging the gun behind him and shooting everything in a vicious sweep.

Somewhere in the distance, Christmas music played. A car horn honked. Stomping footsteps rang out—the shooter's, Cole's, and others in the periphery, stampeding in the opposite direction.

He chased the man for blocks, jumping fences, crossing icy yards, dodging passing cars, and racing down busy avenues. Meanwhile, Dublin 22 stirred to life. And several streets away, the blare of sirens erupted.

The gardai were coming.

Given the fast approach of the sirens, he had thirty seconds tops.

Up ahead, the shooter ran into a wide intersection. Cole trailed him, twenty feet behind. The man abruptly stopped at the center and pivoted, weapon raised.

Cole halted in the street with no nearby cars or trees to take cover. With no choice but to engage in this standoff, he trained his pistol with both hands and met the man's eyes.

Timing was everything.

"I don't want to shoot…" He squeezed the trigger mid-sentence.

His gun clicked dry. Empty.

Oh, fucking fuck.

The shooter tipped his head, and a cold-blooded smirk twisted his lips. He held his gun out one-handed and took a cocky step forward, aimed to kill.

Cole knew his next breath would be his last, and as he drew it into his lungs, the squeal of tires sounded. A motor revved, and a speeding car flew into the intersection and slammed into the gunman. The impact hit him like a freight train, bending him in half. The wrong way.

The body buckled beneath the car, succumbing to the brutal spin of tires and bouncing the vehicle like a speed bump.

His mouth dried, his muscles locked in shock. It took a full second to snap out of his stupor and focus on the snow-covered car.

It skidded to a stop. The tires spun in reverse, and it raced backward, running over the body a second time. Hope swelled in his chest.

Ice coated the windows, blocking his view of the driver. But as the door swung open, he already knew, his feet racing forward, his heart rate exploding.

Lydia poked her head out.

"Cole!" Her neck twisted toward the sound of approaching sirens. "Hurry!"

He slid past the open door, crashing in behind the steering wheel and shoving her into the passenger seat. Then he hit the gas, bouncing over the body and speeding down the street.

She stared at the side mirror, watching the flash of chasing lights, her voice numb. "Are you shot?"

"No."

He wanted to scold her for disobeying him and leaving the house, but under the circumstances, he wouldn't dare. She'd lost her brother and saved Cole's life. Her courage took his breath away, leaving him gobsmacked and awe-struck.

"Where did you get the car?" He pushed the small sedan to its mechanical limits as he squealed around bends and tore through intersections, weaving, dodging traffic, and trying to outrun the gardai behind them.

"I stole it. Where are we going?"

Her voice was wooden, her posture stiff. He couldn't fathom how she was doing. She kept it buried, just like he'd demanded.

"Looks like I lost the gardai." He gripped the wheel, his eyes on the rearview and his neck aching with tension. "We'll dump the car, go to my rented apartment, and stay the night there. Tomorrow, we fly to the states."

Without Mike.

He didn't make promises that everything would be okay. All he could do was hope that when revenge came, it would bring her some sort of closure, something more justified and bearable than leaving her brother lying dead in the snow.

Until then, he would hold her through the pain.

TWENTY-SEVEN

Cole didn't know how to do this, if he was doing it right or making it worse. He wasn't a grief counselor. He'd never tried to console someone through the loss of a loved one.

Watching Lydia suffer and being helpless to fix it was the hardest thing he'd ever done.

She'd held herself together until they reached the apartment. Once they were safely inside, he removed their clothes and carried her into the shower.

That was where she lost it. The anguish pouring out of her tore the flesh around his heart. She cried so hard she vomited. She cried until she hyperventilated. Her pain was all-consuming, strangling her from the inside out.

It made him realize with gut-wrenching misery that when he'd faked his death, Danni had gone through something similar. She'd told him later that her grieving process had been so ugly that she'd drowned herself in grain alcohol for months. He thought he'd understood what she was saying. But he hadn't.

He understood now. Every harrowing tear, each body-wracking sob, the immeasurable, yawning despair that rendered the soul forever scarred—he felt it all with Lydia as he held her in his arms.

Tucked beneath layers of blankets in the bed, he entwined his body around her and cradled her through the night. Eventually, her choking sobs waned, giving way to exhaustion and listlessness.

She didn't speak beyond one-word responses, but he refused to rush her. She needed to go through this at her own pace. When she was ready to talk about it, he would listen.

Right now, his job was to take care of her.

He forced fluids and tried to make her eat. He kept a constant vigilance on the perimeter, overly cautious and paranoid about being followed. Everywhere he traveled, he chose lodging with the best security. This apartment was no exception. But it was no longer just his life he was protecting.

He was responsible for her safety, physical wellbeing, and emotional health.

Hefting the thick mass of her hair in his hand, he laid it against her shoulder, smoothing it, caressing it where it fell in soft waves of satin against her throat and chest.

From roots to tips, he gently finger-combed the strands. Over and over, with each rhythmic stroke, her eyelids grew heavier, the furrows in her forehead flattening out. The hitches in her breaths came with longer stretches in between until they vanished altogether. She was finally falling asleep.

"It's really hard not to love you, Cole."

The feeble sound of her voice startled him, but it was her words that gave him pause. He didn't have to ask why she would try *not* to love him. He knew from experience that love was a risk, its longevity never guaranteed. At any moment, it could be taken away.

Her father, Shannon, Mike—everyone she'd ever loved had been taken from her. Maybe it was safer to avoid all forms of love.

But after eight years of being alone, he knew it was far better to experience all the ups and downs with a partner, to fight together, and spark joy in each other. Loneliness was never a better option.

"Do it anyway," he said.

Her fingers twitched against his chest, her voice a thready whisper. "Did you just order me to love you?"

"Yes."

"I'll think about it."

"Take your time. I'll wait."

Danni had said that love wasn't a choice, and she was right. Love was a chance.

A chance worth taking.

She whimpered and cleared her throat. "It hurts, Cole."

"Tell me what to do." He pulled her tighter to his chest.

"This." She melted against him, accepting his embrace. "Don't let go."

"Never."

Not this time.

She fought the pull of sleep, but at last, her body won out and dragged her under.

Reluctantly, carefully, he slipped out of bed, stepped into the bathroom, and called Rylee. She listened as he updated her on everything that had happened since the moment he decided to walk into Lydia's house.

When he finished, she blew a breath into the phone. "God, Cole. My heart is so happy and sad at the same time. I'm glad she has you right now."

"I don't know what I'm doing."

"She needs you to watch over her and hold her hand while she grieves. Just keep doing that." Her voice softened. "I look forward to finally meeting her."

"This is almost over."

"Matias selected the team for the heist you're planning with the hacker. They're on their way to you now. He's bringing the best. Obviously, I'm not with them."

"You'll be on the next mission."

"I know. Get back to your girl, and I'll see you in a few weeks."

"Night, Rylee."

"Night, Cole."

He made two more calls, touching base with Matias and Romero. If the gardai or Vincent Barrington's men showed up here looking for him or Lydia, Romero would know. The kid was linked into the apartment's security system, as well as multiple security cameras throughout the surrounding blocks.

With that comforting news, Cole returned to Lydia and grabbed some much-needed sleep.

The next morning, he was all business. From the moment they woke, stepped out of the apartment, caught a cab, boarded Matias' private plane, and lifted off the tarmac, every thought in his head and measure he took focused on the safety of Lydia and the team.

It wasn't until they were high in the air that he released a sigh of relief.

Lydia sat beside him in the front of the jet, staring out the small window as they ascended through the clouds. She hadn't spoken much since she woke, and her limbs barely moved. Almost as if she were in a state of catatonia.

"Lydia." He rested a hand on her denim-clad thigh.

She turned to him, the skin around her eyes red and puffy despite not having shed a single tear today. "Don't ask me if I'm okay."

"I won't."

"But you want to know how I'm doing."

"For sure."

"It changes by the second. I feel strong one moment and utterly paralyzed the next." She rubbed her breastbone, wearing the weight of her heart in the shadows on her beautiful face. "I don't want to cry, and I don't want to pretend I'm fine. So I'm balancing on this plateau in emotional limbo."

"It's okay to cry," he murmured.

"There's a time and place." She gripped his hand and squeezed. "I want to do that with you, when it's just us. Which is weird because I'm not a crier. I was a ball of rage when my dad died, and I was a pillar of strength for Mike when Shannon died. But now, God, this is so much harder. It feels too heavy to carry. But I know I can. I will. Because of you." She unbuckled her seat belt and twisted to face him fully, resting a hand on his whiskers. "You've seen me at my worst. As if all the things I did to you in Texas weren't bad enough. Now you've seen me cry for ten hours straight."

"If that's your worst—"

"I puked all over your feet in the shower."

"I was there."

"Exactly," she said quietly. "You were there. You're still here."

"I'm committed, Lydia."

She said nothing and drew her gaze away, her smooth cheeks and pert freckled nose illuminated by the window light. Then she leaned toward him and rested her mouth against his shoulder, her hands curving around his ribs.

He encircled her slight body with one arm and pulled her onto his lap. "I want you to meet my friends."

"They should want to kill me, not help me."

"I told them your drone was a bluff. You already know who they are and what we do. They appreciate a good deception tactic." He stroked along the length of her tumbled hair. "You're exactly the kind of person they want fighting alongside them, not against them."

"I want to meet them."

He stood, taking her with him, and led her to the rear of the cabin.

Matias had assembled a six-person team for this operation. Seven, if he counted Romero, who remained in Colombia surrounded by his equipment. Matias had an elaborate computer lab built for the kid, complete with his own geek squad.

He reached the cabin's lounge area, and six pairs of eyes greeted him, spreading a feeling of weightlessness in his chest. He'd been gone fifteen months, and he fucking missed these assholes.

As he opened his mouth to start the introductions, Lydia beat him to it.

"Matias." She stretched out a hand toward the black-haired Colombian. "Thank you for the ride."

Matias unfolded his hulking frame from the couch and rose to his full height. "It's a pleasure, Lydia." They shook hands, and Matias motioned at the others. "This is my wife, Camila, and her sister, Lucia. The token white guy is Tate."

"I fucking hate this guy," Tate said to Lydia. "If I weren't in love with his sister-in-law, I would've snuffed him already."

Lydia's eyes widened, her lips parting in shock.

Cole smiled at the interaction. He didn't know how much she'd retained from the other night when he walked her through the backgrounds and relationships of all his friends. But she knew their roles and connections to one another. No doubt she'd heard some terrifying rumors about Matias. His brutal, mafia-style code of respect made him the most feared cartel capo in Colombia. But when he wasn't striking terror into the hearts of his enemies, he was annoyingly charming.

"Ignore them." Kate climbed out of the adjacent seat and gripped Lydia's hand, holding on for a long moment. "I'm Kate, the resident doctor-in-training. I'm just here to patch up any injuries."

"Nice to meet you."

"Same. I'll be honest. We've all been so curious about you. Cole's not the most forthcoming guy, so to see him with you…" She cupped a hand around her mouth and stage-whispered, "*with a woman,* well, it's a little tantalizing."

Laughter rumbled through the cabin.

Lydia found his gaze, and he thought if she weren't hurting so badly, she might've smiled.

"This is my husband, Tiago." Kate flicked a finger behind her. "Don't mind his death-glare. I promise his body-count has gone way down in the past two years. He's almost rehabilitated."

A smile slid across the lounging male's face as he yanked her onto his lap and sank his teeth into her neck, making her yelp.

Tiago Badell, the once-notorious Venezuelan crime lord, had to put forth a lot of effort to integrate into their tight-knit family. His past with Lucia and Kate wasn't pretty, and his demeanor radiated an air of cruelty that hadn't diminished with time. But they trusted him. He wouldn't be here if they didn't.

"Here. Sit." Camila gave up her seat and moved to Matias' lap. "Hang out with us. Tell us about your brother."

Lydia stiffened, and he touched her back, trailing a knuckle down her spine.

"You're not ready. I get that," Camila said softly. "I'm sorry we didn't get to meet him."

"You don't have to talk at all." Lucia pursed her lips. "Or you can tell us some of Cole's dirty secrets in your Russian accent. We've known him for years but not the way you know him." She winked.

"We're done here." Cole started to pull Lydia toward the front.

She pulled back and stepped toward the empty seat beside Camila. "Just a warning, I'm not the best company right now. But I'd like to hang out and get to know you guys."

That was a good sign. Any sign of life was promising. He knew she faced a tough road ahead, and there would be days when the grief overwhelmed her. But he liked seeing her among his friends. He loved it, actually. The interaction would soothe her and drive home the fact that she wasn't alone. She also needed to establish trust with them since they were all headed into an operation together.

In one week, they would fly back to Europe and visit the clubs where she'd seen the most Easter eggs.

With any luck, her new dancing skills would lure the hacker into the open. Then this would all be over.

The nine-hour flight from Dublin to Missouri passed quickly, thanks to the nonstop conversation. He had a lot of catching up to do with his friends.

Lydia listened to their stories without comment, her intelligent eyes taking everything in. She wasn't standoffish. She was fighting an inner battle, drowning beneath the gravity of the past twenty-four hours.

He watched her closely and caressed her constantly. Every touch she returned in kind, affirming her strength. She wasn't shutting down. She was fighting through this.

It was after dark when they arrived at the lakehouse. He didn't recognize the black Rolls-Royce Wraith in the driveway, but he knew it belonged to Trace Savoy. The man had a passion for expensive luxury cars.

As he stepped out of the rented SUV and unloaded their bags, Lydia stopped him with a hand on his arm.

Footsteps moved around them as the others collected their things and headed toward the front door.

"It's been eight years." She searched his eyes.

Eight years since he'd seen Danni.

"I know." He brushed a red lock of hair from her face.

"Aren't you the least bit freaked out?"

"A year ago, I might've been apprehensive. But today? With you? Not at all. I'm not excited about introducing my friends to Trace. Too many strong personalities in one room is a recipe for trouble. But they'll behave."

She nodded and stepped into him, hugging his

waist and resting her forehead on his chest. "Thank you for doing this."

"I want this." His blood heated. "Maybe not as badly as you do, but I want revenge for the same reasons. For everything you've lost and for the safety of our country."

"Good." She straightened and twined her fingers with his. "Let's go teach me how to dance."

When they entered the house, Trace met them at the door. Alone.

A glance over Trace's shoulder revealed a vacant living room and kitchen. No Danni.

Goddammit. If she didn't come—

"She wasn't feeling well." Trace read his thoughts and nodded at the hallway. "She's taking a nap."

Tension released from his shoulders as he took in Trace's crisp black suit, six-foot-four frame, and brooding scowl. Always scowling. Predictably broody.

To those who didn't know Trace, he exuded a severe, imposing, pretentious demeanor that reeked of money. His inheritance had made him obscenely wealthy, and he owned The Regal Arch Casino and Hotel, which had grown into a booming enterprise. But he hadn't always been a cutthroat businessman.

He met Trace in the *activity*. They were operatives in the field together, inseparable for years while running dangerous missions. Spending time with someone like that, doing what they did, built a level of trust that couldn't be imitated. They knew each other's weaknesses, fears, dirty habits, every secret. They were brothers in arms. Best friends.

When Trace took a promotion to be his handler—essentially his boss—it had been a great fit. They already had a relationship built on trust. For the next few years, Trace guided him through every operation, and he trusted Trace not to get him killed.

Their work relationship ended when Trace's parents died. He retired and donned a tailored suit. But they remained best friends.

Until Danni.

All those memories came rushing back as he met and held Trace's stark blue gaze. He waited for the blistering resentment to surge with it. The betrayal. The toxic jealousy. But none of it inflamed. Because it no longer existed.

As he stood face-to-face with Danni's husband, he only felt resolution, contentment, and gratitude.

"Thank you for coming." He stepped forward.

There was no awkward shuffling of shaking hands or halfhearted side-hugs. They went straight in for the hard, constricting embrace of old friends, with arms wrapping around each other and fists pounding on backs.

Trace had maintained his lean muscle, evident in the flexing strength of his squeeze. Eight years hadn't physically aged him. If anything, the years made him even more disgustingly handsome and distinguished.

When they separated, Cole turned to the quiet, stunning redhead at his side. "This is Lydia."

Her eyes shone with alertness and curiosity as she shook Trace's hand. "Don't be alarmed, but I know everything about you."

"Everything?" Trace arched a stern brow at Cole.

"All of it." He nodded. "She knows our history, our careers, and every detail of our tangled relationship with Danni. Full disclosure."

Trace looked back at Lydia, his expression softening with something akin to wonderment. "She's the real deal then."

"It doesn't get more real than this." Cole clasped her hand.

She didn't smile, didn't speak. But her fingers squeezed his, clenching and releasing in silent agreement.

He introduced Trace to the team. They knew everything there was to know about one another. They'd just never met in person.

"I'll show you guys around." Tate led the others toward the hallway.

Kate, Matias, and Camila had never been here. Everyone else was well acquainted with the property.

With nine bedrooms and ten bathrooms, it had been designed to serve as his safe house and accommodate large teams of operatives. Plenty of space for this group to spread out and make themselves at home.

"These walls hold a lot of memories." Trace stared after the team, watching them disperse. "Not all of those memories are good."

Eight years ago, he and Trace had brought Danni here and forced her into a decision. They'd shared her in this house. Fought over her. Cried over her. This was where she'd said goodbye to Trace after telling him she'd chosen Cole.

Cole could never live in this house. It wasn't his home. It only served as a safe place to regroup and make plans. That was why he'd offered it to the Freedom Fighters. This property was as much theirs as it was his.

"Why am I here?" Trace clasped his hands behind his back and tipped his head down, his sharp eyes flicking between Cole and Lydia. "I want the whole story."

"You'll get it, but we should wait for Danni."

"I'm here." Her voice drifted from the hallway, followed by the light tread of her footsteps.

His hand went to Lydia's thick red mane, stroking the silky length. He did it without thought, a subconscious gesture of possessiveness, as if he needed to prove that he wasn't available. Which was ridiculous. He didn't need to prove anything to anyone, least of all, Danni.

She emerged from the corridor, her blonde hair falling around her shoulders. The flowy skirt of her Bohemian-style dress rippled around her ankles as she approached, her gray eyes instantly locking on his.

Beautiful, as expected, she glowed with sunshine. Her cheeks rose with a smile, her face bright and shimmering with happiness.

She went straight to him and hugged his waist, and that was when he noticed the change.

"Whoa." He gripped her shoulders and held her away, his attention dropping to the small round bump beneath the dress. "You're pregnant?"

"And miserable." Her smile widened. "Terrible nausea."

If misery gave out a steady light, flushed the skin with warmth and radiance, and stretched the mouth into a permanent smile, then yeah, she was absolutely miserable.

He'd never seen her this happy. It flowed through her expression and bearing and emitted outward in infectious sparkling waves.

That was all he ever wanted for her, and he felt deep pleasure knowing he'd made the right decision eight years ago in this very house when he let her go.

"I imagine there's more to your misery than the nausea." His gaze flicked to Trace. "You're going to be a father." He tsked, shaking his head. "That should be illegal. The poor kid."

Trace's lips twitched, struggling to maintain his scowl.

"Danni, this is my girl." He turned, staring into vast green eyes, where the reflection of trust and acceptance floated atop a fathomless sea of strength. "Lydia, this is Danni, your dance instructor."

TWENTY-EIGHT

"Hi." Lydia pushed the syllable past a tight throat.

She wasn't nervous or apprehensive or even jealous. Cole gave her no reason to be any of those things. When he looked at Danni, there was no longing in his deep brown eyes. No passion or possessiveness. He gazed upon the pretty blonde with kindness and warmth. Like brotherly love.

Like the way Mike had looked at Lydia.

The painful tightness in her throat ebbed and swelled with the vacillation of her emotions. Mike was gone, and while she coped with that insufferable reality, she wasn't in the mood for pleasantries with Cole's ex-girlfriend.

The obligatory exchanges—*Nice to meet you* and *How was your trip?* – where they traded hollow stares, waited for a turn to talk, and skated around the fact that they'd both had sex with Cole—all of it required more energy than she could muster.

But she was here for this. One-hundred-percent. Trace and Danni were sacrificing a week of their time to help her. The least she could do was slap on a friendly face and participate.

"Let's skip the awkwardness." Danni crooked a finger at her and walked through the brightly lit living room toward the open kitchen. "You look like you could use a beer."

"A beer would be great."

The four of them gathered around the kitchen island. Open shelving on rustic wood walls displayed dishes and cookware. The floor-to-ceiling windows on the back of the lakehouse offered a panoramic view of the raw wilderness. The natural rock and wrought-iron terrace off the kitchen connected to a bridge that led to the private dock below.

Inside, the motif was clean, spacious, and monochromatic, as if designed to pull visitors toward the exterior views of the lake and woodland.

It felt safe here. Isolated. Quiet.

"It's weird." She lowered onto a stool at the island, speaking to no one in particular. "For the first time in years, I don't feel like I have to look over my shoulder."

"Do I get to hear what you two are involved in?" Danni set opened bottles of Bud Light in front of Lydia and Cole and poured a scotch for Trace. "Or is this another classified spy mission?"

Cole met Lydia's eyes, his expression grave, silently warning her that he was about to rip off the Band-aid and talk about Mike.

She nodded and steeled herself.

He pulled up a seat beside her, sitting comfortably close with his legs spread around her stool. Then he shared her story with Trace and Danni.

Her father's death, Mike's death, Vincent

Barrington's corruption, the years of dogged determination she and Mike had invested, essential details of her personal life, the operation in Texas, her ugly truths—it was all exposed and so hard to hear.

But as she listened to the narration of her whole existence from Cole's point of view, she didn't cry. She didn't even feel vulnerable. She was riveted. The way he viewed her life was astonishing.

He saw her hopes and struggles as something beautiful and painful and strong and poignant and incredibly human. He didn't perceive her as a thief or a rapist or a horrible villain. She couldn't mistake the raw compassion in his voice. He ached for her. He felt her. He related to her on every level.

That was when she realized that the things she carried around weren't so different from what he carried around.

It was profoundly overwhelming and powerful.

As the night wore on, the others popped in and out of the kitchen, grabbing food and hanging out for a while. Tiago and Kate walked down to the dock. The rest of them eventually went to bed.

After midnight, they moved the conversation to the living room, where Cole lit fires in the hearths that sat on either end of the wall of windows.

Trace lounged on the brown leather couch, looking for all the world like a Viking king in a stuffy suit. Tall and muscled, intimidating scowl, blonde hair, strong features, and a stern brow that, even in its resting state, gave him a brooding mien.

With Danni curled up against his side, he'd shed the jacket, the collar of his starched shirt gaping open. They couldn't have looked more relaxed.

Cole sprawled in the armchair across them as

they discussed Trace's casino business and Danni's leave of absence from belly dancing. She was four months pregnant, her baby bump barely noticeable beneath the dress. But she touched it often, wearing a whimsical smile.

Lydia watched Cole through the night, expecting him to steal looks in Danni's direction. But every time she looked at him, he was looking back, watching her as if she were the only person in the room.

Obsessive stalker.

Beautiful, complicated man.

His presence in her life felt surreal. The whole evening was pleasantly bizarre. For whatever reason, the four of them fell in lockstep with one another as if they'd been hanging out every weekend for decades, as if eight years hadn't separated Cole from his friends. Instead of stiff pleasantries, they spoke openly and honestly, hiding nothing.

"When Cole told me he was going to ask for your help..." She stood beside Cole's chair, running her fingers through his hair. "I was fully prepared to make jokes about the tension between the three of you. But there's no tension. No awkwardness. You're all just...old friends."

"We went through some tough months together," Danni said. "But it worked out."

"It worked out for *me*. From where I'm standing, you made a mistake choosing the uptight, scowly suit over the sexy, rebellious stalker. But hey, your loss is my win."

Trace scowled. Hard. Scary.

Danni burst into laughter.

Cole caught Lydia's waist and pulled her down on his lap. "Are you trying to cause trouble?"

"Just testing the waters."

"You're doing great," he murmured against her ear. Then he looked at Danni. "Your wedding gown is hanging in the armory. Take it with you when you leave. Donate it. Make diapers out of it. You won't hurt my feelings. It's yours."

Danni didn't seem surprised that Cole still had the gown. Lydia wasn't, either. For a battle-hardened vigilante, Cole was remarkably sentimental.

"There's a girl who volunteers at the homeless shelter with me." Danni smiled. "She just got engaged and doesn't have much money. I'll give it to her."

"Your engagement ring is in the River Thames."

Danni nodded, her expression thoughtful. "You've been alone for a long time, Cole." She shifted her gaze, locking onto Lydia. "I was afraid I wouldn't like you. He needs a strong woman, and I didn't think anyone would ever measure up. I'm not sure that *I* measured up. But here you are, exceeding my expectations. I know you're hurting. I *feel* it. I can't even fathom the sheer force you're exerting to keep the tears at bay." She stood, slowly approaching, and leaned down to touch Lydia's chin. "It's an honor to be here, to meet a woman who matches Cole in strength and backbone. It's an absolute privilege to help you avenge the deaths of your brother and father. You already have the beauty to catch the eye of this hacker guy, and by the end of this week, you'll have the moves. Your dancing will be so hot you'll have every man in the club coming for you." She winked at Cole and stepped back. "I hope you're prepared for that."

Cole made a growling sound in his throat.

All Lydia could do was mutter a raspy, "Thank you."

Danni exceeded her expectations, too. It was no wonder why it had taken Cole so long to let her go.

"I'm glad you asked us to come." Trace pushed off the couch and grasped Danni's hand. "We missed you, Cole."

"Same." Cole caressed his fingers along Lydia's shoulder as he asked Trace, "Are you headed to bed?"

"Yeah. The girls have a long week ahead of them." Trace rubbed his jaw. "I want to spar with you. It's been a while."

"Sure, I'm happy to kick your ass. Just like old times."

"The way I remember it, you can't even kick your own ass."

"I'll remind you how it is when you're screaming like a little bitch, and I have to ball gag you."

"The conversation has suddenly taken an uncomfortable turn," Lydia mumbled.

"See you in the morning." Trace chuckled.

It was the first smile she'd seen on his face. Didn't make him look any less rigid.

Shortly after Danni and Trace went to bed, Cole grabbed their bags and led her down the long corridor of bedrooms.

"I'll show you around the property tomorrow." He stopped at a doorway midway down the hall. "This is where you'll be spending most of the week."

He flipped on a light, illuminating the dance room. He'd told her about it in Dublin, saying he'd designed it for Danni but now had no practical use for it.

"We need a sparring room." He shut off the lights and tugged her onward. "After we destroy Vincent Barrington, I'm going to repurpose it."

"Makes sense."

He guided her into the last room and shut the door. Full-length windows covered two perpendicular walls. A massive king-sized bed took up one corner, and an ornately carved wood-burning hearth sat in the other. From the rich wood flooring to the opulent crown molding, he'd invested a lot of money in this place.

As they showered and got ready for bed, she realized how much she didn't feel like herself, her limbs heavy with fatigue and sadness. But every shared look and interaction with Cole felt easy and comfortable. Seamlessly in sync. They'd earned that. After the trials of the past year, they deserved harmony with each other.

"I have something to give you." He removed a small box from his bag and guided her into bed, following her in.

"What is it?"

"I've debated when to give this to you, thinking I should wait until after the mission. But here's the thing. You're so fucking strong you don't need kid-glove treatment. You're not fragile or broken. If you can't handle something, I'll know and tread with care. So I'm going to give this to you. Then I'm going to fuck you." His voice grew husky. "Because that's what you need. It's what we both need."

Her breaths shredded, and her nipples went taut beneath her thin t-shirt.

He noticed, his dark gaze zeroing in as he lifted his hand. Through the cotton, the blunt nail of his thumb dragged over the tight peak.

Heat fluttered her veins. "Let's just skip to the last part."

"No." He took his touch away, grabbed whatever

he'd set behind him, and placed it on her lap.

"What is this?" She lifted the small wrapped present.

"Mike was holding it when he died."

The room grew cold, and her heart thudded in her throat. "I don't want to open it."

"Then don't."

"I have to. I have to confront this head-on, or it will take over my life. If the grief wins, Vincent wins."

"You need to grieve, Lydia. It frees up the painful energy."

"I *am* grieving." She yanked at the red bow on the gift, her vision blurring. "I just don't have to drown in it. I'm channeling it into my revenge. *That's* how I'll free the pain."

She wouldn't fail. She couldn't.

"Mike was such a sentimental gift-giver." She ripped off the glittery paper on the small box. "This is going to break my heart."

"It's not going to break *you*."

With an aching chest, she opened the package and removed a lightweight ball of newspaper. Her hands trembled as she carefully tore away the wrapping and revealed the gift inside.

A hand-painted egg.

"Oh, Mike." Heaviness invaded her limbs as she soaked in the gorgeous, familiar brush strokes. "He made this."

"He painted it?"

"Yeah." Her eyes burned. "He was so artistic. He designed a lot of my tattoos, including the swallow on my chest."

She rolled the hollow, fragile egg in her palm, examining the detailed illustration of the same red swallow sitting on the limb of a cranberry tree.

Searing pain rose through her throat. Her gasping prompted him to inch closer and wrap his warm strength around her.

"The bird..." Her voice broke. "The bird represents my mother, and the cranberries... That's Shannon. Or maybe it's him and me, too. The three of us used to dance around the house, singing songs by *The Cranberries*. Our favorite was 'Ode To My Family.' Shannon loved the band, and though Mike would never admit it, he loved it, too. He always sang the loudest."

A tear trickled down her cheek, and more followed.

Cole positioned her with her back against his chest, holding her and wiping the wetness from her face.

"I really hope he didn't spend his last night on Earth emptying this damn egg and painting it." Her heart hurt unbearably. "He was supposed to get laid." She choked on a sob. "He wasn't supposed to die."

She let herself cry for a moment before swallowing it down and repackaging the gift. "He knew how much I wanted PaulVer to give me an Easter egg. After a year of trying and failing, I was so frustrated with myself."

"So he gave you an egg himself."

"Yeah." She set the package on the nightstand and twisted around, straddling his lap. "I'm okay. The pain feels really heavy, and everything around me has slowed way down, like I'm trying to move through thick mud. But you keep me centered, focused. Thank you."

"Don't thank me. I'm here for you."

"I keep picturing his body lying there in the

snow. He's just lying there alone, cold, abandoned. I don't have any religious or life-after-death beliefs, but I can't bear the thought of him shoved into a refrigerator drawer, anonymous, forgotten.

"His body was moved to a funeral home and will remain there until you decide—"

"How do you know?"

"Last night at the apartment, after you fell asleep, I called Romero. He took care of it."

"How?"

"Digital records. He hacked into the Coroner's Office and changed the orders for the body's final destination."

"Oh my God, Cole." She stared at him, overcome with indebtedness and adoration and…more. So much more.

Deep inside, beneath the sorrow, something was building, thickening, and growing unstoppable.

"Thank you." She framed his gorgeous face with her hands and kissed him. Her pain, devotion, desire—she poured it all into the warm union of lips and tongues.

He groaned, breaking the kiss, and they stared at each other. They stared as if they were both expecting some form of emotional breakdown from her. When none was forthcoming, he curved his hands around her hips and hauled her impossibly closer.

"I want you to be happy." He kissed her slowly. "And naked."

His tongue stroked. Her breaths shortened, and his fingers traveled everywhere. Caressing turned into grabbing. Soft nipping into passionate biting. Heartbeats accelerated, pounding harder, growing louder.

She met him lick for lick. His cock hardened, swelling against her leg as his hands roamed, worshiping, tearing at her shirt. She twisted to tug the garment over her head, exposed and bare.

He looked at her, panting. She looked back, wanting.

She needed his body pressed against her. His warmth. His protection. His talented fingers deep inside her. His beautiful dick. His possessiveness. The taste of his kiss. The heat of his mouth. She needed him.

"I'm addicted to you," she breathed.

"I don't want to be an addiction. I want to be the love of your life."

Then he was on her, his mouth attacking her breasts and his hand between her legs, shocking her with three assertive fingers delving into her wetness. There was no warning, no warm-up. The intrusion bowed her back and reverberated to the soles of her feet.

He bit her nipples and fucked her with his hand. She bit his lips and pulled his hair, trembling, moaning, burning for him alone.

"I love seeing how much you want me." He raised his soaked fingers in her periphery.

She kissed him harder, momentarily shutting him up.

With a firm grip on her waist, he pulled her tight against his erection, withdrawing only to yank her back again in a slow, teasing grind. She whimpered, needing him, wanting him to fuck her, her fingers gripping the striated lines of his muscled back, her breasts aching fiercely.

"I'm going to put you on your back with your knees against your shoulders, and you're going to take it." He rocked beneath her, hips circling, grinding her on his lap. "I'm going to be so deep inside you you'll feel me from your cunt to your throat."

She couldn't wait.

Rolling her to her back, he looked into her eyes and sank into her body, inch by inch, stroking, panting, working himself in. He groaned loudly, and she nearly choked on her own rapture.

With her body folded in half at the waist and her knees on her shoulders, he fucked into her ruthlessly, tirelessly, his eyes fevered and breaths heavy. The pressure on her muscles created a tightness in her pelvis, increasing the sensations with each delicious thrust he delivered.

His tendons and sinews contracted and stretched as he dug into her, deeper, harder, lunging, spearing, putting his magnificent body to work. The position gave her hands access to his ass, and God help her, she couldn't stop groping him, her palms molding to the rock-hard shape, basking in the movement of those round sculpted muscles.

He was a high-performing, wild animal with endless endurance. She dissolved beneath his potency, her legs losing strength in the restraints of his hands.

Once he thoroughly pounded the deepest parts of her, he eased up and gave her a break from the stretch. Adjusting her here and there, he straddled one of her legs and hooked the other over his shoulder, scissoring her in a side-straddle.

Her arms lay boneless above her head, putting the upthrust of her chest into his ravenous reach. His hands kneaded her breasts, his fingers punishing the nipples, and his intense gaze never leaving hers as he gave her the most sublime pleasure with the thick, long strokes of his dick.

He had full control of her body in this position, and he took it, impaling her in fluid, possessing thrusts. Her breaths came faster, his caresses rough and greedy. His hips snapped in a fury.

He rode her with a single-minded focus, parting that jaw, staring into her eyes, and chasing her urgent sounds with growly, winded grunts. Then he drove her into a back-arching, body-shaking, screaming orgasm so powerful that she damn near blacked out.

As she fell apart beneath him, he threw his head back and braced himself on outstretched arms, stiffening, shuddering in the throes of his release.

His roaring, volcanic pleasure was such a glorious sight to witness. She could spend the rest of her life doing nothing else but watching him come.

His dark bedroom eyes looked dazed, lust-drunk, and terrifyingly, thrillingly in love as he stared at her and bucked, jerked, and thrust his way through ejaculation. His lips parted. His neck corded, and his gaze clung. He seemed helpless to hold the smallest part of himself back as he spent himself in an endless climax within her.

She was melting. Slipping. Falling like a feather on the wind. As long as she was in his arms, she never wanted to touch the ground.

TWENTY-NINE

"Touch the ground." Danni rudely snapped her fingers, setting Lydia's teeth on edge. "When you shimmy down, go *all* the way down. Fingertips to the floor. None of this halfway bullshit. And loosen those hips! Start again from the top."

After five days of dance instruction, Lydia wanted to wring the woman's neck. The sweet little blonde from the first night had vanished the moment she donned a leotard. Danni Savoy was a goddamn Dance Nazi.

Every time Lydia tripped, forgot a step, or copped an attitude, she was met with Danni's withering glare. If her spine bent incorrectly, it earned her a stinging pinch from Danni's hand. If she did a butt-wiggle instead of a figure-eight-sway, she got a scolding swat on the ass.

Her feet ached in the heels. Her muscles protested every brutal, repetitive movement, and her heart fought it all, because more than anything, it just wanted to heal.

The days and nights swirled into a fugue of sweating and swaying and tapping and sliding. She was naturally uncoordinated, stiff through the hips, and not always receptive to Danni's criticism.

But she was making progress. Huge progress.

Watching herself in the mirror, she focused on transforming her feelings into movements. Music had the power to connect the soul with the senses, and for the past five days, Danni had been teaching her how to achieve that.

"Let your body loose. Like this." Danni gripped her hips from behind, moving her, demonstrating for the thousandth time how to catch the rhythm. "A stiff frame can't move. Surrender your joints, your muscles, your breaths. Allow the music to control your movements all the way to the floor. See?"

Despite Danni's pregnancy, she had no trouble sweating it out on the dance floor for twelve hours every day. Lydia studied Danni's reflection in the mirror, mimicking the descending, rippling silhouette of Danni's cute body as they undulated together, down, down, down to the ground and back up.

Techno music thumped from the speakers. Just one of the many dance genres she'd learned how to groove to. Different nightclubs offered different kinds of music, and she needed to adapt to each style as the music changed.

And so it went. Hour after hour, day after day, Lydia practiced no less than fifty dance moves and transition techniques.

At her request, Cole stayed away during the lessons. He was too distracting, his gaze too invasive and penetrating. She couldn't work with him stalking the perimeter of the room, consuming her senses, demanding her attention.

But they always reconnected at night amid tangled sheets. With each possessive thrust, it was no longer enough just to hear him roaring her name as they finished together.

She wanted more.

Lovers had come and gone throughout her life. She remembered none of them, never pursued anything more than a five-second fling.

Cole wasn't a lover. He was an unprecedented, decadent experience. His perseverance, dedication, and loyalty was unlike any man she'd ever been with. And let's be honest. There was no one as insanely, unreasonably gorgeous as Cole Hartman.

Whether they were sharing conversation, food, or body fluids, she didn't want it to end. She often caught herself thinking about her life after this mission, and she always circled back to one undeniable truth. She wanted a future with Cole.

Mike would've wanted that for her. On Christmas Eve, he let Cole into their home, into their life, because he *knew*.

Cole belonged to her. He was the one. If she didn't believe Cole's words, she only had to look into his unyielding brown eyes. She would have to cut off his legs if she ever tried to run from him. Until his last breath, he would chase her to the ends of the earth.

He wouldn't need to, for he already caught her, heart and soul.

"Wow. Look at you." Danni danced around her, smiling and snapping her fingers to the music. "You got your groove, girl. Damn, you're on fire!"

She observed her form in the mirror, letting the repetitive electronic beat lift and drop her hips as she slid through the box step.

With each booty shake, she felt less restrained. More confident. With the subtle kicks of her pelvis, her movements glided like oil, more relaxed, freer, sexier. If her feet still ached in the heels, she didn't notice. She only felt the tune, the percussion, and the *music.*

She was so lost in the zone she didn't notice Danni had drifted away until the song ended.

"You're almost ready." Danni leaned a shoulder against the wall of windows, her attention fixed on something outside.

"What's left? I swear I've learned every dance move in existence."

"You've mastered all the techniques and steps you'll need." Danni touched her throat, her cheeks flushing as her gaze remained glued on the window. "What's left is the fun part. I'll teach you how to flirt and…fuck."

"Sorry?" She wiped the perspiration from her forehead and treaded toward the window. "Are you *blushing?* What are you looking at out…? Oh, shit."

Outside, dormant grass stretched from the rear terrace to the surrounding tree line. At the center of the lawn, Cole and Trace rolled across the ground, grappling, sparring, shirtless and sweaty. So goddamn sexy.

Her mouth watered. Her skin caught fire. Her stupid knees went weak.

"Oh, shit," she repeated, entranced by the display of muscle and ferocious power.

They weren't alone. Cole's friends stood on the sidelines, bent forward, shouting, laughing, and cheering on the sparring match. Tiago, Matias, and Tate were shirtless, their workout pants clinging to their muscled physiques.

Lucia and Camila wore exercise clothes, too, with their black hair pulled into ponytails. The sisters looked so similar it was hard to tell them apart.

Kate sat off to the side with a textbook on her lap, cramming for an upcoming exam.

"Trace missed his sparring partner." Danni touched the glass, her expression somber. "I ruined a beautiful friendship."

"*You* didn't ruin anything. Their relationship took a beating and evolved through the hardship. They're still friends. I mean, they still call each other when they're in trouble."

"You're right." Danni nodded. Then she grinned, her eyes glowing with sudden mischief. "Let's take a break."

They shared a smile and slipped off their heels. Then they raced out of the dance room, through the house, grabbing coats and sneakers before heading outside into the chill of January.

The overcast sky draped the yard in a wintry gray. The shirtless guys seemed unaffected by the cold, their grunts and shouts bursting in clouds of steam. Those who stood on the sideline looked just as tousled and sweaty as Cole and Trace. They must've been taking turns sparring.

As she and Danni joined the group, the atmosphere buzzed with energy. Over the past five days, she'd spent more time with Danni than anyone else. But during meals and evening lulls, she got to know the entire group.

Hearing their histories firsthand had given her a whole new respect for this vigilante family. Their experiences in Van Quiso's attic hadn't destroyed them.

It made them stronger, closer, and those unbreakable bonds had formed a team of survivors willing to take the law into their own hands to decimate the most depraved criminals in the world.

They were the personification of justice.

She never had a plan beyond Vincent Barrington's arrest and incarceration. Never let herself imagine what she would do next.

Until now.

The sounds of seething breaths charged the air. A few feet away, Cole held the dominant position over Trace, where they lay on the grass, chest to chest, wrestling for a chokehold.

With Cole on top, he had the advantage, throwing his body weight behind the forearm that pressed against Trace's throat.

Then he looked up, his molten brown eyes homing in on her, softening, heating, then widening as a fist skidded across his jaw and slammed his head backward.

Oops. She winced.

Trace laughed in triumph. Cole scrambled back, flinging a sloppy kick to ward off Trace. They staggered to their feet and circled each other, catching their breaths. Then, with their glares narrowed in determination, they dove back together in a blur of limbs.

"I've never seen that guy get distracted." Tate stood beside her, his crystal blue eyes twinkling with amusement. "It's nice to see him with a distraction. Especially one that puts a goofy smile on his face."

"I hope he doesn't get distracted next week. Did you guys iron out the itinerary?"

"Yep. We narrowed down your list of nightclubs,

using Romero's facial recognition software to identify patterns. There are a handful of clubs between Italy and Romania that are frequented by the same group of men. According to Romero, this group was present on the nights that you spotted Easter eggs."

"Is PaulVer one of these people?"

"We don't think so. We've investigated all of them. They're nobodies. Wealthy, bored nobodies who like to party. No I/T training or apparent computer skills. They're probably just his friends, people who know his schedule and show up to party with him. I doubt they even know he's a hacker. Most of these hackers are in the closet, hiding behind their keyboards, committing federal crimes, and telling no one."

"So these friends…if you know their identities, Romero should be able to track where they are, right? We'll know which city and nightclub they're at?"

"Exactly. Assuming PaulVer goes where they go, it'll be like shooting fish in a barrel. We'll show up where they are. All you have to do is lure PaulVer out of the shadows. Once he puts an egg in your hand, we'll have him."

"Yeah, and while I'm doing that, I'll be luring Vincent's men, too."

"That's why we're here. Cole called us in to protect you while you're dancing." Tate bumped his shoulder against hers, winking. "We're really good at killing bad guys."

"I know, and I'm grateful." She turned toward him. "I mean it, Tate. I don't know how I'm going to repay you."

"We would do this job even if you hadn't lost your family. Vincent Barrington *cannot* become President. Period. And when we take him down, there will be more evil fucks to pursue. This is what we do, and you're part of it now." He smiled, flashing his teeth. "Welcome to the family."

Blood hummed in her veins, circulating a depth of joy that she didn't think she'd feel again without Mike.

A pained grunt drew her attention back to the sparring match. Trace doubled over, and Cole went in for the attack. With both hands, he grasped Trace's head and brought a kneecap to Trace's nose, followed by a kick to the solar plexus. Trace stumbled backward, but there was no blood. No apparent bruising. They were sparring, holding back their punches, not trying to kill each other.

Trace regained his footing, but it was too late. Cole took him to the ground and twisted him into an arm lock, forcing Trace to tap out.

In a blink, Cole was on his feet again, prowling toward her with an impish glint in his eyes. When he reached her, she stepped back, evading the aggressive grab of his hand.

"You want me? Come and get me." She retreated faster, dodging another swipe. "Is that all you got?"

He growled, throwing himself at her. She feigned right, compelling him to move with her, then changed direction at the last minute and broke free.

She took off at a sprint, delighting in the sound of his chasing footsteps.

River-rock streams and mulched footpaths trailed off into the woods. Other paths led to the terrace and exterior doors of the house. She followed the cobblestone sidewalk that curved around the wing of the estate.

The chilly breeze nipped at her cheeks, but the

coat kept her warm. She glanced back, and her pulse ignited. Holy shit, he was right there in arm's reach, shirtless, his expression so intensely hungry her heart tripped…right along with her feet.

She staggered, and his arm swung out, grabbing for her hair. With a yelp, she bolted forward, the strands slipping from his fingers. She picked up her pace, leaping over rocks, laughing, and trembling with desire.

Halfway around the side of the estate, he caught her by the neck and hauled her back, crushing her mouth against his. The kiss split open in a sweep of tongues and searing heat. Her back hit the side of the house, and he moved in, syncing their hips and grinding with the rhythm of their rushing breaths.

He tore her coat open, popping the buttons. Then he shoved her tank top and bra to her neck and pressed his bare chest against hers, burning her skin.

"Cole." She gripped his thick arms, trying to keep up with the impetuous passion of his kiss.

His aggressive lips worked her into a fever, his tongue lashing and twining with hers. God, she loved his sinful mouth, but it was his dimpled smile that stole her heart. He leaned back, giving her a glorious, up-close view of those delicious divots. Then he dove back in, his lips hot on her neck, and his hands running everywhere.

With his body bearing down against hers, they rubbed together, rocking, sliding, and panting. His sculpted physique bunched and flexed against her as the sound of his fervent breaths spun her up and turned her inside out. Every gasp and sizzling exhale confessed how badly he wanted her.

Holy fuck, he wanted her. He was so hard, so

damn long and swollen beneath the thin cotton of his workout pants. He was going to take her right here, outside in the cold, where any of his friends could walk by. He didn't give a fuck, and neither did she.

He yanked her leggings to her ankles and pulled one side completely off, along with her shoe. It freed up her legs, which he lifted and spread, pinning her against the siding with one knee shoved to her shoulder. He held it there as he wrestled down his joggers and freed his cock.

His eyes met hers for the span of a moment, and in that precious space between them, she felt the promise of a future, a beautiful destiny, their hearts fused, their bodies entangled, and their souls forged as one.

As he pushed inside her, he watched her like a man in love, his eyes drunk on happiness, and his dimpled mouth parted in wonder.

Utterly possessed, she captured that mouth and sank into the flames.

He fucked her against the house. Then he fixed her clothes, carried her inside, and made love to her in his bed. Neither of them said the words, but she felt it in every touch, every kiss, every whispered breath.

"Only two days left." She lay in his arms after, stroking the stubble on his chiseled jaw.

"I want to dance with you."

That wouldn't be possible at the nightclubs in Europe. She would have to dance alone to draw in the hacker. The team would take up posts around the perimeter, watching for threats and keeping her safe.

"I have a confession." She made a face. "I hate dancing."

"Okay."

"Okay? I don't think you understand. I'm doing this for my dad. For Mike. When it's over, I'll be happy to never step onto a dance floor again."

"What about slow dancing?"

"With you?" Her chest fluttered. "Yeah, I'd be down for that."

"Good." He brushed their lips together. "I still want a fast, hip-grinding dance with you. Just one."

"Okay." She would happily give him anything he wanted.

As it turned out, he got his wish on their last night in Missouri.

After dinner, Danni asked everyone to gather in the dance room. The entire gang stood around—Cole, Trace, the six Freedom Fighters—watching Danni circle Lydia at the center.

"You mastered the technical part of club dancing." Danni paused behind her, sliding soft, sensual fingers down her inked arms. "There's another aspect of this that isn't dancing at all. It's basically flirting. Grinding provocatively. Fucking with your clothes on."

Across the room, Cole stiffened, his eyes narrowing.

"Calm down." Danni pointed a finger at him and returned to Lydia. "You can do this with the women on the dance floor. Take everything I taught you and make it sexual. Touch them in ways you both like. It's about turning each other on. But there *will* be men, and they're going to flock to you with their tongues hanging out." Danni shifted back to Cole. "Most of the people who frequent nightclubs aren't there to dance. They're there to participate in a clothes-on, fluid-free orgy. Loud music. Simple, mindless beats. Lots of sweaty people who can't hear one another talk. It's a non-verbal, dry-humping fuckfest without the penetration. If you want to succeed in this mission, you will swallow your caveman ego and deal with it."

Lydia burst into laughter. She couldn't help it. Cole looked so miserable.

His nostrils flared. His face turned red, and his jaw clenched to the point of breaking. But after a few seconds, he gave a nod.

"We're going to practice." Danni dimmed the lights and moved to the stereo as she addressed the room. "Doesn't matter if you can dance or not. You're here for the orgy. Lydia needs to test her skills with random bodies rubbing up against her. Let's see some dirty dancing."

Danni started the music—a rapid iteration of electronic beats. It took several seconds for Lydia to loosen up enough to move. When she did, she kept her movements subtle and tight, remaining right where she was, waiting to see what the others would do.

Trace moved first, heading straight to his wife and wrapping his body around her back. They rolled as one, dipping and sliding like they'd danced together a million times. No doubt they had.

Cole stayed at the edge of the room, his hands at his sides, swaying to the music with his eyes locked on Lydia, stoking a fire in her belly.

Someone came up behind her. Small hands rested on her hips. She turned, finding Kate's pretty face smiling back, her body rocking with confidence.

Within seconds, she was surrounded. Tiago, Matias, and Tate favored the two-step side-to-side motion. Simple. Relaxed. Not a hint of awkwardness or discomfort. The women were bolder in their movements. None of them were dancers, but their assertiveness and self-possession more than made up for any lack of technical skill.

This group didn't have a shy bone between them, and sweet Lord, they were sexual.

Through the next few songs, each of them danced with her in turn, rolling their bodies with smooth, deliberate, erotic suggestion, hips to hips, pressing in tight, and grinding with the motion of sex.

Cole didn't lose his shit. He stood at a distance, never looking away. Perhaps he was testing himself, watching her writhe with his friends. Or maybe he was teasing her, making her wait until she was so sexed-up she would explode if he touched her.

As the group slowly paired off to dance with their mates, he approached. She trembled.

He circled her, placing a hand on her waist as he moved out of sight, keeping his touch on her at all times. When he came back around, he edged closer, aligning their bodies chest to chest and rolling his hip. One hand cupped her jaw. The other hung loosely at his side and slightly behind him, making it impossible *not* to grope his ripped physique.

She ran her palms down his torso, tracing the indentations and ridges of muscle through the shirt, and teasing the button of his fly.

"You're beautiful," he mouthed.

"So are you." She smiled, feeling warm and gooey and so undeserving.

She wasn't worthy of this incredible man, but she'd laid her claim and wasn't letting go.

Grabbing his face with both hands, she rose on her toes and captured his lips. He kissed her back and pulled her closer, controlling the movement of her muscles, setting the pace, and letting her feel him.

His body was made for this, hips thrusting, mouth moving against hers, and hands palming her ass. He danced like he fucked, commanding, leading, and she followed without question. She loved his touch on her skin. She adored his breath on her neck. She craved the hard heat of him, and he gave her what she craved, total permission to feel.

To feel with her hands.

To feel with her heart.

To bask in the beauty of their bond.

They danced through several songs, kissing and grinding until her legs burned and her mouth went numb. Slowly, the room emptied, each couple quietly drifting into the hall.

Danni and Trace swayed in their own world, their bodies entwined and mouths locked in passion. Then Trace lifted her, cradling her in his arms, and carried her out of the room.

Cole moved behind Lydia, rocking and molding his hands to her curves and dips. His lips caressed her neck seductively, lovingly, luring her into his hungry orbit.

"I want to strip you down and lick your body from top to bottom," he said at her ear.

Then he led her to the bedroom and did exactly that.

The next morning, they said goodbye to Danni and Trace. It wasn't weird or strained, and it didn't feel final. The couple might not be part of Cole's vigilante world, but she knew she would see them again and often. She would make sure of it.

Her chest filled with nervous excitement as the rest of them packed up and headed to the private airport where Matias' plane waited. As she boarded the plane and flew toward her destination with her hand tucked tightly in Cole's, she recognized that she wouldn't be here without him.

Without him, she would still be in Ireland, financially broke and emotionally destitute. Or dead.

When she started this mission twelve years ago, she had one purpose.

Revenge.

When Cole started this mission fourteen months ago, he had a different purpose.

Rescue.

He'd claimed her in Texas, and at that moment, he'd become her champion. He'd fought against it. She'd fought it, too. But in the end, he laid down life and limb to do what heroes did.

He rescued his girl.

THIRTY

Braşov, Romania
Two weeks later

The nightclub was rainbow lights and primal beats, throbbing like a heartbeat over a loudspeaker. Lydia didn't need the music to rev her blood. She was hyped up on adrenaline and nerves.

Tiago led her through thick swirls of dry-ice smoke and sweaty hordes of writhing bodies. This was their sixth nightclub in two weeks, and she was beginning to think their intel was wrong.

There had been no Easter egg sightings. It had nothing to do with whether she could dance. PaulVer simply wasn't at the venues they visited.

Inauguration Day was in five days.

Five days until Vincent Barrington became the President of the United States, the most powerful man in the world, and utterly untouchable.

She tightened her grip on Tiago's arm as he muscled his way through the throng. The entire team wore disguises—wigs, hats, fake tattoos, and flashy club attire. Her ink lay completely hidden beneath layers of makeup, her wig a vibrant shade of blue.

For the tenth time, she yanked down the hem of her silver body-con dress, but within two steps, it worked its way back up her thighs. The glittery material barely covered her ass and breasts. Cole's expression had darkened when he saw it, but he didn't dare say a word.

The dress did what it was designed to do. It drew attention.

She felt the gaze of every man she passed, despite the danger wafting off her intimidating escort. Tiago wore all black, save for the long, brown fur coat and matching fedora on his head. With his shirt unbuttoned to his belt and his six-pack on display beneath the fur coat, he looked like a goddamn pimp.

She didn't glance around the club for Cole. He would be close. Always within eyeshot. Since they were both targets for Vincent's men, it was safer if they weren't spotted together, even with the disguises.

When Tiago dropped her off at the dance floor, Camila and Lucia were already there, dancing together. She didn't make eye contact as she sashayed past them.

The acoustics in the rafters thundered with the music and the pound of countless feet. Beams of lights crisscrossed over the crowd in an array of blues, acid greens, hot pinks, and gold. The booming rhythm fused with the bouncing bodies, and she joined them, rolling her hips, tossing her head, and miming sex with every person—man or woman—who approached her.

There was no talking, no need to fake an accent. This was all about tactical flirting, eye-fucking, heavy petting, groping, panting, and humping with clothes on.

In the carnal beat of the music, in the heart of the nightclub, a hundred people bumped and writhed in a public gang bang.

While everyone danced to that lustful vibe, she danced for Cole. She knew he watched her. He saw every woman who touched her, every man who humped her, every flirty, grabby dancer who tried to reach under her dress. She kept the unwanted molesting at bay, refusing to give anyone what belonged to Cole.

The dancing lasted hours. Perspiration glistened on her brow. Her breaths labored, and her muscles burned with exhaustion. As the night wore down and the crowd began to thin, she knew it had been another wasted effort.

Disappointment crashed through her, but she kept moving, dipping her hips with someone at her back, dipping with her. Masculine hands molded to her hips. A warm mouth nuzzled her neck. Then she felt it—the sudden chill as he stepped back, the brush of fingers against her wrist, and the round egg-shaped object touching her palm.

Her heart rate exploded, her elation bursting in shimmery waves. She couldn't contain it, her cheeks rising with the stretch of her laughing smile as she thrust her free hand in the air and extended her index and pinkie fingers in the sign of the devil horns.

To anyone watching, she was just waving her arm to the music. But to the team, her hand sign just alerted them that the man at her back was the target.

She spun around, but the man had already turned away, his head down and shoulders hunched around his ears. She glimpsed dark hair and an average-build as he quickly slipped through the jumping crowd.

Cole had demanded she not engage or chase the target for fear he would panic and run off. Her job was to lure him in and mark him. The team would do the rest.

Without any pockets, she reluctantly dropped the egg and glanced around the dance floor, noting the absence of Camila and Lucia. They were already on the move, trailing the hacker. As she turned toward the exit, she came face to face with Cole.

Electricity sparkled across her skin, heating her up. She wanted to scream, *We have him!* But she pressed her lips together and kept herself in check.

Within the shadows of his baseball cap, his beautiful features showed no reaction, no shared excitement. This was his *work face,* the one he wore in fight mode, when he was hyper-focused, detached from emotion, his mindset cold and competitive. She'd seen this expression often during his captivity in Texas.

He pulled her closer and rocked his hips with purpose as he led her off the dance floor. Then he gave her a discreet nudge toward the exit. She walked ahead of him, knowing the rest of the team was focused on the target. They would stay with the hacker until he left the building. Then they would engage.

Since her role was finished, Cole's only priority was getting her out of the venue and somewhere safe. Once they had PaulVer in their possession, Cole would take her to him so she could help plead their case.

Outside, she quickly crossed the busy street, keeping close to the shadows of buildings, parked cars, anything that provided cover. After being hunted for over a year, stealth and concealment had become second nature to her.

Any stranger walking along the sidewalks could

be a hitman.

At the end of the block, she hid in a recess of the building and glanced back. Cole was nowhere in sight, but he was there, somewhere. He would never let her out of his sight.

Their rented vehicles waited just around the corner. She headed there, rounding the bend, and stopped.

A man stood in the empty side street between the medievalesque buildings made of stone and arched windows. He faced the opposite direction, but she recognized his build, his dark jacket, and short black hair.

Twenty feet before him, Camila strutted forward, wearing red leather pants and stiletto heels. The drape of her off-the-shoulder shirt was deliberately baggy, hiding the weapons beneath it.

"PaulVer," she purred, laying on the seductive ruse. "You speak English?"

He stiffened, his shoulders curling forward and hands flexing at his sides. A small satchel hung against his hip with the strap crossing his upper body.

"I don't know that name." His English was succinct, despite the heavy inflection of a Romanian accent.

Lydia's muscles trembled as she flattened herself against the corner of the building, remaining hidden.

Matias and Lucia leaned against their rented SUV, which was parked at a distance behind Camila, well in view of PaulVer. Kate would be inside the vehicle. Tate and Tiago stood in the shadows at the edges of the side street, mere feet from PaulVer's position. Their unmoving forms would be difficult to detect by an unsuspecting eye.

Behind her, people strolled along the main road, coming and going between the bars and nightclubs.

After a moment of searching, she spotted Cole crouched beside the building across the street. He held a gun at his side, his gaze flicking between her and PaulVer.

"I have a proposition for you, handsome." Camila slowly placed one heeled shoe before the other, sashaying her hips as she approached.

"You have the wrong person." He pivoted, revealing a shockingly youthful face before he ducked his head and strode in Lydia's direction, not seeing her.

Jesus, the guy couldn't have been older than eighteen.

As he hurried away from Camila, nervous tension tightened in Lydia's gut. Fourteen months of searching and hoping, and her answer was walking straight toward her. She knew the team wouldn't let him get away, but it took everything inside her not to jump out and grab him. She would do it in a heartbeat if she weren't being hunted by Vincent's goons.

Tate swept out onto the street, walking casually behind PaulVer. Then Tiago emerged, joining the slow, heart-pounding chase.

PaulVer marked them and tucked his hands in the pockets of his skinny jeans, picking up his pace, gaze on his sneakers, and reeking of fear as he inadvertently strode directly into Lydia's path.

He must've decided to head back to the nightclub. In about three seconds, he would turn the corner and see her. She would have to engage him, try to push him back onto the side street and out of view without making a scene.

Something stirred behind her, lifting the hairs on

her nape. She didn't have time to consider who or what before someone crashed into her back. A split-second later, gunshots rang out.

The impact of two-hundred pounds slamming into her knocked the wind from her lungs and sent her pummeling toward the ground.

More gunfire erupted, booming through the side street.

The next few seconds slowed to a crawl.

As she hit the ground beneath the weight of her attacker, PaulVer froze. His shoulder kicked back as if punched by an invisible fist. He staggered. His eyes bulged, locked on her. He reached for his chest, then his arm, and pulled his hand away, smeared in blood.

He was shot.

Oh, God, he was shot.

No, no, no!

A guttural sound barreled from her throat, and her stomach rolled in violent waves. Trapped in the cage of unbending steel arms, she could only watch in horror as PaulVer crumpled to the ground a few feet away. *Lifeless.*

She twisted her neck, her lungs screaming for oxygen, and found Cole stretched out atop her like a shield of flesh-and-bone armor. He'd saved her life *again*, but with that realization spiked a blood-chilling fear for his life. While she lay safely beneath him, his entire body was exposed to the bullets whizzing past her head.

All around her, the team returned gunfire. The deadly exchange of lead lasted a long, agonizing minute. Then the street fell quiet.

"All clear," Matias shouted.

"Cole?" She whimpered, panicking. "Cole, are

you-?"

"Not hit." He dropped a kiss on her temple and rolled off her back.

Three dead bodies scattered the sidewalk behind her. Vincent's men.

She stumbled to her feet, frantically scanning the side street before her. The team had taken cover during the gunfight. Were any of them hit?

The wrath of a million bees swarmed her bloodstream as Cole shouted, "Report in!"

One by one, each person on the team responded with "Not hit."

As she exhaled some of her tension, the blare of sirens broke out in the distance.

"Move out!" Cole crouched beside PaulVer's body and tossed the kid over his shoulder.

She raced ahead, leading him to the SUV with Tiago and Kate.

"Is he alive?" Kate asked from the backseat.

"He's breathing." Cole fell into the seat beside Kate and dumped the kid between them.

Lydia jumped in the front passenger seat next to Tiago, and before she got the door closed, Tiago hit the gas, shooting forward.

The other four teammates sped down the street in the second SUV. Tiago followed closely behind, skidding around turns and running through stop signs.

"Is he alive?" Blood thrashed in her ears as she twisted to face the backseat.

"Yes." Kate bent over the kid's body, eyes narrowed on his shoulder while Cole held a small flashlight on the wound. "It's a graze. Not deep enough to need stitches." She laughed, coughed against the back of her hand, and laughed again. "He passed out from a scratch."

Cole's face broke out in a grin, and within seconds, everyone in the vehicle was laughing, including Tiago as he tore through the streets, outrunning the Romanian Police.

"Search his pockets," Lydia said. "See if there's an ID."

Cole rummaged through PaulVer's clothing in the dark. "No, ID. But this was in his satchel." Cole held up a slim laptop.

His eyes, chocolaty and warm, latched onto hers. They stared at each other, letting the moment sink in.

"You did it," he whispered, setting aside the laptop.

"We did it."

Now they just needed PaulVer to do the rest.

Cole inched forward and gripped her neck, bringing their mouths together. He kissed her softly, adoringly, humming his happiness. She returned the kiss, sharing in his joy, her soul swelling and reaching for his.

"It's almost over." He smiled against her mouth.

"Doesn't feel real."

The trailing sound of sirens faded. Then disappeared completely. They'd lost the police, but Tiago didn't slow. He flew down the sleepy Romanian streets, keeping pace with their friends in the other SUV.

"He's waking," Kate whispered, taping up the bandage.

Cole leaned back, letting Lydia bend toward the backseat.

"Hey, there," she said softly. "Remember me?"

A heavy rasp pushed past PaulVer's teeth, his

thick black eyebrows twitching as he dragged open his eyes.

His dark brown gaze struggled to focus, his eyelashes blinking rapidly, until finally, he centered his sight on her.

"You're my angel," he said dazedly. "My beautiful, perfect angel. Do you like the egg?"

"I love it. Thank you for giving it to me. I've been trying to earn one of your gifts for over a year."

"You…" He was sprawled in the backseat between Cole and Kate, seemingly unaware of where he was. He hadn't taken his eyes off Lydia. "You knew about the Easter eggs?"

"I know it's your calling card, and each night you go out, you give one to your favorite dancer. It's very mysterious. You like that, don't you? You like leaving a trail of mysterious eggs that no one will ever figure out."

His boyish smile appeared out of place with the sexual heat simmering in his foggy gaze. The kid was certainly unconventional and strange. But eccentricity was often associated with intellectual giftedness. As the most notorious hacker in the world, he was undoubtedly a genius.

"How did you find…?" His face paled, eyes widening as he shot up and gripped his bandaged arm. "Oh my God! I got shot!"

"The bullet grazed you. You're fine."

He didn't seem to hear her as he wildly looked around the car, taking in the other passengers.

"Who are you?" He pulled his feet up onto the seat, gasping and scrambling to get away with nowhere to go.

Cole gently held him in place as she reached out a

hand, touching the kid's knee, trying to soothe him.

"We didn't shoot you, PaulVer. We're a vigilante team." She met his terrified gaze. "The shooters were assassins hired by Vincent Barrington. The President-elect is trying to kill me and anyone involved in exposing his crimes."

He stilled, his expression awash with disbelief. Then his breathing sped up, his voice rising in volume and urgency. "Let me out. Stop the car. Let me out of the fucking car!"

Everyone in the civilized world knew who Vincent Barrington was. She couldn't expect him to believe her fantastical claim, and at this point, there was no calming him down.

Matias drove the other SUV, leading them to the rendezvous point. In the meantime, she just needed to tell PaulVer her story and hope he wasn't too scared out of his mind to listen.

"Twelve years ago, Vincent Barrington killed my father in a Russian hotel room. My father was NSA, and the murder was recorded. That recording is in the hands of the Romanian mafia. I need you to get that video file."

He shook his head rapidly, but the pace of his breaths lost momentum. He was listening, despite his fear. He was listening because he was too smart not to pay attention.

She started over from the beginning, filling in details about her dad, her ruse as a swallow in Vincent's employment, Mike's death, her fourteen-month hunt for his Easter eggs, and his ability to bring justice for all of it.

"You're vigilantes." He swallowed, eying Cole with suspicion. "Like...you kill people?"

"We killed the fuckers who shot you." Tiago jerked the wheel, deliberately causing PaulVer to tumble into Cole.

She exchanged a look with Cole, attempting to borrow some of his composed patience.

"We're part of a vigilante team that eliminates evil people." She reached up and pulled off her blue wig, letting him see her natural red hair, her identity. "Human sex traffickers, pedophiles, and greedy, corrupt politicians." She sighed. "Look, I'm only asking if you can hack into the Romanian mafia's network and steal the recording, watch the video, and decide for yourself."

"You won't kill me?"

"Do you traffic women and sell children to predators?"

"No!" He made a horrified face.

"Do you murder innocent people?"

"No. I've never killed anyone. I steal from monopolized corporations and give the money to people who need it." He rolled his lips. "And I like pretty dancers. But I don't…I would never hurt a woman. I just like to give them my painted eggs."

Her chest swelled with hope, but she felt the tension in the car. Everyone was on edge, holding their breaths. There was so much at stake, hinging on an eccentric, fearful teenage boy.

He lowered his feet to the floorboard and leaned toward her, bracing his elbows on his knees.

"I found a back door last year." He raised his dark eyes to her, his accent thickening. "I'm already inside the mafia's network."

Her pulse took off, dancing through her veins. She was so strung out, so anxious and overjoyed she thought she might puke.

"Help us." She lifted a trembling hand to his hairless jaw and let him see the tears welling in her eyes. "Please."

"What will you do with the video?"

"Twelve years ago, it was turned into the NSA. I don't know who saw the footage, but they did nothing. They covered it up and let it fall into the hands of the mafia. I'm reluctant to trust anyone in the government, especially now that Vincent Barrington is five days from becoming our President." She drew a breath. "I was hoping you could disperse it, broadcast it all over the Internet, make it impossible to cover up. Americans need to know who they voted into office."

He leaned back and stared out the window, watching buildings and street signs blur by. "Turn left here and head north. There's a Starbucks up the road. They have a strong WIFI signal."

As Tiago veered left and followed PaulVer's directions, Cole called Matias and told him where to go.

"Thank you." Her ribs expanded with the unstoppable release of years of pent-up emotion.

A tear escaped, running down her cheek, and Cole moved in, gripping the back of her head and kissing away the salty river.

"I'm sorry." She laughed uncomfortably. "It's a long time coming, and I'm emotional."

"A moment I don't want to miss." He touched his forehead to hers.

Tiago pulled into the vacant parking lot of Starbucks and parked behind the building. Matias pulled in beside him.

There, PaulVer sat in the SUV with his laptop and dug through the mafia's network files. She'd given him her father's name and every keyword she could conjure, which he loaded into his software program to scan the mafia's metadata.

Then they waited on pins and needles.

Most of them stood outside the vehicles behind the building. Out of view of the street, they watched and listened for the Romanian police.

The sirens never came.

Three hours later, PaulVer stepped out of the SUV and handed her the laptop. "I think this is it."

She stared down at the paused video, her stomach twisting in knots. "Did you watch it?"

"Yes." He frowned, his face appearing older somehow. "It's bloody. Definitely Vincent Barrington committing murder."

"You don't have to watch it." Cole cupped her jaw, pulling her gaze to his. "Once you see it, you'll carry the image with you for the rest of your life."

"My imagination can't be much better." She pressed play and clutched Cole's strong hand.

On the screen, her dad walked through a hotel room and opened the door. Vincent stepped in as her dad shook his head, speaking rapidly.

"There's no sound?" Her voice shook.

"No," PaulVer said.

Her dad looked calm, albeit a little surprised and annoyed to see Vincent. When the door shut behind Vincent, it happened fast. Vincent pulled a knife from behind him and slashed it across her dad's throat. A clean cut, deep and fast.

He hadn't seen it coming, which meant he trusted the man.

If she had to guess, her dad had set up the video recording because he was expecting a visitor. Possibly the Russian informant he was supposed to meet. When Vincent showed up, he probably didn't want him there because he was expecting someone else.

He wasn't expecting to die. Richard Pictam had taught her everything she knew about combat fighting, weaponry, and self-defense. No one could get the drop on him. Unless he trusted them.

Regardless, the video quality was perfect, the identities on the footage irrefutable.

"That's him." Tears quivered through her voice. "Give it to the world."

Cole wrapped his arms around her from behind, holding her tight as PaulVer switched screens on the laptop and hit a button on one of his software programs.

"It's sending now." He bounced a little on his toes. "It's hitting social media platforms, major news networks, and government agencies all over the world. Inboxes everywhere are receiving the file. It's done."

"Thank you." She pulled away from Cole and flung her arms around PaulVer's neck. "Thank you so damn much."

When she pulled away, the kid blushed and stared at his feet.

She turned back to Cole, and he was right there, waiting, smiling with two gorgeous, irresistible dimples.

"It's over," she whispered.

"It's only just begun." He caught her nape and hauled her in, taking her mouth with pure and vulnerable passion.

In his kiss was heartbreak and risk and choice and chance and a million dreams all condensed into a moment.

A moment hard-won.
In his kiss, she won love.

THIRTY-ONE

Dublin, Ireland
Two weeks later

Lydia visited the house in Dublin 22 one more time. She thought she needed the closure, but now she didn't know. Her heart was a mess.

"I don't know why I'm here." She paced through the small kitchen, looking around for anything she might want to keep.

"Do you want to go through his clothes?" Cole sat at the table, watching her steadily.

She and Mike didn't own anything. No pictures. No clothes worth keeping. Nothing of value. Instead of collecting material objects, she'd collected tattoos. Her memories of him were inked on her body. She had the egg Mike painted, and she kept the image of his lopsided smile safely in her mind. That was all she needed.

There hadn't been a funeral service. No big send-off. After she had him cremated, she and Cole flew to

London, stood on the Westminster Bridge in the moonlight, and poured Mike's ashes in the River Thames.

She let her brother go.

"I'm still trying to come to terms with it all."

"There's no hurry, Lydia. Take your time, and I'll be right here with you, every step of the way."

He hadn't left her side since the night they released the video. PaulVer had done exactly what he'd said. The video went viral, and within twenty-four hours, Vincent Barrington was arrested for murder.

She and Cole had been glued to the news stations for the past two weeks, watching the drama unfold as Vincent was handcuffed and hauled away. The trial would make history. Those in the NSA who covered up his crimes would be named and charged, too.

Vincent Barrington would never see daylight again.

Cole had asked her if she wanted more justice than that. He said he couldn't make promises, but he would find a way to have Vincent murdered in prison.

She didn't want that. Death would be too easy. For a man who had lived so extravagantly off the rewards of his corruption, a concrete cell and penal labor would be the worst kind of hell.

Let him rot behind bars.

She treaded to the window and pulled back the curtain, gazing out at the dead lawn and the quiet street beyond. The snow had long melted, taking the trail of blood with it.

"There's nothing left here but haunting memories," she murmured.

"Then you need a reminder of the good ones."

The chair squeaked as Cole stood, drawing her

attention. He tapped on the screen of his phone and set it on the table. A moment later, a feminine Irish voice sang from the speaker.

Doo doo doo do, doo doo doo do.

Her sinuses flooded with searing, sticky emotion. Her vision blurred. Gasps rose and fell from her chest. By the time the first tear fell, he was in her arms, holding her, rocking slowly as he sang along with "Ode To My Family" by *The Cranberries.*

He kissed her softly as she sobbed out the agonies of her heart. He danced with her in the living room where Mike had slept without complaint. He swayed with her in the kitchen where Shannon had made her magical stew. Then he made love to her in the bed where he'd given himself to her completely and irrevocably on Christmas Eve.

He stared into her eyes as he entered her body as if it were the first time. No regrets passed between them as he stroked inside her, taking his pleasure and giving it back with the devotion of his lips.

He would never leave her. Never let her go. She felt that promise as he looked into her eyes, fucked her achingly slow, and said, "I love you."

"I love you, Cole. Thank you for taking the risk with me."

"You were worth the risk, Lydia. You made me whole again."

He made her whole, too.

She'd lost her family, and though they could never be replaced, he'd given her a new one.

They shared a complicated history, but love was their magic ingredient. With a kiss, it annihilated twelve years of revenge and eight years of loneliness. If that wasn't magic, she didn't know what was.

THIRTY-TWO

Cayman Islands
Two years later

Today was the day. Nervousness might have been a natural response in Cole's position, but he lived for this shit—the tremor of looming danger, the rush of adrenaline, and the thrill in fighting for something meaningful.

It didn't get more meaningful than this.

White-crested waves rolled in from the sun-bleached horizon, lapping at his sandaled feet. He strolled along the beach, hands resting in the pockets of his swim shorts as his eyes moved from sand to sunbathers, from cobblestone pathways to crowded beach-side bars.

The panorama captured the essence of a laid-back paradise along with the elegance of a luxury resort. But he wasn't here to work on his tan.

The warm midday sunshine injected frissons of

energy beneath his skin. He was here to keep his eyes open and senses honed, for today, he would see a year-long dream finally come to fruition.

The blue skies were clear as far as he could see. Even the weather smiled on his plans.

Up ahead, a good-looking guy ran down the beach and leaped in a burst of strength, catching a football midair. His cheerleaders jumped from their loungers and clapped their hands, whistling.

As he turned to launch the ball back to the group, he met Cole's eyes.

Joshua.

He hadn't always been a gun-toting vigilante. Before Liv, he had a promising future as a professional football player.

His green eyes glinted with his smile. There was no resentment there. No misgivings.

With a nod to Cole, he sent a message.

Nothing was amiss. Everything and everyone was in place.

Cole continued on, strolling toward the group. Liv, Amber, and Van watched as Livana raced toward the spiraling football that Joshua passed back. She missed the catch, laughing at her fumble while her gaze made a furtive sweep of the perimeter.

As the only child of Van and Liv, she had big shoes to fill. But Cole had spent a lot of time training her over the years. She was sharp, fearless, and deadly with a gun.

He ambled past the group, smiling a friendly greeting.

Van sat beside Amber on the lounger, leaning in to tease the string on her bikini top. But like his daughter, his eyes were razor-sharp, probing the surroundings until they landed on Cole.

A toothpick rolled at the corner of Van's smirk, cocky and chilling.

Scary as fuck.

But Cole trusted him with his life. He trusted all of them.

While Joshua entertained them with his athletic dexterity, they played their parts as clueless vacationers, lounging and soaking up the sun.

No one knew they were killers. Every single one of them. They were a highly-trained, fiercely passionate team of vigilantes, and they were here to take down a multi-national criminal enterprise that catered to pedophiles.

There were one-hundred-and-twenty child predators mingling at the resort, all gathered for an annual convention. On the surface, it was a fun-in-the-sun holiday for business. But what happened after dark behind locked doors was so sick, sadistic, and inhumane that it called for justice without lawyers and trials.

It called for the Freedom Fighters.

When the team received the signal, they would dig their firearms out of the sand and take justice into their own hands.

Cole veered off the beach and headed into the resort, swapping warm oceanic air for air-conditioned breezeways.

He passed through one of the many indoor bars and spotted Luke, Tomas, and Vera at one of the card tables, playing poker with their targets. Handbags sat at their feet, concealing their weapons.

A hand brushed his arm, and he turned his neck, coming face to face with Rylee's huge silver eyes.

"Hey, handsome." Her cheeks rose with a smile. "Enjoying your stay?"

"Tremendously. You?"

"Everything's perfect." She winked and sauntered off to rejoin the group at the card table.

He crossed through the spa next. Tula, Martin, and Ricky sat in massage chairs, receiving pedicures. Evidently, men did this sort of thing, if he could call their targets *men*.

Old, fat fucks lounged in the other chairs, talking among themselves as women scrubbed and rubbed their feet. They had no idea they were about to die in those seats after spending their final moments on earth getting their toenails clipped.

Fuck them.

They would never touch another child again.

Ricky looked up, grabbing his gaze and giving him a chin lift. *All clear.*

Cole continued his perimeter sweep through the halls, his attention flicking to the shadows, to the opened and locked doors, and other possible escape routes. He and the team had scoured the property from end to end and every dark corner in between. This operation was a year in the making, and he didn't want any surprises.

There were three pool areas with vast spaces for their targets to congregate. He found Matias and Camila sitting at the edge of the first pool.

Camila looked stunning in her red bikini. Her husband, on the other hand, stood out like a douchebag with his floppy sunhat and white sunscreen slathered on his nose.

Fucking ridiculous. But necessary. As the capo of the Restrepo Cartel, he couldn't risk being recognized.

"Nice hat," Cole said in passing, biting down on his smile. "Can I ask where you got it?"

"Yeah, you can pick one up for yourself at..." Matias gave him the finger. "Fuck off."

"Behave." Camila elbowed her husband and glanced at Cole, whispering under her breath, "We're ready."

She rested a hand on the bag beside her, her eye glimmering with excitement.

With a nod, he followed the paved pathway to the next pool. Tate and Lucia stood at a high-top table, drinking colorful cocktails while surveying the area.

Lucia gave him a thumbs-up, and his heart rate accelerated, his blood thrumming for a fight.

He located Tiago and Kate in the final pool, their positions in place and expressions calm.

Everyone was in their assigned zones, locked on their targets.

There were targets they couldn't account for, the ones who were in their rooms or lingering in areas of the resort that required a key. That was where he came in.

And his favorite thief.

He picked up his pace, making a beeline to the outdoor bar at the center of the property. As he turned the corner, the first thing he saw was her fire-engine-red hair.

The thick waves tumbled down her back in lavish, unbridled glory. She sat on a stool at the bar, her spine straight and legs crossed like a lady. But that was where her decorum ended.

She wore an ultra-sexy rockabilly swimsuit, black with a cherry-themed print. The sweetheart neckline and figure-hugging shape drew the eye to her voluptuous tits, where they swelled up and out to here as she leaned toward the man beside her, whispering shamelessly in his ear.

A rush of heat tightened between Cole's legs as he prowled closer, his gaze raking her body, soaking in every dip that he knew so well.

Her beauty was just as bold and arresting as the first night he met her. Only now, he knew that gorgeous face wasn't just makeup and eyelashes. Beneath the cosmetics, she radiated. Her fair complexion, her natural red hair, and those sexy little freckles that dotted her nose—all of that only added to her badass perfection.

He was so fucking in love with this woman he made her his wife last year.

She was his forever. His happiness. And right now, she was instrumental in finishing this job.

Stalking around the perimeter of the bar, he listened to her conversation with the man at her side. Her Russian accent had improved over the years, and she laid it on thick, drawing her target under her spell.

She ordered him another drink, never once making eye contact with Cole. They were so attuned to each other, she knew he was there without lifting her fake eyelashes in his direction.

Watching her employ her seductive powers on her targets shouldn't turn him on as much as it did. But there was something really fucking satisfying about seeing every man in this bar openly gawk at her and knowing that no one could touch her. She was his. Period.

He waited for the moment she would make her move. Her target was the only man at the resort who held the codes to the property's top-notch security system.

Her target owned the resort and ran his multinational child trafficking organization within these walls. He was paranoid by nature, and never removed his fingers from his phone on the bar.

Until she slid a rope of cherry licorice from her purse. She looked away, feigning innocence as she sucked it between her lips, conjuring the image of a blowjob.

Her target homed in, leaned in, his attention on her mouth, forgetting himself, and at last, forgetting his phone.

She held his gaze, licking on her candy as her free hand swapped his phone with a lookalike from her purse.

Just like that, she fucking did it. She had the codes.

His pulse raced as he slipped away from the bar, watching as she started coughing, hacking, pretending she was choking on the Twizzlers.

With a wobbly exit, she grabbed her purse and pounded on her chest. "I'm okay. I'm okay. So sorry. I'm just going to use the ladies' room."

The lookalike phone she left behind was locked and uncharged. It would distract the owner for a while as he tried to power it on. By the time he realized she'd stolen his codes, it would be too late.

Cole stepped out of view, following her at a distance as she made her way toward the beach. Her gorgeous ass swayed in the swimsuit, her gait graceful and confident.

His stomach tightened as he pursued her, waiting for the hand-off. A few feet ahead, PaulVer stepped out of the shadows of a pool house. She dropped the phone in his hand and continued walking, slapping her flip-flops along the pavers.

The night PaulVer had unleashed the shit storm surrounding Vincent Barrington, Matias had offered him a position on the team. The kid hadn't hesitated, and he'd been invaluable ever since. Especially in operations like this one.

Now that he had the owner's phone, he would scrape the codes to break into the security system. In about three minutes, the faces and identities of his team would be wiped from the security footage, like they were never here. The entire system would be hacked, and every door in the resort would be unlocked for their attack.

Cole's chest expanded with the rampant, pounding beat of his heart. He quickened his strides, chasing Lydia to the beach. Their weapons waited there, buried in the sand near Van and Liv.

They had a few minutes before PaulVer gave them the *go*. So Cole stole one.

He stole a moment with his wife, grabbing her from behind and wrenching a beautiful laugh from her throat.

She spun toward him, smiling, showering him in sparks of brilliant chaos. It took courage to walk this dangerous life with him, and she was built for it, born for it. His perfect mate.

"What are you doing?" She leaned up, running her nose along his whiskered jaw. "We have bad guys to kill."

"So bloodthirsty," he growled. "Kiss me, woman."

She tilted her smile heavenward, offering up her glossy cherry lips.

The instant he kissed her, he breathed all the more deeply. Together, they shone brighter. A serenity of souls, fighting in a dark world and reaping their forever.

"I'm in love with you," he said.

"I'm in love with love, and you, Cole Hartman, are all of that."

"Ready?"

"Forever or bust."

"Forever it is." He kissed her again and laced their hands together. "Let's go."

LOVE TRIANGLE ROMANCE

TANGLED LIES TRILOGY

One is a Promise

Two is a Lie

Three is a War

DARK COWBOY ROMANCE

TRAILS OF SIN

Knotted #1

Buckled #2

Booted #3

DARK ALASKAN ROMANCE

FROZEN FATE

Hills of Shivers and Shadows #1

Cage of Ice and Echoes #2

Heart of Frost and Scars #3

DARK PARANORMAL ROMANCE
TRILOGY OF EVE
Heart of Eve
Dead of Eve #1
Blood of Eve #2
Dawn of Eve #3

STUDENT-TEACHER / PRIEST
Lessons In Sin

STUDENT-TEACHER ROMANCE
Dark Notes

ROCK-STAR DARK ROMANCE
Beneath the Burn

BILLIONAIRE REVENGE
Dirty Ties

OLDER WOMAN / YOUNGER MAN
Incentive

DARK HISTORICAL PIRATE ROMANCE
King of Libertines
Sea of Ruin

New York Times, Wall Street Journal, and *USA Today* bestselling author, Pam Godwin, lives in the Midwest with her husband, cats, retired greyhounds, and an old, foul-mouthed parrot. She traveled the world for seven years, attended three universities, married the vocalist of her favorite rock band, and retired from her quantitative analyst career in 2014 to write full-time.

Her interests veer toward the unconventional: bourbon, full-body tattoos, and tragic villains. Equally peculiar are her aversions to sleeping, eating meat, and dolls with blinking eyes.

EMAIL: pamgodwinauthor@gmail.com

www.ingramcontent.com/pod-product-compliance
Lightning Source LLC
Chambersburg PA
CBHW020457310726
48979CB00016B/2691/J

* 9 7 8 1 9 6 6 5 3 7 0 3 8 *